Jackson Joyce was born in Winnipeg, in the middle of the prairies in Manitoba, Canada. He has spent his entire life travelling and living in various countries around the world.

Now 55 years old, he lives in Vienna, Austria to be close to his son and to work on his next novel.

Jackson Joyce

WALK AWAY RUNAWAY

AUSTIN MACAULEY PUBLISHERS™

LONDON * CAMBRIDGE * NEW YORK * SHARJAH

A CIP catalogue record for this title is available from the British Library.

ISBN 9781398404229 (Paperback)
ISBN 9781398404236 (Hardback)
ISBN 9781398402126 (ePub e-book)
ISBN 9781398404243 (Audiobook)

www.austinmacauley.com

First Published (2021)
Austin Macauley Publishers Ltd
25 Canada Square
Canary Wharf
London
E14 5LQ

Thanks to my learned cousin, Nena, who gave me the confidence to continue, and certainly not forgetting my other cousins and family members: Biddi, Bonnie, Janne, Max, Marion and Andrew for their continued support and encouragement.

Thanks to Ian for attempting to keep me on the straight and narrow, both in real life and during the writing of this book.

Thanks to Austin Macauley publishers for taking the time to read an unfinished manuscript and encouraging me to finish. Most of all, thanks to my son, Nico, for being the guinea pig and being the first to read the full story.

Chapter One
Autumn 1979

I am frightened; beyond frightened. I'm somewhere between terrified and panic-stricken, not because I've been *kind of* arrested, that's the easy part. It's the part that's coming causing the distressing tremble to start somewhere deep inside me. The uncontrollable urge to flee is magnified by the inability to do so, until I start to shudder on the surface; shivering uncontrollably. "Pull yourself together," that's what *he'd* say. I wouldn't need to pull myself together if he hadn't put me here in the first place.

The police station is small, the kind you find in little Canadian backwaters that generally only deal with occasional weekend rowdiness or a traffic accident on the nearby mountains-bound highway. I'm at the back of the station. Not at the very back, which is largely unlit and unoccupied, but in cell one. Cell one is the first in a row of four cells, number four being in the deepest gloom, interrupted only by the occasional buzz and flicker of an insect ridden, dying fluorescent tube. I can just see the end cells facing each other, unoccupied; bringing a redundant mood like they've not been used in decades. Through the blinking light, I have the feeling of looking at my life as if in an old black and white film. The whole cell block is a mirror image of four basic rooms with a bed and a toilet. Out of necessity, I have pissed into the toilet from a safe distance, but I can't feel comfortable enough to lie down on the scruffy bed, it would feel like an acceptance of my surroundings that I'm not prepared to embrace. The bars separating me from freedom make me feel claustrophobic and anxious. A cold looking hallway with a nicotine-stained and badly scuffed ceiling lies on the other side of the cage and there is an underlying, strangely nostalgic smell of disinfectant and stale smoke; like the freshly splashed on Old Spice to try and hide the smell of *his* recently smoked cigarette. There is graffiti scratched into the walls of the cell, but I don't want to read it. I don't need to familiarise myself with former occupants. The only name that can't be avoided amongst the etchings is Clive. Clive has been here a lot, and I'm struck by an odd sense of trespassing. I wonder if Clive is arrested now whether I would be moved to a neighbouring cell in order to accommodate him. I bet Clive sleeps on the stained mattress, it's probably him whose stains remain.

The yellowing scratched complexion and dying light in the back contradict the friendlier, glossier front reception area. I can see the reception. I can see the officers, three of them, which is probably the entire quota for the shift. They are giving directions to a couple, an elderly couple who have a huge motorhome parked directly in front of the police station which is large enough to block any view beyond it. It's hiding Rob's beaten up car and hiding the view of The Chief which is a colossal cliff popular with experienced climbers. The Chief takes two days to climb so you can see tents hanging halfway up the giant wall, like gym bags in a kindergarten from invisible ropes and hidden pegs. At night, while the climbers rest before dawn, scattered tents of many colours light up the cliff-like paper lanterns at a Halloween party. The spectacle always impresses me and terrifies me to the point of feeling the sensations of vertigo whilst standing on firm ground. *How do they shit? How the fuck do they sleep?*

The motorhome is impressive. It is the size of a bus with an array of equipment to take the in dwellers into wilderness in commodious luxury. There's a clear dome on the roof, about two feet away from a reasonably sized satellite dish that has been neatly folded down to lie flat on the roof. I'm guessing the dome is over the bed. I love sleeping under the summer night sky, trying to understand our seemingly insignificant purpose within its vastness. Watching shooting stars is always exhilarating. I make wishes when I see one, but I haven't yet lived long enough to see if they will come true. We all dream of miracles happening and we all fantasise about what we would do if they did. I'm looking skyward, trying to imagine the view beyond the paint peeled ceiling and inwardly begging for a miracle right now.

A wintry purple dusk is developing outside and as the light dims, I see reflections on the inside of the station's windows, like an immediate translucent extension has been added to the building. This is when I see Rob's reflection, my best friend, sitting calmly just looking out of the window. He's looking relaxed, arms spread wide on the backs of the chairs on either side of him. He lifts a hand to push his messy brown hair to one side. He looks gangly, awkward in his tall frame, like he hasn't got used to it yet. I wouldn't blame him for leaving. I really wouldn't. Only a few days ago, *he* had held a loaded shotgun to Rob's face. A trembling anger extending all the way to a nervous finger on the trigger animated Rob to slowly retreat, walk away, in reverse from the double-barrel prodding his chest. Looking first at *him* and then at me with a pleading look in his eyes to follow him, but the front door was slammed shut and the weapon was turned on me.

Rob and I have run away. Rob's two years older than me. He's seventeen and has a beat-up old Toyota Corolla which is our getaway vehicle and the reason for our present predicament. Someone, while we were asleep in our motel room, had skidded on the packed snow and crashed into the side of the Corolla. It's still drivable but the damage is extensive and will probably cost more than the value of the car. I suppose we thought that out here in the wild country of British Columbia…the sticks, we'd have no problems reporting the incident to the local police, Rob would get what he needs to get the car covered by the insurance and we would decide what to do afterwards.

By the time we'd packed and readied to leave, the car was being scrutinised by two RCMP officers. Royal Canadian Mounted Police; Mounties. Not local cops. They'd already seen us leave the room before we had time to change our minds and get back inside, so we sauntered casually, trying to be cool, towards the car.

The cops were pleasant and just chatting with us. They weren't looking for us at all, they were only there because the night manager had called in the hit and run. So, having been lulled into a comfortable state, I stupidly parted with my real name and I was subsequently cuffed and stuffed before I finished giving them my date of birth.

He had insisted on an APB (All Points Bulletin). Every cop in British Columbia had been told to look out for me, apprehend me and take me to a holding police station. He will be enraged, unable to control his fury.

The cuffs were roughly clamped onto my wrists and I was stuffed into the back of the police car which still had that pleasantly welcoming new car smell inside.

*

Adrenaline is pumping me full of power. I'm shocked at what I've just done but, at the same time, experiencing a kind of semi relief. We pass *him* heading

9

north as we speed south. Rob and I try to avoid looking at him but can't help peering sideways with strained eyes. We try to turn our faces as far away from him as possible but still, our eyes are fixated, as if connected by some invisible thread; until it's broken and then we simultaneously, nervously submit into mutual laughter because neither of us knows what to say. We are laughing but we're not happy; we're scared and we both know the gravity of the consequences if we are caught. When I looked briefly at him as we drove past, I tried to read his face, but it was devoid of any emotion. The window was half open and he was flicking cigarette ash out of it as he filled the car with smoke when he exhaled. His face remained unyielding though.

Rob and I have no plan. We had no plan in the first place when we decided to leave, but we are completely improvising now... what do you do when you've just broken out of jail?

He will probably be just arriving at the police station to pick me up by now. The mention of it silences Rob and I into our own thoughts about how it will have been received that I'm not there anymore. And that they don't know *where* I am.

*

Although I had been placed in a cell at the station, the local cop who led me through and put me there didn't feel it was necessary to lock me up. In fact, he's right. I didn't need to be locked up at all. I'm not a danger to society and until now, I have only really broken the law by smoking pot or drinking beer when I'm lucky enough to get it.

Nothing but fear drove the adrenaline to make me slide the heavy metal cage door open slightly. It was loud. A low rumble; like a child's first roll of a bowling ball, but I only needed it to open enough for me to squeeze through. The movement caused the mix of insects on the fluorescent tube to momentarily leave the lure of the light, engaging in a lazy short-lived mass hysteria before re-settling back into their semi-comas. Inch by inch I slowly rolled the door, hoping not to be heard.

As soon as I had room, I stuck my head out and Rob immediately saw my reflection in the window. Just outside the entrance to the cells, there was an office to my right with its door closed. To my left, another office, with the door open and I could see the uniformed arm of an officer. The angle of the arm and the relaxed state suggested he was leaning back on his chair, probably having a coffee break. The other two were still in the front of the station preoccupied with helping the motor homers.

With one quick motion, I walked past the office, not daring to even take a breath. I was lucky and the cop lent forward to pick up his cup of coffee, momentarily blocking his view of me and I think I may have closed my eyes as I walked past. Then I had an open reception with the other two remaining officers to negotiate. All in all, about thirty feet between me and the front door. Rob saw the plan and he started to move towards the door. He nonchalantly got up as if to stretch his legs after a long time sitting in one position. He moved towards the door, opened it and I walked towards it, eyes never moving from the goal, not daring to glance at the officers, and I walked out completely unnoticed.

*

"What the fuck are we going to do now?" Rob asks, still half laughing.

"Go to Winnipeg," I say. Not altogether confident with my own decision but I really don't see a better option than to put a thousand or so miles between us and the trouble that is about to follow us here.

We both withdrew nearly all our savings the day before, to fund our escape and we have a total of five hundred dollars between us; a damaged car and fierce appetites. We haven't eaten (apart from water and some stale crackers at the police station) for twenty-four hours and we are ravenous.

Two things need to be done before we leave, and we need to do them fast. First and foremost, we need to eat, and in a very close second place, I need to say goodbye to Jayne. Jayne is the love of my life and I can't imagine leaving her behind for Winnipeg, but I also can't imagine negotiating my way past her dad to take her with me. Rob has a crush on her as well, but he's cool about it. I even snuck up her drainpipe in the middle of the night for a pre-arranged cuddle before she fell asleep not so long ago. It really was a cuddle too. It's important to know that.

Jayne is the (kind of) forbidden fruit of the school that most of the boys and I suspect many of the girls fantasise about in some way. Fifteen, but a woman in every way physically. A very beautiful and sexy woman who doesn't try to hide herself but is unaware of her potential power. She prefers to be a bit of a tomboy, a tough tomboy even, but this still doesn't hide her perfect, firm and well-formed breasts. Her face is still fresh and innocent, framed by wavy, brown shoulder-length hair. Brown eyes, flashing on and off as she slowly blinks, eyelashes performing a melancholic closing ceremony, only to spring back, wide open. Every time she looks at me with her freshly opened eyes, I fall in love with her all over again. She is stunning, but she always carries a deeper look of insecurity and confusion; almost always questioning. Unsure of how to deal with the attention her attractiveness gains, she finds the support, friendship and solace in us: Rob, me and a close-knit group of friends. The misfits, stoners... We've been called them all and we don't give a fuck. Together, we are untouchable. We all drink together, smoke weed together, date each other. We take our first steps into the realms of sexual adventure together. We vary in numbers, but Rob and I are always the steadfast honorary members, if not founders of a group that has become known as the Cave. We always used to meet before school and sit on a neighbouring garden wall that was conveniently sheltered by a large overhanging Laurel bush. From a distance, it resembles a small cave.

*

There is a death-like silence, not only inside the car. Even though we are travelling at around seventy miles per hour, it seems as if all life has literally come to a complete rest for the briefest of moments.

I suppose it could be likened to the calm before a storm... and the approaching storm is about thirty feet below us.

I'm not sure whether to scream, laugh or cry. In fact, I start to giggle uncontrollably as we fly over the road below us. Rob is transfixed, doing a choked kind of laugh, completely at a loss as to know what the car might decide to do now that it's left to nothing more than the forces of nature to manoeuvre it. Gravity is starting to take hold and I'm glad that Rob and I are of similar build because we're descending and we need to stay level.

In this area of North Vancouver, the roads are still constructed using the North American grid system. North Vancouver is built on the side of Grouse Mountain, which stands faithfully looking over Greater Vancouver. The result is that the roads running north to south are, in places, impressively steep. The crossroads that run perpendicular have been levelled up for the traffic to remain horizontal and this creates a very alluring launch ramp for the adventurous teenager, especially when pumped with adrenaline and travelling at high speed.

I'm beginning to wonder if we will ever land. We are on a very steep piece of road and even though we are rapidly losing altitude, the slope of the road delays the imminent impact seemingly endlessly.

I'm looking over rooftops as the decline continues; like a ski jumper, ever descending but never seeming to be able to quite touch down… until we do. With the mix of combined masses, momentum and gravity, we explode onto the tarmac. It sounds, and even feels like all the wheels have imploded in on themselves and are gone forever. The entire bottom of our car erupts in a most impressive show of sparks I have seen. We are submerged in a sea of swirling vibrant reds, whites and oranges as we bounce up for the first time, back in the air, but only for a short time. This time, the landing is softer (wheels still intact) and the sparks not nearly as impressive. Rob hasn't had a chance to use the breaks yet and although the landing will have slowed us down a little, we're still hurtling down the side of a mountain at 60 miles an hour and the T junction at the main road is in sight. My tension eases as Rob gains control of the car and I can see we will manage to stop safely before reaching the major intersection. We're beginning to celebrate our achievement when something catches our eyes in the peripheral, to our right.

The dog is huge. It's like a well-developed over nourished bear cub… and it's running across the road, right in front of us. Accepting its fate, the dog has halted abruptly at the sight of the car.

As it happens, the enormous dog does most of the necessary stopping for us. We stop virtually dead and my knee crushes the plastic dashboard on impact. The dog rolls down the road like it's playing roly-poly; like it's a game. When it stops rolling, it gets up, shakes itself and goes and sits quietly by the side of the road. No sign of any panic. Rob goes to the dog while I look at the newly added damage to the already decrepit Corolla. It's not good. In fact, I'd say we're fucked.

Fred is the dog's name. He's a St Bernhard and it's not often you see one without a barrel, even if it's only decorative. Inside the barrel is a little tightly rolled up piece of paper with Fred's name on it and his owner's name and address. The owner is apologetic and seemingly unperturbed as if it is a daily occurrence and Fred trots into his home as if he's just been for a play in the park.

Back at the battered car, Rob turns the key to fire the ignition. It starts and it's running. The odd rattle and whine but it seems okay. It is okay, all the way to Jayne's house, and then the wheels fall off; literally, not metaphorically.

13

The front axle had apparently been split on the earlier landing but manages to hold out for five minutes before simply breaking into two halves, freeing up the two front wheels to go in any direction they wish. Like reaching the point of no return whilst doing the splits in socks on a polished floor, they spread apart, and the car still rolls on, wider apart… and then bang, the front end of the car slams down onto the pavement, still driven by momentum, ever slowing but not enough to stop us sliding side on, onto Jayne's front garden. Jagged bits of metal cutting through obsessively manicured lawns, ripping out small shrubs within neatly cut borders.

Jayne comes running out as her father is calling 911 from the phone in the hallway by the front door. We're fucked anyway, so the only thing I ask of her is for a bite to eat before the storm hits.

She looks flustered. "What the fuck, Kev?" She's shaking as she speaks.

I shouldn't have come here. Fuck, I didn't think about the shit storm I've brought Jayne now. Sirens.

Here they come. But not before *he* comes screeching around the corner, very nearly on two wheels, totally out of control but still coming, fast. Very fast. We turn to run, not from the police but from the four-wheeled missile heading straight for us. We turn directly into the face of Mr T and he, in turn, greets me with a furious gaze; a rage on the verge of being exposed.

Momentary darkness, pain, stars in my eyes… he's here. I'm on the grass, face laying half turned to see the impeccably polished shoes of my father.

My head is sore and when my vision clears, I see the briefcase. I see blood on it, my blood. They are picking me up as the police cars arrive in unison; their sirens winding down, quietening through a dissonant chord and fading to an exaggerated quiet.

My father is viewed by my friends and their parents as a ridiculously strict man. They call him Victorian Dad. They think he's a cut and dried authoritarian but, he's everything but. He has no idea what he is himself. He has told me so many versions of his own life that I don't think he even remembers who he is anymore. He's a follower. He learns by watching the people he feels are worthy of admiration and transcribes it into his life pretending it's always been him at the helm.

Again, had he stuck to one person as a role model to mimic, this would have passed as acceptable, but he changes like the wind changes direction in an Autumn storm, from one overt devaluing narcissist to the next. The only constant median that has always run through our household is simple; his house, his rules. Mum, ever quiet.

For the second time that day, I'm cuffed. Not stuffed this time. I'm not allowed to leave this situation without some sort of public humiliation. The cops are explaining to my father that putting me in handcuffs isn't necessary and it looks like we've both been through enough.

"Put the little shit in cuffs and don't worry if you hurt him," my dad spits at them.

"And put that bastard in them too!" he follows up pointing at Rob.

Rob's parents have just arrived and are immediately intervening. Stopping anything unnecessary happening to Rob and taking him away from my father's venom.

As requested by my father, we are all now sitting in the living room of Jayne's house. I'm sitting directly under Jayne's bedroom, the bedroom where a week ago I felt so in love while she let me stroke her back. She said it was okay to stroke her back, but I'd have to wait a while before I could see the front. I didn't care. I was in Jayne's bed, stroking her back.

Next to me, on my left is Rob and to his left, his mum, then his dad. To my right is my dad, sitting up on the highest chair he could find. Not only to compensate for his five-foot-eight stature but also because he went on a seminar where he was taught that sitting above everyone else will automatically make them look up to him and follow him. Mr T then ups the stakes and switches himself up onto a bar stool, giving him the new alpha position. My dad stands up and walks into a nearly full circle comprising Rob, his mum, his dad, Jayne, her mum, her dad, four RCMP officers, my mum and my father who has now taken centre stage. He is red in the face and screaming at me.

"Stand up," he bellows. My father's voice takes on a kind of guttural tone, it's like he moves everything he's saying a bit further back in his mouth before he releases the words. It's his authoritative tone and it's horribly embarrassing for me to watch him humiliate himself by using it publicly. He also has a telephone voice; he mimics how he perceives the queen to answer the phone.

A voice for his friends and family from Leicester; for his Rotarian friends, for the Vicar, for his patients. He adapts and changes his behaviour to suit every surrounding, but I have never seen *him*.

I just see daily, even hourly facades to constantly present himself as the best in whatever situation he is in.

I see where this is going. He needs to show his dominance, his power, his unparalleled parental brilliance.

"Stand up I said, insolent boy!" in his best Victorian Oxford English. He *is* from Leicester by the way.

It's not only me this amuses but Rob doesn't manage to suppress his snort. If Rob's parents weren't there, I'm certain the briefcase would come out again for Rob's disrespect. Some of the parents are also stifling sniggers. Mr T isn't paying attention to the game going on in the centre of his living room and is talking with two of the younger police officers. He calls Jayne over and I could see him looking more agitated, and Jayne's looking guilty.

Rob doesn't move under my father's glare and even though I know my dad terrifies him, he looks him straight in the eyes and forces him to return his attention to me. By now I'm standing, simply because one of the officers gave me a nod to get up. He wasn't threatening, just wanting to get this over with now no doubt. My father swings his body (he hates that I'm taller than him) threateningly towards me and bellows at me with the Victorian voice again:

"Sit down!" Only his vindictive smile visible to me as he says the words.

"Fuck off!" I say, knowing full well this will aggravate him further, and this time, Rob bursts out laughing... and his dad can't help but join him in an inappropriate chuckle.

My father moves to hit me but thinks better of it.

"You will do as I say and sit down now, boy," he looks at the others apologetically as if to say I'm sorry my son is so bad. He's trying to and believes he will gain their support. There is none but he continues.

"This really isn't solving anything," says one of the officers, intervening. He's the oldest of the four and about twice the age of his partner.

"What he needs is for you four to take him outside and beat the shit out of him. That'll teach him a lesson!" My father is losing control now.

Mrs T is joining Mr T and Jayne with the two young cops. Mrs T has always been nice to me. Mr T is looking irate but that is common. He's a diluted version of my father. Jayne is so cute. I wish we were upstairs again in her bed, feeling the first taste of love. I felt intensely alive when I was touching her, like every sense was enhanced, which lasted long after being with her. Like that moment was going to be one of the most memorable nights of my life.

One of the young cops who was talking to the T's steps into the centre. Now, two RCMP officers are in the centre of the room; easily usurping my father. I'm happy that part is over. I'm looking at the front door weighing my chances. Slim, at best.

"The fact is: the only person with any need for our presence is the homeowner and he has decided not to press charges," says the young cop,

"Can't you lock him up anyway?" The cop just ignores the comment from my father.

"There was a report from a neighbour about a young lad climbing up a drainpipe a little while ago. Jayne's already given us her version. Do you know anything about it?" he asks, clearly knowing the answer himself.

"Yes, it was me. I'm sorry," I say. Mrs T smiles as I look nervous about what will happen next. Mr T is showing restraint.

"Why did you climb up the drainpipe in the middle of the night?" the cop pushes, doing his job.

I just keep thinking to myself why is this such a big deal? Isn't it fucking obvious? I only wanted to lie next to a person who had given me a glimpse of love. I wanted to feel that feeling of warmth; that nourishing feeling of an invisible void being filled that only Jayne can do. I only wanted to fall asleep in her arms.

"Because I wanted to sleep with Jayne!" I blurted out…

Chapter Two

I'm awoken by a cold drip of water that lands directly in my ear. Slowly coming out of a drunken slumber, I feel it's drizzling. It's more like a mountain mist than rain but the accumulation of water on the branches above me occasionally roll together into one crystal clear ball and fall. The first drop that woke me up is followed by another; and another. I'm wet, cold and I have a hangover from hell.

My head hurts to the point that even the tiny droplets landing on me send vibrations to encourage the violence happening in my head. I turn to look up to the source of the drips. I open my mouth to let single tears land in my mouth at irregular intervals soothing my sore tongue and dry throat. I try waiting a little longer each time to let more water build-up in my mouth to satisfy my growing thirst. A stirring nearby shifts my focus. A shuffling of undergrowth and an awakening groan. I turn my head to see Rob slowly coming to with a similar disorientation I had just recently experienced. Lisa is still asleep in his arms. Dennis is already up and pissing over the edge of the ledge we are on, using no hands to guide the flow, while trying to light a half-smoked cigarette with a damp book of matches. The fire from the night before is still smouldering and regardless of the damp autumnal air, it's still giving off a little warmth. There's still a hint of mushrooms in the air but it's overwhelmed by the smell of fresh damp pine mixed with the pungent smell of fading embers. Dave, Chris, Randy, Gary, Dee, Donna, Mark and Scott are still sleeping; scattered masses of muddy clothes and damp straggly hair under unevenly distributed jackets for warmth.

"Let's go to Denny's!" Dennis announces enthusiastically, as his freshly lit stub falls from his mouth into the forested canyon below us.

"Fucks sake!" He balances precariously as he sees if he can retrieve it. "Anyone got a smoke?" he asks looking desperate.

To be fair, Dennis does not always have the greatest of ideas and some have ended up in us trying to get out of some difficult situations but this is a good idea. We're all wet, cold and in need of nourishment and Denny's *is* the best place to get it all for free on occasion.

"Okay. Let's go!" I say. Thinking more about the warmth than the food.

"You better lie low, Kev. Don't you think?" Rob says, with his hand feeling up Lisa's left breast.

He's right. If I go anywhere outside of this hideaway, I'll be delivered right back into the hands of my father probably within the hour.

After my faux pas in the living room arena the evening before at Jayne's house, it all turned a little ugly…

It was a mistake; a bad choice of words. It was nothing more than that. I genuinely meant I wanted to do nothing more than fall asleep with Jayne, but it was like my ill-chosen sentence had unleashed the ugliest beast from the deepest depths of hell. Mr T went an odd colour; a kind of blood-red mixed with plum purple. His head literally looked like a badly bruised fruit before his hatred was unleashed on me. I was ushered to safety, outside the house by the police as he charged at me, seemingly literally wanting to kill me. Jayne was screaming and crying at the same time and not for the first time, I felt guilt. Three police officers were struggling to hold Mr T back as I was led by the oldest of the four cops outside. Then, my father was out of his depth and seemed to temporarily retreat until the storm settled and he could rise again victorious, later, in private.

Because of my badly chosen words, Mr T had added breaking and entering and harbouring of a minor to the list of formerly dropped charges. I stood in disbelief as the officers asked me if I understood.

"I understand," I say. But I don't. I don't understand any of it. I don't understand why my word is worth nothing and I can be pushed around in any direction anyone wishes depending on their mood. The charges against me have serious consequences and I could go to juvenile detention centre for a considerable amount of time, simply because I nervously chose the wrong words to try and start explaining that I genuinely love his daughter. I didn't even get close to the part where I was going to apologise to the prick because he just turned into a mindless torso of murderous rage.

The ride home from Jayne's house was gut-wrenchingly silent. Both mother and father looking ahead through the windscreen. I was leaning my forehead against the side window trying to gain some momentary relief from a splitting headache by rolling my forehead slowly over the cool glass. As daylight waned, I gazed into the lit rooms of homes I knew nothing of, each one of them looking more inviting than the one before. A little taste of paradise for all to see before the curtains close on wealthy middle-class suburbia.

By the time we had pulled into our driveway, all my fear had passed and what energy remained was just meandering around my body in a dull numb acceptance. I stepped out of the car head bowed, exhausted and defeated. Then I saw the cigarette lying on the ground, right at my feet. It was a sign. It was a Russian cocktail cigarette. This message was to say they're there for me. I looked around, without alerting my dad, and then I saw Mark's old Chevy van parked up just down the street.

I was marched into the house like a prisoner of war; father in front, mother behind. The keys were thrown aggressively onto the table which slid off and landed in the dog's water bowl which caused further irritation for my father.

"Sit!" he bellowed, pointing towards the table.

"Can I just go to the bathroom first?" I asked, just wanting to get out of the room that didn't seem to me to be anywhere near as warm as the homes I was looking into on the homeward journey. I was followed all the way to the bathroom by both parents and I was wondering if they might even come in. Once inside, I could breathe again. I could feel the adrenaline coming back, the survival mode was kicking in again. I turned on the taps, opened the window, climbed out, and without a second thought, I hung from the windowsill and dropped two stories onto the hard pavement below. Nothing hurt, I walked briskly around the corner just as the front end of Mark's van appeared at the end of the driveway. The side door opened, and I rolled into the plush purple velvet stud padded out the interior with my best friends already there. Mark sounded his air horn which his trucker dad gave him, Dennis stuck his bare arse out of the side door and the last thing I saw through the living room window was my father running towards the bathroom…

With the van full of beer and weed, we headed for what we simply called the Ledge.

*

Everybody's awake now and Dave is trying to get the fire going again. Dave is Dennis's brother; his twin but they are nothing alike. Dennis is a lean, tall guy, over six foot with military short black hair. Dave is bigger; stockier. He's still tall but looks very different from his brother, and he's much quieter than Dennis.

They both share the same Mediterranean dark complexions but that's about as far as it goes. Dave seems happy to live in his brother's shadow and enjoy wherever he leads him, and I have never seen them argue; in fact, I rarely see them interact at all but if anyone crosses either one of them, the other is immediately his ally.

Regardless of being wet, cold and generally dishevelled, we are all in good spirits. Dennis is hungry and growing impatient about the trip to Denny's so he's fabricating an unelaborate harpoon with which he intends to catch us a 'hearty breakfast' in the creek below. Rob is doing his level best to lose his virginity with Lisa, and it looks like that moment isn't far off. Mark is smoothing Donna's hair. She has the reddest hair I have seen, with the palest of skin. She wants to be an air hostess and to see the world. I'm worried about Jayne. Her father's reaction wasn't normal and it worries me how much control he has over her. I miss her, and I hope she's okay.

"BEAR!"

"BEAR!"

"BEAR!"

"FUCK! FUCK! RUN!"

Randy is running and shouting at us, panic-stricken right at us, pants around his ankles, which trip him up on his final approach to the camp and he face plants with his ample pink bare rump, face up right in front of us. We all rally into motion and look towards the direction of the bear, none of us sure what we will do if it comes for us. Randy remains frozen in the position he arrived, not even daring to move to cover his arse. A rustle just out of sight but close enough to scare the shit out of all of us. Then a movement of undergrowth, I can see the fucker and it's coming straight for us.

"Grr…" says Dennis as he pokes his head out from behind a wayward rhododendron.

Evidently, Randy had gone for a quiet contemplative shit in the woods when Dennis spotted him on his way to the fishing hole.

"Fuck me, the moon's up again," Dennis says pointing at Randy's butt.

"Fuck off, needle dick." Randy's standing up now and pulling his pants up.

I slip away behind an outcrop of rocks looking for some temporary shelter from the strengthening drizzle and Dennis carries on in the direction of the creek, singing one of his military songs he's so fond of as he goes.

"I don't know but I've been told, I don't know but I've been told, Eskimo pussy's mighty cold..." etc.

Normally, it's a call and repeat song but Dennis is quite happy singing both parts himself as his voice slowly trails off into the woods below us in the valley.

"If I die on the Russian front, If I die on the Russian front, bury me in a Russian cunt."

Whether he's just stopped singing, or he's faded from earshot, we are reprieved the repeat. He's not a bad singer really though, even if his repertoire is limited to regimental marching songs.

Randy is a calm, quiet soul. He's a big guy and if he weren't playing on the high school football team, he would probably be the target of bullying for being considered tubby. He's a gentle giant, but he will wreak his revenge on Dennis, when Dennis, and everyone is least expecting it. We all know it's coming. Dennis knows it's coming but only Randy knows when.

I don't know how long I've been asleep but I'm aware that the weather has shifted from a drizzle to a steady downpour, and it's the sound of the rain on Mark's leather jacket covering me that wakes me up. I'm no longer uncomfortably cold, thanks to the scattered garments of clothing covering me. Donna's woollen shawl is keeping my body warm enough to appreciate her sweet perfumed scent while I slowly move to get up. The Ledge is deserted, even the fire has finally given up against the rain and I'm disappointed I let it go out. It will be a nightmare to get another one going with nothing but wet wood. I have one match left and I really want a cigarette, so I weigh up the odds of getting a fire going with one match, choose the most sheltered area away from wind and rain and carefully light up a slightly bent cigarette behind cupped hands.

This is wilderness. I'm sitting, literally within walking distance of one of the largest cities in Canada and I can't see one man-made object in any direction. It's beautiful; serene. A blue-green oasis bordering an ever-greying, ever-growing suburban sprawl. I sit down on the edge of the ledge and look down into the deep valley where the creek runs. The salmon will be running upstream now which is something to see.

At this time of year, the ordinarily deep, emerald-green pools will be obscured by a shimmering layer of burgundy red just under the surface. It's the closely packed bodies of Coho salmon returning to their spawning grounds to deposit and fertilise their eggs – then die. Imagine being born and your parents are already dead.

A bald eagle soaring along the valley draws me out of my thoughts and this touches the sense of freedom I crave. I'm close enough to see a flash of pale-yellow eye focussing on any movement as it scans the ground for prey, gliding effortlessly, relaxed and elegant. Her need to hunt to survive reminds me that we are never truly free; we are always a slave to something. We cannot just exist.

I should imagine Mark has arrived in the usual parking place about a mile along the logging road below. We always park there and then walk off track the rest of the way, so we keep our hideout a secret. As far as I know, we are the only people that come to the ledge. It's out of sight of the logging road and there are no obvious paths leading to it, and I only stumbled on it by chance when I went on one of my more adventurous fishing trips. I'm sure the odd hunter might pass by occasionally but apart from that, there has never been any evidence of anyone else using our personal piece of nature.

I head for the sound of the horn that frightened the eagle away. I know they will have supplies that need carrying up the mountain and I'm guessing Mark sounded his ludicrous air horn to get me to help... and do they have supplies! Beer, food of varying descriptions; including some left-over Denny's, tents, sheets, tarps, sleeping bags. It's like a team of Sherpas walking to Everest's base camp. And Jayne. I see her carrying what looks like a battered old oil lantern she probably scavenged from the un-used camping supplies in her basement. She's walking with and talking to Lisa who's clearly freshened up. It turns out that they have all decided to sit it out up here for the long haul. It seems the explosion in my life has ignited a united rebellion, and we all share the same desire to say a big fuck you to everyone and everything in our own lives for our own reasons. We are going to establish a camp and we will have the best freedom party the world has ever known. Scott throws me a beer and says, "Let's fucking do this."

We have music. Ted Nugent is playing Wango Tango on Scott's ghetto blaster as we set up camp. We're drinking, getting high, singing and we feel untouchable, unreachable... free! We have a base. A fireplace with a covering tarp that's high enough to avoid the flames but low enough to keep the rain off us as we sit around the crackling burning pine, sharing stories and playing truth or dare. Jayne opts for truth and Lisa asks her if she loves anyone here. Jayne says she loves everyone here. Lisa presses her and asks if there is anyone, she loves more than everyone...

"Yes," she answers, looking shyly at me.

Lisa smiles and I have the feeling of a million butterflies in my gut. Jayne didn't say any words, and I have never heard the words I love you said to me, but that look told me that she does love me and I don't need to hear the words. The fact that she openly admitted her feelings of affection towards me in front of everyone else makes me feel an intense feeling of pride. I think it's pride. Maybe it's love... I think it's love.

Jayne has brought her guitar and I hope she sings that Anne Murray song sometime. I've been with her in the recording studio a few days ago, listening in from the control room and I love to listen to her sing. I like going with her in the studio, but the main engineer doing the recording is a complete dick. He keeps stopping Jayne and making her sing the same lines repeatedly even though they are perfect to begin with. It's always perfect the first time when Jayne sings, she's a natural. I did tell him to shut the fuck up and let her sing a while ago and he's only just forgiven me and let me back in. He promises that she will be a star one day but, I've seen the way he looks at her. He probably sits at his desk making her repeat songs so he can maintain his perpetual erection for her. She knows it; even plays on it, but I still want to punch him.

Randy is hanging his mac jacket on a stick which is supported by another stick, by the fire to dry and I'm wondering if any bits of Randy float up into the ether with the steam that's coming off it. Endless joints are being passed around the fire and we are all starting to relax into our new life, thriving on our united insurrection. The mix of alcohol, weed and solidarity gives us the bravado to laugh in the faces of the parents that are probably presently searching for us, and none of us carry any regrets.

"Got one!" We all turned to see Dennis... I'd forgotten all about him. He's standing proudly just outside the campfire area holding a fungus ridden, half-eaten and most certainly long dead, remnant of a fish; his makeshift harpoon sticking precariously into one of its rotting gills. He carries the fleshy offering into the campfire area and holds it over the flames. The stench is intense and it's amplified further when the rotting gill flakes away, the fish tumbles down onto Randy's jacket which is knocked into the heart of fire with the offending fish landing on top of it.

The stench is repugnant, but apparently only to us because it has attracted the inquisitive nose of medium-sized brown bear which is slowly lolloping up the hill for an easy late lunch. Dennis is still oblivious to the bear, no doubt shitting himself over what Randy will do to him. I remember that when you see a bear, it's best to make lots of noise which will frighten it away. If that doesn't work, then play dead and hope for the best. I have had vivid nightmares about the latter so I would prefer to avoid it if I can. I start clapping my hands and shouting at the bear and this is when Dennis turns and finally sees it.

"FUCKS SAKE!" he shouts.

"BEAR!" Dennis is practically screaming the word as he runs completely out of control and starts to climb a tree. Climbing a tree is never a good solution to escape a bear as they can climb like monkeys or will simply shake you out. A human can't outrun, outswim, outclimb but can, on occasion, outwit a bear. The best solution would be to shoot it if it attacks, and most people who spend extended days in the forest are armed for the purpose, but currently, the only means of defence I see around me is Dennis's harpoon and I don't really fancy my chances. Dennis is really quite a long way up the tree now and the noise and commotion we are all creating at the camp is having no effect at all on the encroaching unwanted visitor. The bear is no more than twenty feet away and its pace is accelerating. I grab the rotten fish by the tail and haul it out of the fire. The fish literally falls away from its own rotting body and I have just the tail in my hand. I throw the remains of the flesh in the direction of the bear and it seems momentarily satisfied with its snack. The smell coming from the rotten salmon is making me want to wretch, but Rob and I keep hurling bits of meat at the bear. Then we start to circumnavigate the huge imposter and start a fish trail leading it back in the direction of the creek. Not surprisingly, the bear is more interested now in the contents of the camp than a bitter rank fish.

We stand below and our friends stand above as we watch the bear sniff, claw and eat its way through a good proportion of our supplies. It would be a good time to leave but the bear doesn't seem in the slightest bit interested in us; it certainly isn't frightened of us. A bear will generally only attack a human if its cubs are threatened or if it's very hungry; like if it's just woken up from a winter's hibernation. It looks like this bear is having a good final top-up before his own hibernation and I'm grateful he prefers ketchup flavoured crisps over human. Appetite and curiosity sated the bear merely carry on in its lolloping way, away from the creek; away from us in the direction of the logging road, closer to suburbia than people would like to know.

"You useless, vacant void of a whore's CUNT!" Randy shouts at Dennis.

Dennis remains silently hiding up the tree and Randy settles quietly in his own knowledge that Dennis will pay dearly.

We all knew that Randy was going to wait for Dennis to come down from the tree, pretend to be asleep and when Dennis slept, he'd get his hand placed in a bowl of water, so he'd piss in his sleeping bag. It's childish, but it's still funny. Dennis didn't come down from the tree until he knew everyone was firmly asleep and we all woke up to see him snuggled up, sharing a sleeping bag with Dee. I suspect more as a way for his own protection than anything romantic.

I think we all know; Dennis and Randy would be lost without each other and their friendship couldn't exist any other way. It's just the way it is, and we get our entertainment from it too. I don't really know how long they've known each other but it feels like a long time.

*

The days blur into one. We are tiring. The rain is merciless and the temperature is dropping continuously, to the point of the rain turning to sleet at night with occasional full-on flurries of big, wet snowflakes. The cold nights have been mostly spent around the fire and we are taking shifts maintaining a perpetual cycle of wood to fuel it. It's burning so hot now. It always fascinates me to stare into the raging hot embers and remember how difficult it was to get a simple little flame to ignite in the beginning. It's satisfying building a furnace capable of burning ample tree boughs from nothing more than a match and a piece of paper.

We're out of beer, low on weed and we have only enough food for a measly breakfast ration each of corn flakes without milk. Mark is dosing in his sleeping bag which has been zipped together with Donna's and he doesn't ask any questions when I ask for his van keys and Rob doesn't ask any questions as he follows me on the walk to the van.

Rob drives, simply because he can. I don't have a license yet, but I would have driven, had Rob not insisted. First stop: the bank. I have one hundred dollars left in my account and I need to get it out. My bank is located on a quiet high street in a sleepy village-type suburb of North Vancouver, which also happens to be directly opposite the entrance to my father's dental practice. I have lost track of the days, but I know it's not a weekend because the last one doesn't seem distant enough. I'm guessing it's probably a Tuesday and I can see that the bank is open; as is my father's practice. Good. At least he's getting on with his life.

My father's surgery overlooks the high street from the second floor of a two-story building offering him a direct view about midway into the bank.

Wearing one of Mark's baseball caps that are lying around the van and Rob's black leather jacket, I start walking down the high street, head tilted face down on my father's side of the road, lessening his chances of him seeing me by overexposing myself. Just before reaching his entrance, almost as if my anticipation of it happening causes it, his door opens fast and wide which freezes me to the ground. It's Kiera, his assistant and if she's leaving the building, they must be on a break which isn't good for me. I was hoping he would have his head buried deep in someone's mouth doing whatever it is dentists do in there. Now he could literally be anywhere. Still, I've got this far, I'm not going to retreat, so I walk, pretending to be confident like I own the road across to the entrance of the bank and I join a line of three people waiting in front of me. Then, almost immediately two. This won't take long. One more to go and then it's my turn.

"How would you like the money, Kevin?" asks the friendly teller. Her name badge tells me her name is Wendy. I always think it's a shame they don't put their phone numbers on those badges as well.

"Dollar bills, please."

Rob and I thought small bills would be better and raise less suspicion when being spent. A 15-year-old with big bills lifts eyebrows.

Wendy is agonisingly slow and diligent when counting out the one-hundred-dollar bills and it's starting to irritate my frayed nerves further. I just want the money and to get out now.

As she counts, I'm recalling the story of this bank being robbed only a week ago. I wonder if Wendy was held at gunpoint; if she was looking down the barrel of a gun thinking a simple pull of his finger and it's all over. She seems very calm now.

"Buying yourself something nice?" Wendy asks with a cosmetician's smile.

Beer, food, some weed and a cheap room for the night most likely, are my thoughts.

"Uh…yeah, a little treat." I don't know what else to say.

"Seventy-eight, seventy-nine, nearly there—Oh, look, your dad's coming." She's still smiling like some sort of malfunctioning robot, breaking the rhythm of counting.

"Where was I— seventy-eight or seventy-nine?" Still smiling! Fer fucks…

"Please don't let on to my dad I'm here!"

"What?" Still smiling but with confusion flooding into her eyes.

"Can I just *please* have the money, I'm really in a hurry – the money's for a surprise present for my dad so, shhh… please," I say putting my finger up to my lips. The confusion in her eyes drains and the general dazzling blue emptiness returns to normal. I smile at her and she gives me a wink as she slides over the money as if we are doing a covert drug deal.

Nearly outside now and *he's* about to be served by Wendy also…

"Bye, Kevin. Have a nice day." In her excitement of being part of a covert plan, she forgot her lines in the instant, but I guess it seemed like she'd be abandoning a faith if she didn't say them before I left.

"Really?" I mutter, and then I run, once again throwing myself into the safety of Mark's van. Rob had seen my dad crossing the road and heading for the bank so in anticipation of me doing exactly what I did, he'd pulled up nearby, so I didn't have far to run.

*

The bank had been held at gunpoint by three gang members from Manitoba; the fourth was in the getaway van. The van didn't manage to get away, nor did the gang. The police arrived and seized their toy guns before they'd pocketed a dollar. We were all shocked but not terribly surprised when we heard about it and who the robbers were.

We first encountered the four a few months ago. They were in their late teens or early twenties, smoked weed and liked Frank Zappa. They were fun to hang out with and I guess we felt cool hanging out with older guys, even if they were a bunch of red necks from the prairies; in fact, maybe that made them even cooler. There was something a bit troubling about them though. Something that was hard to pinpoint, but a niggle, nonetheless. They're a bit too hardcore perhaps. Although they were only playing with replica guns, it was still unnerving and the menace in which they were played with, made us all uncomfortable. We are just a bunch of teenagers trying to figure out what the fuck life is all about. These guys seemed more like they've given up on life altogether and they live by their own rules. They carried an element of danger about them but it was devalued by their combined stupidity.

They had absurd names like Pugwash, Three-way and Spud. The fourth was Rusty; the self-appointed leader because he had been to prison and was considered the toughest. We were hanging out together one night by Cleveland dam which is an impressive sight and a popular tourist destination by day. At night, it's largely unoccupied and we were sitting around a picnic table drinking beer and getting high. The dam is one of those places that I sometimes go to by myself. I love to look over the precipice down the vertical hundreds of feet, watching the water roar off a ramp at the bottom of the dam into the flowing current of the Capilano River, momentarily ruffled and then continuing on, as if unperturbed by the preceding fall. It's thrilling to throw sizeable rocks, the size of footballs and watch them fly seemingly forever as they are propelled by the fierce flow of water; a strong reminder of our own fragility. I often wonder if other people contemplate death as often as I do. Death and our knowledge of its inevitability is the reason I question life itself being a gift. It's a mighty gift to be given only to be told right from the beginning that it's only temporary and it will be taken away again at any point, with or without warning. Yet we are programmed; almost drugged into reproducing and most of us will continue the cycle like hamsters in a wheel without asking the obvious and simple question, why? The other oddity to me is that I'm not even permitted to enjoy the gift I have been given in the way I wish. I am to be moulded into a version of the man who I have no wish to replicate and fit into a society/regime that seems alien to me.

I could hear the thunderous turbulence of the falling water as I walked, feeling very stoned towards the lookout point in the middle of the dam. I could also hear something else…

As I got closer, I could see that what I heard was Lisa getting fucked hard from behind by Rusty. He had bent her over the edge of the dam, pushing her head down to look into the deadly abyss below while he pounded her relentlessly. He stopped as soon as he saw me and pulled up his jeans quickly; nervously. Lisa was distraught.

"She wanted it," Rusty said over-enthusiastically, "she was fucken begging for it," as if to bolster his earlier comment.

"Are you okay?" I asked Lisa.

"Yeah, I'm okay, Kev. Can you take me home?" she asked and looked pleadingly at me.

"I'm telling you, man; she was begging me for it." Rusty looked defiant, eyes darting all over the place like a speed freak. He was still fiddling around with his fly, but his eyes were firmly fixed on mine as I made a lunge for him. He didn't have time to get his hands up to block my punch which had enough anger in it to produce the most satisfying crunching sound as my fist connected with his nose. He went down to the ground and I kicked him in the nose again until he laid down on the ground, sobbing – crying like a child. It's hard to imagine he was in prison if he can't take a punch from a teenager. It was the first time I had really connected a punch with true anger, and it wasn't until the adrenaline had dissipated that I noticed the pain in my right knuckles. A dull pleasant reminder that his face will be hurting a whole lot more than my hand.

"Let's just please go, Kev." Lisa let out a little sob as I put my arm around her. We left in the direction of her home. We walked for about half an hour without exchanging a word but never removing our arms from around each other. She looked at me in the eyes on her doorstep. Imploringly, she said,

"Please don't tell anyone about this, Kev," and she kissed me on the cheek and went inside.

None of us knows anything about Lisa's home life. In fact, most of us don't really talk a lot about our lives at home. It is a subject we're all happy to avoid for our reasons; real reasons. Not just teenage angst but we all share a deeper understanding of one another without words being exchanged. We aren't sure what was wrong with our lives and we don't know how to express the words, but we all understand each other's' pain. I hoped Lisa has someone she could turn to inside her house that night, but it's probably unlikely.

I told no-one. It was never talked about. I don't know if Lisa talked to anyone else, but I tried to push it to the back of my mind. I never saw or thought about any of those idiots again until they decided to execute their embarrassing bungled attempt at a bank robbery. I hope Lisa can have some peace in the knowledge she will probably never have to see her attacker again and that he'll probably not fare well behind bars.

Orange and black Halloween decorations are starting to fill shop windows. Soon, the smell of dead wet leaves and pumpkin pie will be here. It's one of my favourite times of the year. Suburban freshly-raked lawns to match their neighbours, provide the fuel for the numerous back yard bonfires across the neighbourhood. It's always a pleasant smell to me. We are in the pharmacy, looking for some aspirin. There's a sign on the wall with diagrams depicting the level of a man's fertility which can be assessed by putting the semen between a thumb and forefinger. When you pull the digits apart, the length of the semen before it snaps indicates the level of fertility. If it's buttery, thick and breaks, then apparently the chances of having children are slim but if it stretches, like bubble gum stuck to a shoe, then it's safer to cover up if you don't want kids.

I didn't know what kind of semen I had until an odd occurrence that happened in the summer. It was such an arousing encounter that I had to ride home on an uncomfortable racing saddle for about five miles with a throbbing erection being severely chaffed. As soon as I got home, I went straight for a bath and spent a good half an hour coaxing it to do something, *anything* that it's supposed to do to ease the aching in my balls. That night, it happened; and it freaked the living shit out of me. As soon as I felt a very strange sensation of something new rising, I panicked and let go. The next night, I didn't... and that has formed a fairly regular pattern since.

It's time to move from the ledge now. The rain is becoming more of a steady sleet and at this altitude, it won't be long before we're waking up to a foot of snow. As romantic as that sounds, we're not prepared for winter camping and we are all perpetually tired and never free of feeling damp. It's really time to either move on or give in. I'm certainly not ready to concede yet and neither are the rest. We're having our taste of freedom and we love it!

The motel isn't in the best neighbourhood. It's on Vancouver Eastside, but it is warm, dry; has a games room with a pool table and a heated outdoor pool. Most importantly, it has the owner on-site who turns a blind eye to us being there if we behave ourselves. He also turns the same eye many times a day and night for the working girls that are appreciative of his hourly rates for rooms one through six. We are in room seven.

School has started again so only Rob, Dennis and I are at the motel during the day. Rob and I have been expelled from school, mainly for underachieving, but being caught with both of our lockers lightly stocked with Columbian Gold marijuana during an impromptu police search on the last day before summer holidays didn't help. Dennis has been suspended for the first month for an incident that happened at the same time.

During a short film in English, Dennis fabricated one of his huge spitballs that he is infamous for in the school. We were watching a film that had captured my interest, about a man who was publicly hanged from a bridge for a crime he hadn't committed. During the film, Dennis launched the wet soggy mass of spit and paper in the direction of Scott. It was just harmless Tom foolery really but, unlike Dennis, his technique wasn't on form and rather than reaching his intended target, the ball flew off the side of his ruler that he used as a catapult, in the direction of Ms McPherson. She screamed as the offensive projectile stuck to her blouse right above her right breast. This, of course, caused the class to erupt with laughter, heightening Ms McPherson's embarrassment. She knew the culprit, and Dennis was immediately suspended. So, we find ourselves free of the mundanity of the education mill and learning about life in an hourly rate motel downtown.

I love Jayne. There is no doubt in my mind that I have very strong feelings for her but seeing the working girls and hearing them fucking next door is testing my loyalty. I still haven't had the pleasure of a woman fully, and knowing I'm surrounded by extremely sexy women who will do anything for the right price is making me very horny. In fact, the distraction is almost unbearable and the need to know what it feels like to be inside a woman is even more overwhelming than the usual constant yearning. Dennis is actively looking for some way to peep next door while trying to see if we can club together enough for an hour each. He has a particular interest in a slim blonde in flared faded jeans that pull in really tight over her butt to advertise her strong asset. The best part is, most of the customers only last a couple of minutes and occasionally, the girls will take a little time out in the pool. Although the three of us are extremely tempted to blow all our money on our neighbours' skills, we decide to be sensible. We don't have much and we don't know what's around the corner. The room is cheap, but we need to save what we have left. With this decision made, Dennis goes to the pool.

In the evening, after school and dinner at their homes, Mark turns up with his van and the rest of our friends. It looks like Mark and Donna are now permanently together. They seem happy together and complement each other. Mark is a little wild and unpredictable. All the kids at school give him room and never want to aggravate him because of his reputation. He's big and he likes a fight. Donna is so quiet that I don't think anyone knows anything about her except that she wants to travel the world. We only found that out because we all went to have our palms read, and she confided briefly in us because the psychic had said if she becomes an air hostess, she will die. I was told I will be rich, have a beautiful home and live to a ripe old age. Donna was genuinely upset by the prediction offered by the creases in her hand and was crying over her shattered dreams. Thankfully, the psychic was exposed as a fraud within the week, and Donna found solace in this but she remains a closed book. She's very shy and the only person she really speaks to is Mark. She doesn't really drink, or smoke weed, so never has the boosted courage to open up. We all love her though; we love each other. If someone wants to talk, any single one of us will listen, but nobody ever pries. We all know better than that.

We had asked if anyone could bring us some swimming stuff because, unlike Dennis, Rob and I are a little uncomfortable going to the pool in our underpants. I'm in a pair of Randy's oversized running shorts which, in my opinion, still look less ridiculous than a pair of purple Y fronts with an orange trim, which Dennis is dressed in. Randy is bigger than he looks. The drawstring on his shorts is barely long enough to secure them safely. The girls are all in bikinis and look every bit as sexy as the girls next door. My earlier thoughts of wayward straying, forgotten and my horniness has returned with a painful vigour that only a virgin teenager can feel. It's the first time I've seen Jayne in a bikini, and I have become transfixed. Her body is so perfectly proportioned and beautiful. A body to be proud of and worthy of admiration. Jayne is uncomfortable though and is sitting on the edge of the bed, arms folded beneath her bent torso; trying to hide as much flesh as possible. I am nervous to approach her because it all seems so different when she is barely dressed. She has drawstrings holding each side of her bikini bottom together in tidy bows and I can only think of how it would be to pull one open. Dennis is in the bathroom and Jayne asks him to throw out a towel. Rather than just pass her a towel, he does what is his impression of a stripper; pulling the towel unerotically between his legs and impersonating a stripper grinding on it as he thrusts his orange and purple pants towards Jayne's face. Dee giggles.

"Is it wrong that he's turning me on?"

"Yes, Dee, it's very wrong," says Jayne laughing.

Dennis ignores her and heads for the pool before us. I don't know why Dennis shies away from Dee. She looks really good in her tiny blue bikini. She's tanned, toned and very cute, with long, brunette, wavy hair and big brown eyes, which are following Dennis's pants out of the door. Dennis is not exactly having much success with women generally, so I'm perplexed by the relationship between them.

Jayne has wrapped herself in the motel's stiff white towel which is accentuating her summer tan and it looks like she's just stepped out of the shower. I imagine her naked under the towel and I realise that even though

Randy's shorts are loose-fitting, I'm starting to show evidence of arousal. I stick my hands in the pockets to push the fabric away from my growing situation, but the movement of my hands down there does nothing more than encouraging the problem. I'm at a loss as to what to do next and the only thing I can do is sit down on the other side of the bed from Jayne, facing the opposite direction. Jayne and I are sitting almost as if we are a mirror image; both trying to hide our modesties. The problem is getting awkward now and they are all getting up and making a move for the pool.

"I'm just going to roll one before I come," I say, trying to play it cool.

"Already ahead of you," says Rob, pulling a joint from his inside jacket pocket.

Fuck…

"Okay, I'll meet you there. I just need a piss." This seemed to work, and they all left… Except for Jayne.

"Not going for a swim?" I ask her.

"I'll wait for you," Jayne answers with a wry smile.

I am so nervous now; I don't know what I should do. Should I just sit here and hope that things return to normal in their own time; should I…

Jayne's body is behind me. I can feel her breasts on my back already, I feel her getting closer and closer until she has me in a tight embrace. She kisses my neck and strokes my hair. Long, thick, reddish-blond hair that I hate. One of her hands moves around to the front of my body and she is kneading my chest as she continues kissing my neck and back. What hope I ever had of losing my erection, long forgotten and now wholly appreciated. She pinches my nipple which sends an extraordinary tingling sensation cascading all the way down my body to my feet. I start to feel an excitement that is new to me as her hand moves slowly down the front of my body, stroking me; caressing lovingly; over my stomach, and down until her fingertips are touching the top of my shorts. I can't believe this is happening and I never want it to stop. Her touch makes me feel real and loved but at the same time, it's alien to me and I don't know how to respond. For me, love and sex are two different entities and I don't know how to combine my desire for Jayne with my utter love for her. I feel like I'm betraying her; if I cross this line, it will never be the same. I love everything about Jayne and I don't want to fuck it up. What if I'm crap? What if my cock is too small to satisfy her? What if I cum before we even get there? What if she hates me afterwards? Sex should be for the girls next door; it doesn't matter if that's fucked up.

For the first time in my life, I have the hand of another person on me. She is shy, inexperienced and nervous, but it's the best feeling I can ever remember having. She is stroking, giggling and playing with me and I am having a feeling so intense, it's euphoric. Pure lust now; and an animal desire to be inside Jayne makes me turn and kiss her passionately on the lips. She responds hungrily and I start to lean into her, and she slowly falls back onto the bed. I need to slow this down because I don't want it to be over too fast but at the same time, my carnal desire to fuck her is strong.

However strong my desire, it's overwhelmed by the high-pitched scream coming from just outside the door. It is a hideous sound; like a feral cat being violated and it sounds worryingly serious.

Quickly pulling up my shorts as Jayne dives under the covers, I head for the door. As I open it, I see all the outside security lighting is on and glaringly bright. Once my eyes adjusted, I can see Dennis standing in the spotlight, trying to pull his pants up whilst whimpering and holding his groin. I quickly go back in the room and tell Jayne to get out and get away. Quickly.

The motel owner is still in his office, but his gaze is fixed firmly on Dennis. Jayne slips out through the back window and I start flushing the weed.

This is Vancouver Eastside, so it takes no time for the police to arrive. Downtown Met cops.

The cuffing and stuffing are brutal. We daren't speak to each other on the ride to the downtown police station, as much as I am dying to know what the fuck is going on. I'm sitting in the back of a Met cruiser with two very unfriendly looking cops and I feel naked in only my shorts – Randy's shorts. Dennis is clearly in real agony and it doesn't help that he can't soothe his injury because he's cuffed.

At the station, we are treated very much as criminals. It is not what I had experienced in the last jail I was in. This time, the cell is locked. Dennis is in another cell at the other end of a large block. We have been purposely separated so we can't talk to each other.

"KEV!" Dennis shouts down the corridor separating at least twenty cells on each side.

"SHUT THE FUCK UP!" There is a guard. A fucking guard. And apparently, we are to remain quiet.

It's cold in here. I'm still in my shorts, there is no blanket; not even a mattress on the bed. Just bare, dangerous-looking rusty springs. The toilet smells of disinfectant but with an underlying permanent stench of old piss and vomit. I don't know how long I've been here, but it feels like at least a night and I still don't know why I'm here. The cops didn't even check for weed floating in the toilet and I was only trying to defend Dennis by saying he'd had too much to drink. The motel owner told the cops that we were together and that we must have broken in because we're too young to rent a room; the next thing, I'm downtown mixing it up with the local Hasting's Street winos in the drunk tank.

I hear the percussive jangling of keys and the rumble of a cell door sliding. It's not mine, but it *is* Dennis's. The guard is walking him through the security door into the police station.

Four hours later, he's still not back and I'm worried about him. Around another two hours pass and the guard comes to tell me that they're keeping me for twenty-four hours at the request of my father. Dennis has gone home.

"What the fuck. I don't even know what it is I've done." I sound truly perplexed.

"It's out of my hands, I'm afraid." I really do feel a little sympathy in his last two words.

I don't believe this.

"I'll tell you what I know," offered the guard, "your father was called to collect you, but he insisted on you staying the maximum length of time without charging you."

"I haven't done anything."

Almost sounding defeated now.

"We know about the motel owner and his side-lines. We know he's renting out rooms to juveniles and we know you didn't break-in."

"So, let me go."

"Because he is pressing charges, we are obliged to question you and your friend. Because you are wanted for questioning, we can hold you here. We were prepared to release you but your father has asked for us to keep you."

I'm not surprised by this. I'm also slightly relieved, and now that I have a nicer, cleaner cell with a mattress on the bed, I'm not terribly unhappy and it's nice to drift off into a much-needed deep sleep.

I must have slept for many hours and my peace is abruptly, almost aggressively interrupted by the unlocking and rolling of the cell door.

"Your dad's here to get you." The guard is ushering me out of my cell as he speaks.

Randy's shorts are long gone and I'm wearing jailhouse overalls as I'm taken through to meet my dad for the first time in over three weeks. He doesn't look pleased or relieved to see me, but I am pleased to see my brother, Colin, with him.

I love my brother. He's different, quirky, nervous as fuck all the time and completely uncoordinated but he's a perfect big brother. He's fourteen years older than me and has the most impressive hardcore pornography collection any fifteen-year-old could hope to have access to. He lives with us now. He hasn't always; in fact, he left home when I was seven and we have only reunited six months ago. It wasn't planned for him to leave home. We were living in England at the time and Colin went on a field trip with his agricultural college to Manitoba, he met up with his old friends in Winnipeg and we never saw him again for seven years. He turned up at our house in Vancouver in the coolest, beat-up old red Ambassador convertible (a huge American tank of a car) with the tatty white roof down. He told us that he lost the exhaust somewhere in Saskatchewan and that he was burning more oil than petrol. I was so excited to see him, and I couldn't wait to go for a spin in his Ambassador. However, what's cool and exciting for me isn't reflected in my father's eyes and the Ambassador was towed and scrapped before I even sat in it.

Colin was almost as dilapidated as his car when he first arrived; long, unwashed straggly hair that was thinning out on top to show a shiny red sunburnt crown. His beard was nicotine-stained and carried remnants of an old meal; probably a service station hot dog. His glasses only had one arm and one lens, both of which were held together with a grubby plaster, and when he smiled, it was slightly reminiscent of Stonehenge, with more black voids than teeth. His shoes had holes in the soles and the toes which revealed his bare feet because his socks were essentially non-existent. He had on a button-down shirt that was probably quite expensive a couple of decades ago and I should imagine it was bought at the same second-hand shop as his stay press trousers. He smelt like he hadn't bathed in weeks and if he were a stranger in the street, I would probably have given him more room than normal. But he's my brother and I couldn't contain my excitement at his return and I ran to him and hugged him, and it felt good to have him hug me back.

Colin had it worse than me. He's nearly thirty years old now and still fears and tries to appease our dad. It was not long before he went on his college trip when an argument erupted at the dinner table between Dad and Colin. My dad's fist flew past my head with tremendous aggression to connect with my brother's nose. He fell, headfirst onto a glass-topped coffee table, breaking it into a thousand pieces with his head. Colin was pleading for my dad to stop and as my mum led me upstairs to my room, I could hear the continued beating and cries from Colin. That was when I started to see my dad in a light that was dimmer than my previous adoration of him. It was soon after then that Colin left home. My dad went to pick him up from his trip to Canada and he wasn't there. He simply didn't return and it was never discussed. I missed him terribly and wished, almost daily that he would come back.

I can see it's raining outside and by the way people are dressed, I'm assuming it's cold as well. Thankfully, the police let me wear the jailhouse overalls home on the condition that they were returned and I was grateful for this, considering I was arrested wearing swimming shorts. The drive home was long and made even longer by hitting rush hour traffic. Although I love Colin, he does tend to still try and make my dad approve of him, so he begins laying into me about going off the rails and that I need to get my act together. I simply stay quiet and say nothing as we slowly creep through downtown traffic. My father has said nothing at all to either of us during the entire journey so far and I break the silence:

"What happened to Dennis, is he okay?"

"You have bigger concerns than Dennis." The words were threatening; menacing even, and Colin tried to give me a reassuring look, but it didn't work. I know I'm in deep shit, I just don't know how deep yet.

"Col, do you know what happened?"

"I don't, Kev, sorry." I believe him. He doesn't really know much about my friends apart from what my dad tells him, so I will have to try and find out myself somehow what happened to Dennis; and why I spent a small part of my life in a drunk tank.

Pulling into the drive, I feel a little as though I'm an imposter arriving at my own home, and the moment I step through the door, Dad reinforces the feeling by picking up a walking stick that he uses for walking the dog and whacks me really fucken hard, right behind both knees, making me buckle and fall. Then he hauls me up and does it again… and again. I'm in intense pain and it feels like some serious damage has been done to my legs, and then the walking stick comes down hard on my head. I am momentarily stunned and very close to being unconscious but at least he seems to have finished with me for now. One thing is for certain: I'm not staying around to see what's coming next. I haven't even seen my mum yet but I hear her preparing dinner in the kitchen as if all is fine in the world and we will all sit down to a nice family meal and discuss our days. Colin looks at me sympathetically but is too frightened to do anything and I don't blame him.

"You have a choice. You can either smarten up, obey the rules of the house, or you can leave and never come back. If you walk out that door now, you will never be welcome in this home again."

It is a stark warning, considering I have no money and nowhere to go, but I open the door, turn to face him and simply say, "Fuck you!"

As I limp painfully away from my family home, Colin runs after me, pleading with me not to go. Telling me that things will get better if I just do as I'm told.

"I've got this, Col. I'll be okay. I just can't live with him anymore and I would rather just go. I'll call you bro and do yourself a favour and get the fuck out too."

With no money, battered, painful legs, a splitting headache and still in the jailhouse overalls, I head in the direction of Dennis's house.

The feeling of abandonment is strong; it hurts to be flung from my nest that I've only known so far in my life. Even if I didn't like it there, it was something that has always been there wherever we were in the world. The anger, frustration and adrenaline are still strong, but a wave of realisation and fear is creeping in. I'm homeless, penniless and although I'm living in the most temperate climate in Canada, the prospect of winter around the corner is just another thought that is flying around my confused and frightened mind. I stop. I'm midway between home and Dennis's house and I feel as though the next step I take in either direction, will be the final step of acceptance. I accept my father's rules and become a replica of my brother or I continue to walk away and try to figure this life out by myself. I'm on the verge of tears, I'm shaking not only from the cold, and I feel bile rising in my throat as I take the final step away from my family.

Chapter Three

It's late in the evening and the day is fading into a crisp autumnal night. At least the relentless rain has stopped momentarily but I am still soaked through to the skin. Dennis's house is in darkness. It's too early for them to be in bed already, so I'm assuming they've gone out for the evening. His parents own a restaurant downtown and sometimes the whole family are working there, so it could be that they won't be home for some time. I walk around the house and let myself in through the side gate, which is always unlocked, around the covered outdoor pool and head for the pool house which is also unlocked. There is no heating in the pool house, but at least it's dry. It also has various items of clothing lying around which have been discarded and forgotten after many pool parties. A Frank Zappa T-shirt that is most likely Dennis's is chosen, along with a pair of jeans that were a little loose fitting and frayed but still wholly better than my overalls. I still had my own trainers that I am trying to dry out without much success. I put them next to the pump for the pool which is constantly whirring away with periodic gurgling noises. I lay down on a sun lounger and cover myself with about half a dozen towels which slowly start to help warming me up… and I feel myself drifting away into an uncomfortable slumber.

I wake up shivering and shaken from a dream where I was falling to my certain death from a great height, and I see that lights are on in the house. I don't know what time it is but I'm guessing it's late; too late to ring the bell. Dennis's bedroom light is on and I see a shadow moving behind the curtain, so I pick up a pebble from the garden and gently lob it to his window. The first one misses and lands in the gutter but the second one catches his attention by finding its way through the narrowest of gaps in a slightly opened window, to hit a bell on top of his Noddy and Big Ears alarm clock. He nearly soiled his seemingly only pair of purple underpants as he jumped to the window to see me. He nods, smiles and points to the pool house, indicating we'll meet there.

Dennis hugs me hard and says sorry about ten times in a row. I don't blame Dennis for anything and I let him know that he owes me nothing other than an explanation. I genuinely want to know what the fuck happened while I was about to lose my virginity to the most beautiful woman in the world.

"We were playing truth or dare in the pool," he tells me. I already have a feeling I know where this is going now because Dennis will have chosen a dare over a truth; he always does.

"Rob dared me to put my cock through the letterbox of room six."

Dennis would do this without a second thought. It's a lame dare for Dennis, considering the things he does for fun anyway. I'm sure he would have tried his chances that way voluntarily had he thought of it first.

"It's really embarrassing, Kev, and I'm so sorry you got the worst of it. I did the dare and I panicked as soon as I did it and the fucken letterbox is one of those spring-loaded things. I couldn't pull the fucker back out again and the girl in the room caught sight of it."

At this point, I can't stop smiling which is slowly turning to an uncontrollable laugh.

"It's not fucken funny, you asshole."

This just makes me laugh even more.

"So, what happened then?" Still chuckling.

"The stupid cow used her lighter and burnt the shit out of my bell end and then I ripped the shit out of it as I yanked it from the letterbox. I'm tellin' you, man, it hurts like fuck."

My stomach and sides hurt from laughing so hard and Dennis is laughing at the absurdity of it all as well.

"What are you doing here anyway, Kev?" Dennis asks in between still chuckling and groaning in discomfort.

"The old man gave me a choice; stay or leave, so I left."

"Fuck. What are you going to do? Where are you going to live?"

"I was hoping I could stay here for the night if that's okay with you."

"Yeah, of course. The folks are in bed now so come up and sleep in my room. No trying to sneak in on Cora though."

He's grinning his huge roguish face at me because he knows I fancy his sister – fancied her – before I fell in love with Jayne. She's much older than her twin brothers... and me, and she is ridiculously hot. We all fancy her, but we hardly ever see her. She's always working at the restaurant or dating another dick with a cheap wannabe muscle car. She prefers to remain very aloof from her brothers' friends, and that makes her even more desirable. I would never sneak in on her though because she terrifies me.

"Ha! Yeah, no worries. I'd prefer to remain in one piece, thanks," I say, but I still can't stop myself from imagining Cora in bed with one of those skimpy see through things that I've seen in the lingerie sections of catalogues as we walk past her room. I wonder if women masturbate as well.

The thought of going into a warm home is inviting and has reminded me that I'm still frozen to the bone, so I don't hesitate in accepting his offer. In his room, there are more pairs of purple and orange Y fronts scattered on the floor, so at least I know he does at least rotate them.

"I've gotta piss," Dennis announces.

"Okay, buddy. Thanks for the info."

"Actually, it's not really that okay and I've been putting it off for the best part of the day and I've drunk fuck all to avoid it. It burns like I'm pissing vinegar with bits of broken glass in it."

This makes me visibly wince and grab my own groin protectively. It also puts the pain in my legs and head into a different perspective. Dennis does make a rod for his own back, but I can't help feeling sorry for him.

When Dennis comes back, he has a sleeping bag for me and he gives me one of his two pillows with which I make myself a makeshift bed on the floor, by the side of Dennis's bed. I'm warm, comfortable and after a bit of banter and forced competitive farting, followed by inevitable infantile giggles, I soon feel myself drifting off to sleep. The former brief giggles not diffusing the hollow ache of uncertainty and insecurity that's always there, especially just before I fall asleep.

The morning comes soon enough and I am surprised to feel the sun on my face which is shining through a six-inch-wide gap in the curtains. As I move to get up to open the curtains further, my mind is returned to the sequence of the events of the prior day by very sore and bruised legs. It reminds me of the time when I was given six of the best at a very tough all boy's school in the industrial heart of an already very industrial Birmingham in England. Six of the best were three whacks across the palms of both hands with a four-foot-long cane, rendering them useless to do any writing or any other schoolwork for a week. I hope this pain will subside sooner, but instinctively, I know it will take time to heal. As I push the curtains apart to let the sunlight in, Dennis stirs, and his door opens at the same time. His mum looks momentarily surprised to see me there but is pleasant. She's one of those middle-aged Mediterranean women that are still exotically attractive but just on the cusp of starting to look old. She carries herself with confidence and grace, and always seems composed and beautiful.

"Oh, hi, Kev, I didn't know you were here." She puts down a cup of steaming hot coffee on Dennis's bedside table and immediately asks if I would like one too.

"I'd love one, please. I'll come down and help you." Dennis has fallen back to sleep and I doubt his coffee will be drunk, at least not while it's still hot. I hadn't taken off the borrowed jeans and Zappa shirt, so I slipped out of the sleeping bag and went downstairs to help Dennis's mum. They're Yugoslavian immigrants, restaurateurs and the smell of good coffee drifting through the house is welcoming. She pours me a cup, sets it down on the breakfast bar and asks if I would like something to eat. I can see she's in a hurry and I know that she and Dennis's dad work pretty much all the time, so I tell her not to worry and I'll get something myself when Dennis gets up. My parents and Dennis's parents have never met but I know they know about my father and they have never approved of his ways or ideals, so she doesn't need to ask why I'm there and she doesn't do or say anything to make me feel unwelcome.

"It'll literally take me five minutes to rustle up some scrambled eggs," she says, already reaching for the fridge.

It might be because my recent meals have been of drunk tank quality and that I missed dinner last night, but these are the best scrambled eggs I have ever tasted and I express my real gratitude as Dennis's mum leaves for another long day in the restaurant. Dennis still hasn't stirred, so I pour myself another cup of coffee from the percolator and sit down on the couch. Next to me is an out of date newspaper with the cover story being about the recent bank robbery. Apparently, the gang of Manitoban losers have a long list of crimes and they have been on the run for many months. It doesn't look like we'll be seeing them for a very long time on our streets again.

For a big guy, Dennis is very quiet and I had no idea he was behind me until he started coughing up a loose bit of morning phlegm from his premature smoker's lungs. He is still in nothing but purple Y fronts and is drinking his now cold coffee as he sits down next to me and even though his hair is too short to be bed ruffled, he still looks half asleep and dazed by the reality of morning.

"What's the plan for the day, big guy?" he asks as he's rolling up his first joint for the day.

It's a question I have no idea how to answer. If I had money, I would suggest going bowling or to the pool hall.

"I think I need to get a job," I answer and to be honest, the idea gives me a rush of excitement. A true independence. My own money which I've earned, and I can do as I wish with it.

"I could ask my mum and dad if they need help at the restaurant if you like."

This is a good offer and I know they are always busy and need help. Dennis hands me the paper I was reading and points to an ad looking for someone to work part-time in a local hardware rental shop. I know the shop well, it's in the village one street over from my father's practice.

Within two hours of reading the ad, I'm in a tiny room at the back of the shop beginning my shift. My job is to wash the dishes that are rented out for large dinner parties for the North and West Vancouver residents. I don't mind it, it's a job and most of the customers send back the dishes already washed so I just load them into a dishwasher, dry them and load them back into boxes ready for the next party.

John is my boss. He's not the owner but he runs this shop. The main shop is about four miles away in West Vancouver and the owner spends most of his time there. I haven't met him yet but John says he's a good guy. A straight talker who takes no shit and rewards well for hard work. The pay is crap but it's not as though I'm in a strong position to pick and choose my employment. John has a lot of coffee breaks and always goes into the back alley to smoke a cigarette with his coffee. To be honest, he could do the dishes himself in the amount of time he spends drinking coffee but I'm grateful for his addictions because I need this job. The shop has a narrow frontage but is very long from front to back and is packed with all kinds of tools from screwdrivers to heavy-duty building equipment, and there is a section dedicated to gardening with the latest chainsaws, petrol-driven rotor tillers and in the corner, there is a huge rig that looks suitable for drilling for oil but John tells me it's for making holes in the ground for fence posts. It's Monday and the busiest day for washing dishes after the weekend parties and weddings. The last dishwasher walked out without warning a few days ago and apparently, John has been too busy to keep on top of the dishes, so as I'm battling my way through the backlog, more and more boxes of dishes are brought through, never allowing me to feel like I'm making any headway.

"Smoke?" asks John, offering me one of his Lucky Strikes.

"Yeah, I'd love one. Thanks."

"The boss doesn't like us smoking in the shop, so we have to go out back," he says, already walking in the direction of the back door. It only seemed a few minutes since he was out there the last time, but I'm quite happy to follow him.

When we get outside, he gives me a cigarette and as I take it out of the packet, I see a few ready-rolled joints in there.

"Shall we spark one of these up?" I ask looking at the joints.

"Sure, if you like. Weed or hash?" he asks.

"I've never tried hash," I tell him and he starts telling me about its benefits as he's lighting it up.

Hash tastes very different. It almost has a slight chemical taste to it, either way, it has certainly given me quite the buzz from only one toke, so I take a couple more and hand the joint back to John.

John seems cool. We're living in a time of change and even though the Canadian music scene has been changing from a steady diet of west coast American rock and Rush to a mix of new wave and disco, John is clearly an ardent rocker, with frayed jeans, biker boots, white T-shirt and a black leather jacket; long, dark-brown hair that is a good six inches below his shoulders and a little tuft of facial hair growing just below his bottom lip. I'd say he's in his late twenties but still struggling with having to grow up into adulthood.

"Are you into Zappa by any chance?" It's the tuft of facial hair that prompted me to ask him because it's Frank Zappa's latest look on his new album cover.

"Fuck yeah, man. Zappa rules. He's coming to Vancouver next year," he announces excitedly.

Of course, I knew this, and like everyone else, I'm waiting for the release of the tickets which will be sold out within minutes. I've been into Zappa for a while now and whenever I mentioned his name before the release of Joe's Garage, nobody knew who I was talking about, but this latest album of his has caught the attention of many Canadians; enough to make him come to Vancouver and I will surely be there.

We finish the joint and go back into the shop. I can honestly say that I've never felt so high and the task of the boxing up crockery and cutlery takes on a whole new perspective as John and I start to sing in unison the lyrics to Catholic Girls.

"Can I use the phone, John?"

"Local?" he asks. To be honest, I don't think he really cares.

"Yeah, I just need to call a friend down the road."

I have been wanting to call Rob since I left home but haven't had the chance yet. I filled him in on a few details of the past couple of days briefly and he said he would meet me after work. I asked him if my father had been in contact with him, which he hadn't, so it looks like he's given up all hope of me conforming to his regime. This leaves me feeling both free and oddly disappointed, I suppose, like with every argument, I'd hoped he would come around to my way of thinking and respect that I have my own views at least a little. This is never the case though. Opinions of people he regards as lesser beings than him are swiftly discarded as liberal rubbish and should never be talked about in his house. I have been severely chastised for using the word sex at the dinner table, even if it was used in the context of referring to the opposite sex. *How does Colin accept this without question*? From day one, Colin has felt the pressure to be number one at everything. If he didn't stand out as the best in every situation, he was simply punished and reminded constantly of how disappointing and useless he is as a son. Consequently, Colin just stopped believing in himself and thinks everything our dad says is right. Sex is considered a filthy thing for my dad and sex before marriage is just totally unacceptable. So, although he's only a few days away from his thirtieth birthday, my brother has still not had the pleasure of intimacy with a woman… or (in my father's eye) God forbid, a man.

The day passes quickly and I've enjoyed my first day of employment. John closes the shop at exactly five in the evening and heads out into the back alley where he has his custom dodge van parked. It's a nice-looking van; jet-black with a custom paint job of flames behind the front wheel arches, wide chrome wheels, chrome thrush mufflers and small bubble tinted windows near the back on both sides. I haven't seen the inside apart from a chrome chain steering wheel that can't be more than six inches in diameter, but I bet it's nice. He offers me a ride home and I'm glad I'm spared the awkwardness of having to explain that I presently don't have one, as Rob's lanky shape comes walking towards us.

"See ya tomorrow, washer upper," John laughs as he climbs into his van and starts it up. It sounds as good as it looks.

"Nice Van," Rob says as he hands me fifty bucks.

"What's this?"

"It's what's leftover of our funds. I reckon your need is greater than mine right now."

I am extremely grateful for the unexpected money which will see me through to payday at the end of the week and I invite Rob for a Chinese dinner in the *café* around the corner.

"Donna's gone." It's the first thing Rob says as we sit down.

"Gone?"

"Just disappeared. Mark is going fucken crazy. He's calling her every five minutes and has come very close to beating her door down, but nobody is answering... it's totally weird. He's apparently in trouble at school as well because he's beating the crap out of anyone who knows her to find out where she is."

"Ha, good ole' Mark and his diplomacy."

The last time we were in this restaurant we were kicked out because of Dennis so I'm glad they didn't recognise us. To be fair, it was Randy really. When Dennis had gone to the toilet, Randy took off the lid to the glass sugar dispenser, laid a serviette over the top on which he piled up a good few spoonsful of salt and then screwed the top back on again. When Dennis took a gulp of his coffee that would normally have been heavily sweetened, he immediately spat the sour contents all over the owner's daughter who was politely serving us some dumplings. To be honest, I really felt sorry for her. She just looked so awkward and clearly embarrassed. Because we all knew it was a successful practical joke played on Dennis, we couldn't contain our laughter which made me feel even more guilty. The owner was furious with all of us equally and had no reservations in manhandling us all out of his restaurant, and I don't know why Dennis would think the situation would improve by singing *Ying tong iddle I po* in a Chinese accent as we were removed.

Finishing up our sweet and sour pork, egg fried rice and two cans of Coke, I quickly pay the bill and we start walking the ten-minute walk to Mark's house.

Doorsteps are decorated with deftly carved pumpkins lit by candles on the inside, giving a lantern-lit romantic feel to the streets; much more so than the intended spooky atmosphere. The carboard ghouls at doors, designed to scare demons away, in fact, do the exact opposite and any doorstep displaying even the weakest attempts at decoration are considered to be participating in the custom and should therefore have ample sweets on offer. It's one of the fun times of the year with its own personal character and nostalgia attached to it; like Christmas and Easter. Historically, it's one of the times of the year my father lets his guard down and becomes momentarily fun; likeable in a way... so very likeable it's convincing and hoped it will last. It's like he gives himself brief holidays throughout every year from being an arsehole the rest of the time. I expect he and mum will be getting ready soon for the Halloween ball that his Rotary club put on every year. A flamboyant masquerade ball. He'll be going with that Japanese couple whose names I can never remember; actually, I have never really understood them when they've introduced themselves, so I've just let it go. Whenever my dad mentions him or introduces him to anyone (his wife is very secondary), it's clear that his pronunciation is off by the reflex wince and the following bigger wince when my dad immediately follows up the introduction with an insight into his career as the first violinist of the Vancouver Symphony Orchestra. An achievement worthy of my father's admiration and sycophancy.

Soon, the kids in the neighbourhood will be stuffing their faces with an assortment of sweets and chocolates collected from the annual door-to-door scavenge on the last day of October. It's a strange custom but I like it and it doesn't seem so long ago that I was collecting my own arsenal of candy.

Mark really isn't in a good way and his mum is worried about him. He's pacing up and down the living room in his house like a lunatic in an asylum. His emotions are clearly a mix of anger, sorrow and there is an element of fear too. His knuckles are scuffed and look sore from his fights at school and I can't help feeling sorry for his innocent victims. His face is an angry shade of red which makes his shortish light blond hair look even lighter, he's shaking through the mix of emotions out of his control and he's clearly completely at a loss as to what to do next. Rob and I have no idea either. The only thing we are here to do is to offer some support. We don't have answers; which Mark is only looking for.

He leads us down into the basement where he has his chilling room. It's a part finished basement and Mark has thrown in a bunch of bean bags, an old television set and a small fridge which he always keeps stocked with beer. Rob sits in one of the bean bags and rolls a quick joint.

"Light up, sit down and let's work this shit out," Rob says handing Mark the joint to light up.

Mark gets irritated by people asking for a beer and prefers us to just help ourselves, so I grab a cold Molson, flick the cap off with my lighter and we all start to relax a little, although Mark is restless; agitated.

"When was the last time you saw her?" Rob asks.

"Two nights ago, but we arranged to meet after school yesterday and she didn't turn up. It's not like her, so I asked around and nobody's seen her for two days." Mark's rubbing his knuckles as he speaks.

"And there's nobody at her house? Maybe we should try again and see if someone's home now," I say. I doubt the situation has changed but I can't think of another suggestion to seem as though we're doing something to help.

Mark always drives fast and hard in his old van but now that he's pumped full of alien emotions, he's out of control; not stopping at stop signs, running red lights, honking and hurling abuse at anyone who gets in his way. Dennis's house is on the way to Donna's and I want to ask if we can call in quickly so I can update him on what's happening but I'm getting the feeling Mark isn't interested in a social house call, so I keep quiet.

"Get that piece of shit Buick out of my way, you decrepit old cunt," Mark shouts out of his window at a perfectly innocent driver waiting at a red light.

In fact, it isn't a single decrepit old driver. It's a group of three men in their twenties and the driver just flipped Mark the finger.

At the best of times, giving Mark the finger is like a red flag to a bull and Rob and I groan when Mark flings his door open and struts, fists clenched towards the Buick. Mark walks up to the car as we sit in the van to see how it will unfold. It's quite clear how it will unfold but we both prefer not to get involved in punch ups if we can avoid it. I don't avoid fights; I just don't particularly like them.

Mark opens the driver's door, grabs the man by his long hair and hauls him into the street, punches him twice hard in the face at the same time telling him to get the fuck out of the way. As Mark is walking back to us, the man he punched is following him and the two other passengers get out of the car and follow too.

At this point, Rob and I have a simple choice: we can jump in and help Mark in a situation that neither of us would have caused just out of simple loyalty to a friend, or we can keep the fuck out of it, stay safe and avoid unnecessary injury or even possible arrest and let Mark deal with his own consequences.

My beaten legs from the day before hurt as Rob and I run towards the messy scrum of men and flailing fists. Simultaneously, we launch ourselves into the fray and I manage to elbow one of the three strangers in the eye as I land on top of the two men who have Mark pinned to the road. I wind myself when I land, and I roll off the pile of fighting bodies to momentarily recover which unfortunately gives the man I elbowed the opportunity to kick me hard right on my bruised legs. This might not end well for us and my feeling is confirmed when the same boot that kicked me on the back of the legs has just connected very hard with my balls. I don't even have time to register the pain before the second kick comes in. Then, I feel the pain. It feels like my balls have imploded in on themselves and an excruciating, ringing, throbbing intense ache radiates through my entire torso and I feel vomit rising rapidly; like the pain is flushing my system out. This time, I'm happy to hear sirens in the distance because the three men run off, get in their car and speed off. I'm still writhing in agony and puking when Mark and Rob haul me to the van and throw me unceremoniously in the back. Mark gets behind the wheel and floors it, wheels spinning enough to spew burning rubber smoke into the faces of bemused onlookers.

"You okay, Kev?" asks Mark.

Am I okay? I've just had, what felt like some substantial boots send my family jewels to a region of my body that might need to be surgically removed.

"No! I'm fucking not okay, you oversized punchy asshole."

There's a momentary silence. Then Mark starts to laugh, which starts Rob laughing. I'm still holding my very sore balls as I turn to look at them both. They are pretty beaten up and the laughing is making it more painful for them.

"Assholes."

This just makes them laugh more and now that my pain is subsiding a little, I begin to laugh with them, until the three of us are wheezing, coughing and crying with laughter, as Mark continues on his way to Donna's house.

I know we're close even without looking because Mark always likes to deliberately slide the back end of the van around the hairpin bend just before her house; screeching the tyres and burning more rubber.

"A light's on," Mark says excitedly, accelerating towards the destination when most people would be slowing down.

"I don't see a light," Rob says.

"Me neither," I say. There isn't a light on. It's pitch black.

"I'm telling you, there was a light on; in Donna's room." Mark is adamant as he slams on the brakes and skids skilfully to an abrupt stop right up against the curb outside the house. Rob and I are still getting ready to leave the van as Mark's already halfway up the drive and he's ringing the bell before we close the doors. My legs are stiffening up as they slowly heal and my bollocks feel like a duffel bag carrying two hand grenades about to blow, so my progress up the driveway is slow. Nobody's answering the door which isn't surprising because regardless of Mark seeing a light on, the place is in complete darkness. I think Mark mistook the house in his optimism. He keeps ringing the bell and banging on the door. Each time holding the bell button longer and banging on the door harder.

"Let's take a look round the back." Rob's already walking around the side of the house as he's saying the words.

The back yard is lit by the dim glow of orange suburban lights so it's easy to negotiate the garden furniture which has been stacked neatly against the side of the house in preparation for the coming winter. Rob tries the back door and all of us are surprised to find it unlocked. If someone is home, why won't they answer the door? Nobody goes out and leaves their house unlocked in North Vancouver anymore.

"Hello?" I don't know why, but this makes me snigger when Rob calls out the words.

"Fuck hello!" says Mark as he barges past Rob.

"Donna? Are you in here?"

Mark turns on the kitchen light and that's when we all see the mess. Contents of the kitchen cupboards have been tossed out all over the place and there is broken crockery all over the floor. Mark quickly dashes to the living room and turns the light on to reveal a similar situation. In the hallway, I can see the television set that should be in the living room along with a brand-new stacking stereo system put together by the bottom of the stairs.

"What the f—"

"Shh. They're being robbed." I whisper. "And I reckon the fuckers must still be here. Turn off the light."

The private joke I shared with myself earlier about this seeming like a corny horror movie is turning into an uncomfortable reality, and in real life, it's really not quite so amusing. I now believe Mark did see a light on, but it wasn't who he thought it was. It wasn't Donna; it was an unwelcome stranger, or strangers invading Donna's home. Again, my thoughts are drawn to the cliché of thrillers, and the obvious thing to do is get the fuck out, but when you're in the situation and it has personal value to you, it's not so clear cut; plus, I have no idea where the imposters might be now and we might walk straight into them while trying to escape them.

"Fuck this." Mark walks over to the wall and turns on the lights, then he goes marching through every room in the house doing the same, as we tentatively follow behind. The house looks unoccupied and Donna's window is wide open. It's an easy escape from there onto the garage roof below and then off into the night. The burglars are long gone. They've probably managed to stash some small swag in their pockets but at least we saved a television and stereo from being lifted.

"We better leave...like now," I say to the others.

"Don't you think we should call the cops? It *is* our friend's house," Rob answers.

"It's a nice gesture, Rob, but our fingerprints are all over this place and I doubt the burglars left any behind."

Mr T is temporarily holding back on pressing any charges for my earlier mishaps but I'm close to being fingerprinted and I don't want this being added to the list.

"Fuck. I didn't even think about that."

"When you're a gnat's cock away from going to juvey hall it plays on your mind."

"You're not going to Juvey, Kev. You've done fuck all," Mark offers positively.

"Tell that to Mr T, and who the fuck knows what mood he will be in tomorrow... or the day after."

"He really doesn't like you trying to tap Jayne's ass, does he?"

Even though I would have preferred Mark to have chosen the words a little more respectfully, he's right. Mr T hates that I'm dating his daughter; passionately!

"Shh." Rob puts his hand up.

Sirens in the distance. It's probably nothing to do with us but it motions us to get moving. The three of us are sitting in the front of Mark's van now waiting for him to finish fumbling in his pockets for his keys. Worryingly, the sirens are getting closer.

"I can't find my keys. I must have dropped them somewhere." Mark is opening his door to go and look, as the sirens get louder. Rob and I are out also studying the ground and when we see the flashing blue and red lights of the police car rebounding off the houses in the vicinity, we all simultaneously flee in our own directions.

I painfully haul myself over the low fence at the end of Donna's back yard, being very careful not to injure myself further; especially trying to avoid aggravating current impairments. There is about thirty feet of mature Spruce woodland between the fence and a small creek; one of the many mountain tributaries that flow into the Capilano River.

*

I was looking after the neighbour's three kids for a day while their parents had to attend an all-day seminar. We all soon got bored hanging around the house, so I took them up this same creek trying to catch crayfish and rainbow trout. It turned out to be a memorable outdoor adventure for all of us because the moment we had finished building a lean-to bivouac (That somehow the four of us had managed to squeeze in to), its strength was tested by an earth tremor. It was only small, but it still shook the kids up; me too. Then a bang, followed by what can only be described as a wave; like one end of the earth had been lifted and shaken like a quick flick of a duvet. As the wave passed under us, the whole ground thundered and shuddered. Although I was supposed to be the guardian of the three kids, I felt completely helpless; vulnerable to an ungovernable energy. Nobody was hurt and I complimented the boys on their building work. Shaken and all a little deterred, we headed home. I don't know about them, but I was hoping the big one wasn't on its way right then. Geologically speaking, this part of North America is pretty fucked and it's more than likely that Vancouver Island will drop off into the Pacific Ocean at some point, along with a large chunk of the west coast of Canada. I suppose it's the trade-off for living in paradise; a very long game of Russian Roulette for being able to ski in the morning and sail in the afternoon. Vancouver *is* a paradise and my life is slowly returning to colour after living in England for six years. The weather was grey there but my memories are a deeper shade than the ever-attending clouds and fog; more like a graphite smudge trying to block out a stupid answer on a school test. It's a time I prefer to try and forget about and hopefully, one day, it will all go away from all memory and the grey will be whitewashed over and painted with bright and different colours.

Reading about the earthquake in the newspaper the next day told me that according to the Richter measurement, it was only classed as a small quake – nothing more than a tremor really. Earthquakes are commonplace here and we have all been taught what to do and have had regular drills at school in preparation for one. The key message was always not to panic. In the event, it was all too shocking and bemusing to panic and it felt as though it had been a bit more like a free ride at a fairground; had it continued, I would have liked to get off though. The only difference being; none of us was sure if it was merely a prequel to something bigger.

*

I'm still not certain the police were heading for us and I don't feel as though I'm being pursued, so I'm in no panic as I accustom myself to the woods and creek. Although it's dark, the city glow gives me enough light which is an odd sensation when I'm walking towards a bivouac in a forest. The temporary shelter, if anything is left of it, is only about a minute away, downstream and as soon as I reach that, there is a simple path to follow which will bring me out on the road by the side of the school, not too far from the cave. Once there, it's a bit of a hike to Denny's, but that's the ultimate destination. It's pretty near the top of our list of rules: if we get split up for any reason at any time; meet at Denny's.

It's busy at the diner and I'm scanning the heads looking for two that I recognise. Unexpectedly, I see what I'm sure is the back of Dennis's head. Dennis has very short hair which defies the trend, so it stands out. Once I see him, he turns his head slightly to look out of the window, I see him taking a draw on his cigarette in his unmistakable style. Dennis started smoking while he was in elementary school, which earned him the nickname, Nicfit, among his peers at the time. If anyone calls him by that name now, it's basically an invitation to receive a good hiding. He still hangs onto the old habits of exaggerating every step of the smoking process; pulling the cigarette aggressively away from his lips, his hand moving as if he's waving someone beneath him away. He inhales deeply and loudly to show that he's a real smoker and not one that just sucks it in their mouth and quickly puffs all the offensive smoke away. He holds in the smoke longer than usual and without exception, exhales through his nostrils.

I flick his ear as I walk up to him and ask if anyone is occupying the other seats…

"Only my imaginary friends," he smiles, "And they're nicer than my real ones." He stands up and we give each other a quick hug. Dennis slides back into the booth and takes another drag on his cigarette. I slide in opposite him, so we're both sitting next to the window overlooking the carpark, facing each other. I owe a lot to Dennis. He is the first person I'd met who taught me that parents aren't always right. He taught me to start believing in myself.

"Did you hear about Donna?" I ask him. He hasn't, so I fill him in on the story almost to perfect timing because as I'm explaining why I'm at Denny's, Rob and Mark walk in.

"Nicfit!" Mark announces, grabbing Dennis's cigarette and taking a drag on it. Mark went to elementary school with Dennis and he is the only person given leniency towards using the name, but Dennis is still perturbed.

"Go fuck yourself, punchy," Dennis retorts.

"Any trouble?" I ask Rob and Mark.

"No. Nothing. You?"

"Nope. I don't think the cops were coming for us."

The waitress comes with coffee and to take our orders. I'm still full of the Chinese from earlier so I just order a side of fries, as does Rob. Mark orders a huge burger and Dennis asks if it's okay if he has the mega breakfast and if she could unbutton another button of her top. She ignores the comment politely. To be honest, it looks like the button is in its last moments anyway. The blouse is already stretched to full capacity over her ample bosom and I can see the outline of her bra pinching slightly into her breast through the gap where the two sides of her top just can't quite meet. When I manage to pull my gaze away, I see the others also focussing their eyes on her tits. Her slightly awkward movements and seeming lack of hurry to leave, suggests she is enjoying the attention her fabulous, probably recent developments are getting.

"You really do have an amazing set of jugs," Dennis says exhaling smoke from his nostrils straight in her direction. There's a strange custom where if you blow smoke into the face of another, it's the same as saying, 'I want to fuck you but without having to say the words'. She looks flustered and shy, but she doesn't budge and stays long enough to breathe in a little of Dennis's smoke before a little upturn of her lips at the corner of her mouth suggests that even with momentous odds stacked against him, Dennis might get laid.

"Might get some action there," Rob says, winking at Dennis.

"Yeah, she'll have to wait. My cock's still swollen and not in a good way. It looks like it's been overcooked and dropped from the barbecue. It doesn't even get hard anymore, man… I'm worried it's totally fucked."

"It's not as though it was really overused before though, was it?" Mark throws in.

"I'm not telling you again, you knuckle bare orang-utan," Dennis retorts with fake anger.

Mark leans across the table and Dennis leans back in reflex, but the banter stops as Mark peers through the window.

"I'm sure that's Donna's mum's car," Mark says as he moves closer to me to get a closer look out of the window. He smells of a mix of cigarettes, beer and diesel with an odd underlying whiff of baby powder.

The car is pulling into the Diner's car park and the passenger door opens first to reveal Donna's dad getting out of the passenger seat, clearly very drunk. Then her mum gets out of the driver's side and takes her husband's arm as they walk slowly towards the diner, with an anguish to the core in every movement they make.

Chapter Four

For two weeks now, we have been searching for Donna, although after the first week, I think most of us started to recognise the futility in looking too hard. If the police aren't concerned to a great level, then maybe she really is okay anyway.

Her parents had been out looking for her on the night we saw them at Denny's. They'd been searching every neighbourhood in the city for forty-eight hours non-stop. They decided to go home to get some sleep and found that they'd been burgled and that's when Donna's dad grabbed a bottle of Jack Daniels from his sideboard and proceeded to drink most of it before they'd got to Denny's and ultimately the motel just behind the diner. I could see what little bit there was left of Mark disappear behind an almost tangible veil when the news was divulged that Donna had secretly been seeing a much older man for weeks. Her parents didn't interfere and watched from afar, hoping the flame would burn out and she would see sense. They saw her climbing into his white pick-up truck with Saskatchewan plates one night and that was the last time they saw her. Mark has never stopped looking. It's his only mission in life and he's chosen to hit the road and follow it wherever it takes him in his search for Donna… and an explanation. Whatever Donna's reasons may have been for lying to Mark, it's a certainty that the man from Saskatchewan will be subjected to extreme pain.

I've mainly been staying at Dennis's, although this is unofficial and not really talked about because his parents would prefer to avoid an altercation with my father. Sometimes, I've crashed at Rob's and on a couple of occasions, John has wanted to leave work early and he's given me the keys for the night to lock up. There's still a camping cot in the backroom from when the owner was going through his divorce and the subsequent aftermath, so I've slept there a couple of times. I'd been working in the shop in West Vancouver with Ron, the owner for the past four days. He's opened a bottle bank around the back in the yard and it's been my job to give out cash to customers for their empties. I ended the days stinking like an ancient brewery, but the perk of the job was that about one percent of the thousands of bottles that were returned had never been opened, so this made for a good Saturday night with my friends. Ron knows, in fact, he generally takes a few for himself, proclaiming a dislike for wastage... especially for good Canadian made beer. It's a good gig and I felt lucky to have been given the chance. His words to me during my training session were: "You can clean the drains out with the American mosquito piss, but don't waste the good stuff."

I was happy with the way things were going. I considered John and Ron to be my friends as well as my superiors and that's why I was really pissed off when Jamie fucked it all up. I was out in the yard helping a guy unload his truck of about a year's worth of collected empties while Jamie was smoking his pot pipe in the area where all the bottles are stacked. Ron doesn't care about anyone smoking weed and I suspect he's a toker himself, but his one rule is: no smoking at all, in either of his stores and that includes the bottle bank. I liked my job, respected Ron and was gutted to the bone when I was fired over it. I saw John the following Monday and he told me that Jamie is now working in the bottle bank. This, added to the fact that I gave the cunt twenty-five bucks to get me some weed, is going to take some strong convincing from someone for me not to severely impair the two-faced thieving arse kisser. But first, I need to get another job because I haven't exactly been preparing for this particular rainy day. I'm a little jaded on the north shore and work prospects are slimmer over here than downtown in the main city of Vancouver.

There are many buses that will take me over either of the two bridges crossing the inlet separating the north shore from the lower mainland and a couple of sea buses that will take me right into the heart of the city. I choose to walk though. I have never walked over the Lions Gate Bridge before and it's freeing to have a day without rain and I'm enjoying the glimpses of occasional sun. Vancouver is often likened to San Francisco and I wonder if the Lions Gate Bridge, which has the official name of the First Narrows Bridge has been nicknamed to its sister in design, the Golden Gate Bridge. Both being amazing feats of similar engineering and architecture and having both been completed within a year of each other in the 1930s does suggest a unique parallel between the two cities. As you head mountain bound on the bridge, on a clear day, you are treated to the wonderful view of the twin peaks of the Lions rising behind the undulating foothills of the coastal mountain range. This is from where the bridge, the local football team and many other attractions take their names from.

There's a fresh breeze pushing the faint smell of pine mixed with shellfish through the air as I start the incline to cross the Burrard Inlet. Even though the suspended part of the bridge is less than a half-mile span, the entire length of the bridge is approaching a mile from the north shore to Stanley Park on the lower mainland. As I continue my climb, I can feel the shudder of the bridge as the continuous traffic rumbles over it. The trucks and buses create a much more noticeable mixed kind of turbulence as they pass by me; a warm, thick polluted air mixed with an odd bouncing sensation as I walk. I'm looking down, over towards Ambleside beach where in the summer, I had one of those erotic experiences that will probably arouse and taunt me forever.

*

She was awkward, clumsy and immediately caught my attention as she left an office building on Marine Drive in West Vancouver. I spent a lot of my summer riding my bike aimlessly exploring the area and always having an underlying horniness. She wasn't dressed sexily, nor did she move gracefully, but she captivated me and I slowly followed her as she walked towards the grassy area next to the Capilano River, close to the mouth of the river as it meets the Pacific Ocean ebbing and flowing in the inlet. She knew I was following her and she had already looked back and smiled at me but I didn't know how to approach her. As she walked ahead of me, she crossed her arms below her waist and grasped the hem of her summer frock. With a slow, awkwardly attempted teasing movement, she lifted the dress over her head. If she hadn't caught a strap on a hair clip, it could have been very graceful, but it was still ridiculously erotic. Having witnessed my brother over many years in similar predicaments, I have seen the familiar clumsiness and the inability to recover from a setback. Once the scene is set and wheels are in motion, it will usually end in a minor catastrophe. This particular catastrophe came by way of a little wobble on her right wedge sandal that led to overcompensation on her left, which resulted in a rapid face plant to reveal an odd sight. She had on a skimpy black bikini, which was a nice thing to see but for some reason, rather than removing her underwear first, she had tried (unsuccessfully) to conceal it underneath a garment that was about five sizes smaller. With this sight of oversized underpants lumping up and sticking out the side of her bikini bottom, I grew immediately hard.

Still, without a word being exchanged, I was lying next to her on the grass, both of us pretending to be sunbathing but the sexual tension was tangible. The back of my hand brushed against the side of her left thigh. I started to nervously move my hand as if it were a twitch; testing the water. *Will she move her thigh away?* She didn't. I moved my hand up once and swiftly down again; a micro stroke. She still didn't move away, so I started to stroke her continuously, without moving any other muscle in my body. She was the same. Both rigid, staring skyward, the only things moving were my hand and the painful twitching of my erection.

"Kiss me."

It was a whisper. I had smoked a joint a little earlier so I could have imagined it.

She turned her head and I turned mine to look at her. She is much older than me, around twenty-four.

"Kiss me."

Still a whisper but this time clearly not an auditory hallucination. *She wants me to kiss her. I really want to kiss her.*

I had absolutely no reservations about the age difference, experience etc… I just wanted to kiss her deeply and passionately and fuck her right there on the grass. The kiss was deep, and it was passionate. A kiss that I was lost in, not caring who saw; not caring about anything other than getting inside her. She kissed me back hungrily and I could feel her need for passion, for love; however brief and random. My hand was moving up her inner thigh until my fingertips touched the edge of the bottom of her bikini, and when I ran my hand along the edge, I felt the bunched-up mess of her knickers which excited me so much I couldn't help myself from slipping a finger under the fabric, just enough to feel a wisp of soft pubic hair. Our tongues were doing an erotic dance inside our mouths and I was feeling unbelievably ecstatic about what was happening.

"Stop," she whispered as I was about to slide my fingers a little further towards her damp warmth.

"I have to get back to work," she said, sitting up and slipping her dress back over her head. Her hair is a complete mess and her lipstick is totally smudged but she just carries on getting up and starting to walk back in the direction I first saw her.

Riding next to her, she puts her hand on the back of my saddle and walks beside me silently.

"Can I see you when you finish work?" I ask, eager to finish what had been started.

"No," was the simple reply.

"Can I see you again another time?"

"Have you ever been with a woman before?" she asks.

"No!" I tried not to sound desperate.

"Your first time should be with a girl you love, a girl your own age." She didn't have to wink at me when she said it.

Frankly, I've never been particularly bothered about the emotional aspect of sex and I was trying to put my point across as she just turned and walked away. She still looked a complete mess when she turned to blow me a kiss and then she disappeared behind the mirrored glass of the office block.

*

I'm looking at that very same office block from the bridge now, feeling aroused by the memory and frustration for not having tried harder. I wonder if she still works there.

The sight of a huge cruise ship heading into the inlet revivifies my step and I'm nearly at the point where the whole bridge is suspended from the cables which seem very thin considering the payload. From a different perspective, at night, I see the bridge functioning in reverse. It looks more to me like the bridge is holding up the decorative lights that draw cameras from around the world, rather than the deck being held up. The two supporting cables swoop down, almost touching the deck from the top of one abutment, which is twice as high again as the deck I'm on, forming part of a perfect circle as they rise back up again to the other abutment nearly half a mile away. From the other side of both abutments, the pattern continues in a reducing symmetry until the ends disappear and nature takes over again. The supporting cables at the top, which seem nearly two feet thick are really a mass of cables all strapped together. It's a stranger and more uncomfortable feeling looking up than down, especially when a truck passes by. Now that I'm suspended by only the cables above me, the traffic creates more bounce and even though it's only subtle, it's a little disorientating as I'm noticing heights still seem to make me feel uncomfortable. A cyclist shouts at me to watch out as he comes full speed towards me, seemingly having gathered maximum momentum from the top of the bridge. His elbow clips mine as he's calling me an asshole and he's out of sight before I start gathering my thoughts together. Smoke a joint. I'll smoke one… fuck, I haven't got any. By the time I'm resting against one of the towering abutments, I'm starting to get into a rhythm of just counting my steps and looking straight ahead. It's okay but I still see the void to my right tangentially and it doesn't correspond to my forward movements. It's disorientating and the more I try to block it out, the more I'm drawn to noticing it. I'm thinking about turning and retreating but I'm nearly at the top anyway and I honestly don't think I can let go of the handrail long enough to make the turn. I certainly couldn't turn by putting both hands on the rail because I would then be facing my nemesis head-on. Keeping my right eye closed helps as I keep getting closer to the top. It becomes much easier near the top because the footpath becomes encaged; a solid steel floor and wall to about a metre up the sides and then a caged roof. I even manage to divert my mind to glance at RIP notices scratched into the paint on the steel wall. RIP SB. We miss you.

As I acclimatise myself to the height and start focussing on the huge ship about to pass underneath, my fear starts to subside. I'm grasping the cage so tightly with both hands that my fingers are uncomfortable and my knuckles are a bluish shiny white. I'm at a height which makes me feel very distressed and makes impressive sized yachts look like tiny corks floating in a bathtub, but the bridge of the ship seems almost touchable as the floating hotel passes underneath me. I can literally see the crew on the bridge, all doing their part to navigate what could almost pass as a small town into the port of Vancouver. It will probably stay a few nights in port because Vancouver is a favourite destination amongst cruise ship holidaymakers. Then they will either head north, up the inside passage towards Alaska or south, towards California.

I start to enjoy the decline down the other side of the bridge towards the gate of Stanley Park. I'm much closer to the ground again and I've managed to free myself of the handrail as I'm walking over the steady stream of roller skaters and joggers creating a perpetual moving ring around the full perimeter of the vast park. The sun brings Vancouverites out in droves. It's such a rare sight through the late autumn and winter months that any opportunity is seized to enjoy it, so the park is bustling with both locals and tourists, with full Greyhound buses being the main traffic negotiating the narrow park roads.

I find a quiet footpath to follow. It's going in the direction of the city and looks easier and quieter than the sea wall. The forest is full of red squirrels which seem quite happy to share their woodland with me, so I take a seat on a stump of a recently chopped down pine tree. Judging by the size and rough count of the rings, I would say it was about a hundred years old when it was felled or fell.

The squirrels are incredibly tame, and one has climbed up my jeans to sit on my right knee to eat a nut he's scavenged from somewhere. Another one climbs the other side of me and rests on my shoulder. I know people liken squirrels to rats but I just don't see it. Squirrels have character; humour, and in my opinion, an altogether different appearance from that of a rat. There is no way, even with a considerable payment that I would let a rat sit on my shoulder. The squirrels cling to me and seem in no hurry to leave me when I get up to carry on walking. They eventually jump off and the brief encounter with the little creatures has lifted my spirits for the walk into the city.

After spending most of the day approaching any business that I thought would be interested in employing a fifteen-year-old, even if only part-time and having absolutely no success, any previously heightened spirits have now dissipated. I spent the last of any loose change I had on a burger, chips and a watered-down coke for lunch and now, I'm hungry again. I don't even have enough change to catch a bus to the north shore. I would go to Dennis's parent's restaurant, but they have gone to Yugoslavia and closed it down for their annual return to their homeland, leaving Dennis's older sister in charge; which basically means Dennis and Dave can do what the fuck they want. The downside is that she doesn't want to get into trouble with my dad so says it's best not to stay there while they're away. Local calls are free so I could call Rob from a payphone but again, I don't want to inflict my problems and my father onto his parents.

Granville Street is a good place to try and get some money. The male tourists and businessmen gravitate to this part of town as it's the edge of the red-light district and has a few strip clubs up and down the street. They have a few beers in the strip clubs and return out into the open with a new bravado and they like to show off their wealth to the girls working the street by donating generously to the beggars that are scattered around the area. I know this because we came to this area on occasion during my confirmation course last year and the reverend told us that the homeless like this street for that reason.

"Spare some change?"

I feel shame, extreme embarrassment but above all, I feel like a fraud. I have the choice to live in the affluent part of the city in an impressive suburb with mountain streams running through gardens. My father's aspirations of my predestined life of greatness seem very severed from reality right now. Although professionals with prior impressive careers can and sometimes do end up on Granville Street, I think my father had hopes of me mingling with them as my peers at dinner parties rather than sharing a bottle of cheap Rye whisky with a man called Jim. I think his name is Jim, it could be John and although I asked him to repeat it, I still didn't quite catch it. He's drunk, speaking with slurred words and the words seem to be muffled further by the bushiest and filthiest beard I've seen. He's not really helping my chances of getting any money but I'm glad of some company in strange surroundings… and he looks like he knows the lay of the land well. A young man gave Jim or John half a joint which he didn't want so he gave it to me and I put it in my pocket for later. I can't understand a word he is saying but he seems happy in his way, and harmless so I laugh politely when he laughs, and he keeps passing me the bottle.

The combination of an empty stomach and more alcohol than I've ever drunk before is debilitating. It's hit me like a blast of wind from a high-speed train and I can barely sit up straight. Jim/John is still talking at me and laughing as he speaks. I start laughing with him, with not a clue what I'm laughing at other than him laughing. A brief enormous spin of my surrounding world and then nothing.

I feel the same cold in my living body as I felt in my snowy dream when I start to come to my senses. It's so cold but it feels like there is something else; more internal, making me shiver. The quivering of my body forces up a stream of projectile vomit which blasts across the pavement with surprising force. Orange coloured puke has spattered a pair of tatty baseball boots that are about two feet away from my face which is resting uncomfortably on its side on the concrete. *Why is it orange?* I'm too frozen to the bone to move and I feel like I really could die at any moment. The nausea doesn't abate and another stream of warm puke splashes onto the sneakers. Then, more shoes start to crowd around me. The puke spattered baseball boots are disrespectfully wiped off on me and as I try to get up to defend myself, the other shoes start coming in rapidly and connecting with force with my body from head to toe. They scatter when a doorman from one of the strip clubs shouts at them and starts running towards them. He quickly checks if I'm okay and then advises me to get the fuck away from here because he doesn't want to be saving my drunk ass all night long.

It's a different feel downtown from on the north shore. Vancouver isn't a huge city, but it *is* a big port which is useful for drug traffickers. It's also becoming a favourite location for shooting movies, so the actors that were struggling in Hollywood have migrated north to struggle here instead. Gang-related crimes are on the increase and prostitution has exploded onto the downtown streets. A couple of blocks over from Granville street is the heart of the red-light district and is, for some reason, the direction I'm gravitating towards.

The ten-minute staggered walk here hasn't warmed me up in the slightest way and I feel really fucken awful; so awful that death wouldn't be unwelcome. Through my muddled vision, I can see the neon lights of an all-night diner which seems to be a popular meeting point for some of the girls working the streets here. Beyond that, I can see a tiny spire of a little chapel, an old run-down timber building like a lot of the buildings around me. Sunday school every Sunday and a religious upbringing that has only recently been openly rejected leads me to what I've always been taught is a sanctuary open to all, especially to those in need.

It's closed, firmly. It has even been chained through the handles with a hefty chain and substantial padlock, all of which have been covered in the random colourful paint of the graffiti that covers a lot of the whole building. Some of the art is very good, with obvious skill and thought put into it. Most of it is random scrawls of initials and names and phone numbers written on with marker pen inviting people to call for a good time. The chain-link gate around the side of the chapel is also firmly locked in a similar manner to the front door and has barbed wire over the top of it. They really don't seem very open to visitors at all. I can see through to the back and I see steps leading up to what is most likely a covered porch. If I can get over this gate, I would at least feel safer and hopefully be able to find something to warm me up... anything. I'm so cold and my ribs are killing me so I can't physically bring myself to take off my jacket to throw over the barbed wire but there is an old cardboard box littering the pavement at the front of the chapel; probably a discarded temporary shelter from one of the many homeless people that roam these streets. The box will be useful for not only getting into the back of the chapel but also as an insulation against this biting wet cold that is getting even colder. It wouldn't normally be difficult scaling the gate but it takes every last bit of reserve energy I have left and every step drains me further as I cautiously drag the box up the wide wooden paint-stripped steps to the deck. It's unoccupied, no homeless people that might get territorial towards an imposter. This will be my home for the night. There is an old camping mat that has been left behind, indicating I'm not the first person to seek safety here.

I have an old, slightly damp cardboard box and a camping insulation mat as bedding for the night. The cardboard is lain out as a mattress and I roll myself up inside the mat like the meat in a sausage roll. My legs are still exposed to the cold, but my upper body is starting to feel a hint of body heat being reflected on itself and my fatigued body is rewarded with sleep.

The awakening in the morning can only be described as a living hell. My throat is so sore and swollen it's virtually impossible to swallow. My head hurts beyond any headache I've experienced in my life and the pain is making me wretch within seconds of waking up. I'm trembling uncontrollably which is reminding me of my battered body and I just dearly want to go back to sleep. I can literally feel the cold in the bones of my legs.

"You can't stay here."

The words pulled me out of a semi-slumber that was verging on returning to a peaceful sleep. A man in his mid-thirties with a thick sheepskin-lined denim jacket, open just enough to reveal his white rigid clerical collar is pouring out coffee from a thermos flask into a flimsy-looking plastic cup. He hands me the cup of hot coffee and even though the thin plastic offers no protection against the heat of its contents, I relish in the warmth and wrap both hands tightly around the cup. The steam from the hot drink is both stinging and soothing my sore blood dried nostrils but I need to wait for the drink to cool a little before I attempt to swallow anything. I know having the warm drink inside my body will warm me up quickly, but I can barely swallow minute amounts of saliva. The vicar sees me shaking and places his jacket over my shoulders, and then walks away, down the weather-beaten steps and around the corner out of sight.

I try my first sip of coffee, a tiny sip, barely even a drop; certainly not enough to feel any warmth from it but at least I could swallow it. The second one is easier and then the combined warmth and moisture start to ease the dryness in my throat. Enough to thank the vicar when he comes back around the corner with a different jacket on and a blanket which he places over his jacket that he's already covered me with. He offers me more coffee and pours one for himself, sits down on the edge of the deck with his feet on the top step. He takes a big gulp of hot coffee, apparently immune to the heat and swivels around to face me.

"What's your story? You're young to be facing winter out here. I'm Alan, by the way."

"Kevin," I manage with a distinct lack of voice. I give him a very brief account of how I ended up here and he gives me a brief account of how he still lives next door trying to tend his flock even though the church was condemned two years ago. The coffee is going down easily now and I'm starting to feel a little better. In comparison to my general health though, I'm very much feeling on the wrong side of shit. Alan offers to buy me breakfast and even though I haven't eaten anything for nearly twenty-four hours, I can't imagine anything other than fluids passing my lips for some time yet, but I accept his offer happily.

It's agony walking to the diner, even *if* Alan is walking slowly to accommodate my limping, the pace is too much for me to keep up. It's not so much the bruising from the kicking, it's a deeper ache than that and it's draining the energy out of me to just breathe.

We're sitting in the diner I saw last night. It's much quieter; almost deserted during the morning. There are girls working the street corner nearby but the line of beautiful girls I saw through blurred vision last night is vastly diluted this morning. I see a woman in the distance with flame-red hair. Half a dozen girls sporadically placed along the street and the red hair stands out brightly as it quickly disappears down an alleyway.

*

Confused and disorientated but warm. I'm feeling a little hungry and I can smell freshly baked home-made apple pie drifting past my nose... Mum's home-made apple pie. I'm home, in my bed; surrounded by about half a dozen hot water bottles. A brief notion passes over me questioning whether it has all been a bad dream but the pain in my side along with other pains starting to materialise as I completely wake up confirm the reality of my life.

*

I remember sitting there for what seemed about an hour with Alan, rarely speaking and I think we both liked it that way; forcing myself to pick at a bacon sandwich which was the only thing on the menu I felt I could stomach. Then, it all became a bit of a blur, as if my mind had altered a little. I was sure I saw my brother walk into the diner but dismissed it as a trick of my dazed mindset, and from then my only disjointed memories are of feverish dreams.

*

I have never appreciated the smell of my mother's baking as much as I do right now. It's just something I've learned to take for granted. Monday's baking day. Always has been and always will be. I'm certain it was Friday night when I was on Granville Street getting drunk on whisky, so I've lost two days. Literally, two days of my life have vanished from all my knowledge and I have no idea how I got here either. If it's Monday, my father will be at work, so I feel safe venturing out into the hallway and it shocks me that I'm out of breath just leaving my bedroom. I catch myself in the hallway mirror and I'm pleased to see some serious attempts at facial hair growth. It makes me momentarily ponder whether my penis will grow anymore... or if this is it.

"Kev!" Colin's getting up excitedly and coming towards me.

He works nights, driving trucks downtown delivering fresh salmon. He had the job of filleting the fish until he nearly lost a few fingers on his second shift. He went upstairs to the men's toilet to wrap what was left of his fingers in toilet paper and a Safeway bag and went back to his station to finish his shift. I think because of this, and the fact that he turned up the next night for his shift again, his boss gave him a driving job. He even managed to turn one of the trucks on its side at a major intersection just before morning rush hour in Vancouver during his first week and as soon as it was upright again, he carried on with his deliveries. A work ethic drummed into him over many years.

As he's hugging me, I'm looking through the living room window towards a beautiful brand-new Mini Cooper, special edition with wide wheels and everything. You can't miss the huge wedge-shaped speakers fixed to the back-parcel shelf. They look too big for the car, but I bet they sound awesome.

"It's good to have you home, bro." Colin is genuinely excited to see me but I'm still too bemused by my situation and I still have a bit of a fever brain to reciprocate emotionally.

"That is one nice car parked out front," I say patting my brother on the back.

"Thanks." He looks at me smiling.

"Seriously? When? How?" I am stunned. I loved the old Ambassador that he arrived in but that's because it was an old wreck. He managed to save a bit from his job to buy himself a piss green Fiat with a floor that had rusted out on three sides. That really was a piece of shit and it pained my dad every day to see it on the driveway. This is a brand-new gem though with a lot of credibility on the streets. A European import, custom-built left-hand-drive edition so it wasn't cheap.

"Dad bought it for me."

That is the thing, right there that always keeps us coming back for more. When you're on his good side and appeasing him, he is very generous.

I can hear Mum doing her Mum stuff in the kitchen and I know I'll be greeted with a very poor dressed down version of what my father would say, so I save us all the embarrassment by just walking up to her and giving her a hug. I feel no warmth in her. I feel no return of a hug. She almost reminds me of a tiny rag doll who can be manipulated to do anything her owner wants her to. But no matter how hard you try, that ragdoll will never say what you want to hear. She turns away brusquely as the timer for the oven starts a half ringing-half tapping sound; as if the hammer can't quite reach the bell sometimes. She spins the timer swiftly to stop the noise and deftly removes the perfectly baked pie, decorated with four pastry leaves atop a golden-brown pastry lid over what looks like coarsely chopped apples and blackberries from an autumn harvest. I used to enjoy those days out when I was younger but the older I got, the more of a chore it seemed to turn into. On the rare occasions that Colin and I were together on those blackberrying excursions, we would be master under achievers together. There were infinitely more interesting things to do like looking for frogs or playing hide and seek... anything but picking blackberries. As far as I was concerned, every time I went to the freezer, for as long as I can remember, it's been stacked to overflowing with blackberries, so I appreciate the time spent with Colin by having fun exploring and playing stupid games with him rather than getting scratched to fuck for berries that will likely end their days with freezer burn anyway.

I'm feeling weak and very sick but I really want some hot apple pie with ice cream melting over it and that is exactly what is put in front of both Colin and I as he is in the process of defeating me rapidly at a game of chess. I have never once beaten Colin at chess and the more he plays as opposed to my never playing at all, just widens the skill gap between us and I'm sure he must find me boring as a competitor. Still, he's setting up his pieces for another game as he dives into his apple pie. He's a noisy, messy eater, with a good amount of food finding its way to the floor and ultimately the dog. Ice cream is smudged around his mouth like a three-year-old not caring about the mess, just enjoying the treat. He moves a pawn, but before releasing it from his grip, he lifts it to his mouth to suck off remnants of ice cream and syrupy berry juice before placing it in the intended attacking position.

"What's that? Germ warfare or something?" I say, pointing at the saliva covered pawn.

"Ha Ha. I don't need any tricks up my sleeve to defeat you." He's right, and even though I accept my defeat even before the game starts, I enjoy playing with Col.

Just as he puts me in checkmate which occurs before the pies are finished, I feel the pull back towards my lovely warm and cosy bed. I've slept for two days but I still feel very weak and sleepy, but I need some gaps filling in. I'm still very confused and my memory of the last few days is very foggy, every memory just out of grasp by a thin opaque veil, like my mind wants to forget the whole experience and move on without any fuss.

It turns out it was a chance meeting at the diner. I wasn't hallucinating before I'd passed out. Colin apparently goes there every morning after he finishes his driving shift. I should imagine eyeing the girls on the street. He's happy to observe but he would never go so far as to defy our dad by employing one… I just know this. As much as it frustrates me to watch my brother live the way he lives, I understand why he does. He's had too many years of being moulded into what he is and even though he doesn't possess the same streak as our shared father, he tries in every way to appease and emulate him. I learnt that I've already been in the Mini Cooper, but I don't recall it. Colin and I bear little resemblance to one another but we both share physical stamps from our father's side. It wasn't hard for him to persuade Alan that he is my brother, so he forwent his breakfast and took me home. He said I walked (unsteadily) to and from the car, but I don't remember any of it. Colin took me in and put me to bed on Saturday late morning and then he kept changing my hot water bottles. Mum has been checking in on me and dad has apparently not said a word about me being there to anyone. He'll be home around six and I would prefer to be fast asleep for his arrival. If I had the strength, I would probably run again but I'm so sick, it exhausts me to even go to the toilet.

The doctor has been around to see me this morning and says I am slowly recovering, but most certainly not out of the woods from a combination of pneumonia, hypothermia and I hadn't even noticed myself, that I've got frostbite in the tips of my big toes. How do the homeless survive the winters in the prairies? It can get down to a blood-freezing fifty below zero there. I was born in the prairies, in Winnipeg which is commonly known as Winterpeg in Canada. I don't remember the cold, in fact, as short as they might have been, the hot summer days, drinking Cool-Aid and running after the guy on the tricycle selling fudgsicles, the smell of barbecues, running through the sprinkler, frightening flash thunderstorms that would leave puddles to ride our trikes through and the frequent trips to the local outdoor swimming pool are the memories that stay with me most. As many months as we spent under snow all year, I have few memories of doing much in it. Maybe I don't remember the winters so well because most of life was spent inside warm insulated homes. Funny, one of the useless pieces of information that I retained from social studies is that in a recent survey, around eighty percent of Americans think Canadians live in igloos. I wonder if they think all Mexicans snooze under a cactus with a sombrero pulled down over their eyes.

The comfort of my home around me makes me feel warm, but I feel far from secure. I'm very anxious about my father coming home and although I need this respite in my mess of a life, I cannot change how I feel towards him and I cannot simply say yes to keep the peace. I really hope I'm asleep soon. Sleep is my interim escape from a reality I prefer to avoid and I welcome it at any opportunity. I climb back into my wonderfully warm bed and relish in its downy comfort. Even though thoughts are spinning around my head, it's hard to grasp onto a singular one, and there is a notion that feels just out of reach; it's there. A faint memory but not enough to grab onto and within five minutes, I'm asleep.

"Wake up. Dad wants to speak to all of us." Colin looks sympathetic but at the same time is nervously rushing me to get up.

"Now? Really? Can't it wait? I feel like total shit." In truth, I am feeling a lot better since my sleep, much better than this morning but I still feel awful.

"He told me to come and get you." Colin is clearly anxious to get back to the family meeting so as not to irritate our dad.

"Yeah, okay, I'm coming." I have no choice.

Father is sat at in his usual place at the head of the dining table and mum is sitting opposite him at the other end. Colin takes up the place on the side nearest the window at the front of the house which leaves me sitting next to the partition between the dining room and kitchen. Colin looks nervous, more so than usual. Next to me on an occasional table is a framed photograph of Colin and me on my confirmation day. Ironically, it was the day I decided that I didn't believe in God; not in the biblical sense anyway. Dad had bought Colin a suit for the occasion but regardless of the garments, Colin will always look clumsy and scruffy. In the picture, he has a cigarette in one hand and the other in his trouser pocket. Even though his suit jacket is buttoned up, it seems rucked up, as if the buttons and holes don't match up, probably because he's wearing a thick woollen jumper underneath it. He has new glasses on in the picture, the same pair he has on now and in both scenes, they never sit on his face straight. They're even more bent now than when the picture was taken and one of the lenses has dropped so low on his face that I doubt it barely has a function. We're both uncomfortable in front of the camera and both our sets of lips are contorted into brief fake smiles, probably saying cheese. I remember how nervous I was when the picture was taken because it was before I had to read a long passage to a full congregation. I was both nervous about public speaking which my father had already told me is very disappointing to watch… and trying to display a level of authenticity towards the faith.

"I've booked you in to see a psychiatrist," Dad says, taking off his glasses as if expecting me to launch a fist at him.

"Okay. Great!" Everyone is surprised at my reaction, but for me, this is the perfect opportunity to prove that there isn't anything wrong with me, even *if* my father seems to think some medication might keep me under control.

"Okay. It's the day after tomorrow at 11 am for an hour and a half. You should be feeling well enough by then." With that, he walks away and grabs his coat and the dog's lead. He believes the rest of us don't know that the frequent ten-minute dog walks are his excuse for sneaking in a swiftly smoked cigarette.

"We think it's for the best," Mum says robotically.

"I know you do, Mum, and so do I."

She smiles at me unreassuringly and the three of us start to clear the table. Her look hurts me to the core. It's not a look of disappointment, nor one of anger. It's a look of not even caring through Valium deadened eyes.

Colin wants to play another game of chess, but I want to just go back to bed and be alone. My parents think I'm insane. They're not sending me to a shrink to *help* me, but to get a diagnosis so they can be exonerated of any responsibility. This realisation hurts me more than frustrates me, it hurts me more than any pain I can remember.

I glance in the mirror in the hall again. The facial hair really is starting to take on a manlier look with more robust, thicker red hair than the blondish downy fluff that has been there a few months now. My hair looks ridiculous; a thick bushy mass of wavy thick hair that seems capable of defying gravity forever and instead of growing further over my shoulders which I would like, it just seems to keep getting thicker and bushing out sideways. I will get it cut soon. My eyes have faded from a mid-blue to a dim blue/grey, my skin is pale, and I have a crop of angry-looking pimples about to flourish on my chin. I better get myself cleaned up before I think about seeing Jayne; if I ever get to see her. Her dad is chaperoning her everywhere. He even sits in on her recording sessions which he never does usually. He is literally never letting her out of his sight.

I'm feeling a lot better in the morning. The fever has passed and I have regained some colour to both my skin and eyes. I'm still far from a hundred percent but I'm well enough to be looking forward to the appointment with the shrink tomorrow. I'm looking forward to finally putting this illusion that I'm insane to bed. Mum says I'm looking a lot better. Colin isn't home from his shift yet, he's probably having his breakfast at the diner where he found me right now. I'll have to ask him if he's seen Alan again.

I'm not at all nervous before the appointment and I arrive exactly on time. The doctor is dressed smartly but casually, leaving the tie at home for more formal occasions but is still wearing a smart blazer. He's not trying to be young and cool in a vain attempt to try and help me relate to him; it's just his way and he seems genuine to me. His office is quite bare, with a picture of what I assume is his wife and two daughters in a lean-to frame on his tidy oak desk. I don't recognise his daughters who are a similar age to me, so I guess they go to one of the many private schools around here. I like him and at the end of the appointment and as we're exchanging handshakes and goodbyes, I have the feeling he likes me as well. The hour and a half spent with him was nothing like what I had expected. I was prepared for tests and a deep evaluation, but it was really nothing more than an informal chat which left me wondering what it was all about.

It left my father in no doubt though that I had somehow managed to trick the psychiatrist into thinking I'm normal when he gave my dad my clean bill of mental health.

"Well, you must have lied your way out of that as well," were pretty much the only words he said to me.

I don't remember there being anything I felt the need to lie about during the appointment. It was just general chit chat and occasionally talking about my current situation. There's no point in arguing with my father though because he's already made up his mind that the psychiatrist is incompetent.

"Go to your room," he says with his back towards me.

"No," he swings around, struts towards me, grabs me by the hair and drags me by it to my room. He shoves me in and slams the door, then I hear him walking away, back down the hall.

I feel the fight draining away. I feel the sense of defeat, a feeling that this is a battle that can never be won for as long as he's alive. It's his belief that nothing short of greatness is worth achieving. But it can only be the greatness that is understood by him. The boundaries of his understanding are very limited though and any dreams of living a life of love, fun and creativity are disregarded as communist idealistic rubbish.

Two days later (having managed to completely avoid my father), at 7 am, I'm woken by Mum to start my first day working at his dental practice.

Chapter Five

I'm seeing Jayne tonight. I can't wait. I haven't seen her for ages; since the incident at the motel. It's just been impossible. My dad forbids me to see her and her dad forbids her to see me, driving an ever-thickening wedge between us. I'm swallowing a lot of pride and adhering to the rules of the house to gain momentary solace in my life. If I obey the rules, I'm virtually left in peace; even at work, in the back room at his dental practice, I'm left to my own devices as long as I keep quiet and show willing. He hasn't always been a dentist. He was a dental technician until he was forty and then decided to move to the UK, his country of origin to obtain a full grant to study dentistry at Birmingham University. I have heard umpteen variations of his success as a dental technician and he likes to still have a small laboratory where he can maintain his former skills. This is where I work. I pour plaster models from the impressions taken of the patients' teeth and trim them up on a wet and dry grinding machine specifically made for the task. It's okay work but it's not any more interesting to me than loading a dishwasher and I had more fun stacking empties and meeting different people. I tend to hog the communal toilet, which is shared with the office next door and take momentary unnoticed naps throughout the day. I just curl up on the floor and have a quick sleep. It helps to break the monotony of looking at teeth… or lack of, in most cases. I graduated to being allowed to work with wax and a Bunsen burner, but again the work is tedious and repetitive. The wax is more fun than plaster though and instead of taking naps, I start to play with the wax and make obscure sculptures with it. I don't focus on making a specific object, like a dog or a cat. I just see what happens as I warm it, add to it and knead it. This afternoon, I had been 'sculpting' a few pieces of six-inch-long by four-inch-wide sheets of pink wax. Pink is used to resemble gum tissue for denture try-ins. As I added bits to and manipulated the wax, it took on a very strong resemblance to an erect penis. The intricacy that I put into the wax cock from only memory even astounded me and I'm now sat having a coffee at

Denny's deciding how to answer Randy who has very unexpectedly offered me a dollar for it.

"Quick. Before anyone else gets here," he says, putting a buck in front of me.

"A buck says Jayne's dad drops her off here," I say putting the money Randy gave me for the wax dildo in the middle of the table.

"That's a given. Five bucks you get laid tonight."

"Doesn't that mean I'm betting against myself getting laid? Fuck it, I'm in anyway." We're laughing and Randy is stuffing the cock into his inside pocket as Dee turns up with Dennis slowly swaggering behind her, blowing smoke through his nostrils over a table occupied by four teenage girls, probably a couple of years older than us. One of them looks tough and unimpressed by Dennis's attempts at suaveness. He can't help himself though. He just can't stop being an arse around women and since his near success with the waitress here, Dennis feels all women are invincible to his nostril fumes and it's noticeable that he's pretty much chain smoking just in case.

Rob and Lisa arrive together and squeeze in, so we have six in a four-person booth. Randy's waiting for his date to arrive, who we haven't met. He doesn't seem nervous that she's not turned up yet, but I am getting worried that Jayne hasn't arrived. She's been allowed out tonight, as have I, both under the strict rules that we are where we say we are and that we will be home by 9 pm. This sounds early, but we will take what we can and accept our curfew. She's still not here, and I'm hoping Mr T hasn't had a change of mind, again. It is very possible and my spirit is sinking. It's ten past four on Saturday afternoon and we have a packed schedule of movies and bowling ahead of us and I really want to make the most of my freedom. Randy's date has arrived and she's cool. Hot too. I've forgotten her name, but she clearly likes Randy. She can't keep her hands off him.

Jayne's mum eventually drops her off and I suspect there's a story behind why, but we are all half walking half running towards the cinema, so I don't have time to ask her. We're going to see a film called Little Darlings with Tatum O'Neil, Kristy McNichol and Matt Dillon, not for any other reason than it being the only film that is showing within our given time-frame and still leaves us enough time to shoot some pool and play some ten-pin bowling afterwards. It's liberating to just have a few teenage carefree hours together, with the closest people in the world to me. We all feel the rush of being free and being together at the same time as we excitedly occupy a row of eight seats in the back row.

Jayne went in first, followed by me so we are sitting at the back in the right-hand corner of a large cinema. The type that is used for blockbuster releases to accommodate larger audiences in the first few days of hype. We're halfway through the adverts when the only other people to join us, sit in the row directly in front of us. A couple in their thirties. He's enormous, both in height and width. She is tiny, even smaller than my mum, all four-foot-eleven *and three-quarters* of her. Dennis and Dee are at the other end, with Dee being closest to the end of the row of twelve seats, all her view of the screen blocked by the bulk of the giant sitting directly in front of her. Dennis hasn't noticed so doesn't understand why Dee wants to move to the other side.

"Sshh," the huge man says looking angrily over at Dee who is still trying to persuade Dennis to move.

"You Sshh, you fucking gorilla."

Dee stands up and empties her iced coke over his balding head. When he stands up, he has ice cubes falling from his matted straggly hair; matted on the sides only, the baldness on top has been accentuated further by the widening of the parting caused by the coke flowing down... now onto his brown suede brogues. Even though Dennis is now standing, he still looks small in comparison to the huge man bearing down on both him and the seemingly insignificant Dee.

"Dude, the place is fucken empty. Why park your fat ass right in front of me fer fucks—"

Dee's words trail off as the huge man squares up to Dennis.

"You need to muzzle your bitch," he says, with no hint of humour.

Dennis laughs... then punches him. And then about half a dozen employees come rushing in wearing their peaked hats without tops to evict everyone. Before they turn on their torches to clear the agitators, Jayne and I slip down the outer edge of the rows of seats, next to the wall. We lay there quietly until all the commotion has passed.

The film is still running and now Jayne and I have the whole cinema to ourselves. This time we grab the best seats in the house right in the middle. She rests her head on my shoulder, her hair is tickling my neck and when I turn a little to face her, I can smell the comforting smell of her recently shampooed hair. She smells good; her neck smells sweet, and when I kiss it, I let my tongue taste the saltiness. *She tastes so good*; I want to devour her; every inch of her but this is more than a simple sexual desire. This is an all-consuming yearning to be as close to her as I can possibly be; to be inside her. I want to be completely inside her, so I know what's going on in her mind so our minds can mould together… forever. Inseparable. It's difficult to judge the situation. Half of me is enjoying just being with Jayne and feeling her next to me. The other half of me remembers with a renewed vigour that we nearly went all the way the last time we were together. I wonder if Jayne is remembering the same and if she wants me to make a move. It's a delicate balance and I don't want to ruin an already good feeling. I'm enjoying just sitting with her and as I move an inch closer, she does the same and then she laughs at a scene in the movie. I've already lost the plot through distractive thinking but turn to face the screen which is beautifully decorated with a scene of Kristy McNichol in very short shorts and very long socks. I'm glad Jayne's enjoying the film. It lifts the pressure of wondering what I should do, and we both sit as tightly as possible to each other as we watch a scene in which Matt Dillon steals a school bus and we both start half dancing in our seats as the soundtrack of the piano solo in Supertramp's Crime of the Century helps to drive the bus full of rebellious kids away from summer camp. It was just another confirmation that teenage rebellion is normal and that rebellion against unreasonable authority is even more understandable. Had my father seen the film, it probably would have been forbidden for me to see it, along with playing Pink Floyd, Led Zeppelin, Joe Jackson, Queen, ELO, and especially Frank Zappa in the house. Creative rebellion and sticking the finger up to society is unacceptable for him and it doesn't help that he has no interest nor understanding of music. It's tiring to try and explain that just because the word fuck arises in a song, it doesn't have to undermine the entire song/album/artist. What my father fears, he won't accept. If he doesn't understand something, he will turn it to not tolerating something. He doesn't want to lose face by allowing someone else to understand it; especially his subordinate son. He used to put on Barbara Streisand for dinner parties until she released a song that started "It's raining, it's pouring. My love life is boring me to tears." Because she had mentioned the words "love life", the song, along with its now disgusting artist has found its way to the banned pile.

Jayne and I aren't even ushered out and when the credits come to an end and the reel spins empty. We finally release our tight embrace of one another and walk to the exit with both of our hands in each other's back pockets. I can just feel the outline of her knickers through the thin fabric of her tight jeans and I'm wondering what they look like. *I wonder what colour they are.* I've seen all kinds of underwear and studied them to detail over many hours in home-shopping catalogues and I certainly have my favourites. I've never really understood why there should be such a big difference between ladies and men's undergarments and I'm equally perplexed by the bra. I can only say that in my very brief experience, I hope they make something a whole lot easier to grapple with than present-day designs in the near future. I slide my hand up over Jayne's arse, up her back and under her jacket to feel *her* bra. I've seen Dennis flick one or two open (one-handed) through T-shirts on unsuspecting young women on buses (not always on a dare), but I fail to seem to grasp the concept, and it usually ends with whoever I'm having a rummage around with unclamping it herself. I run my hand over the clasp of Jayne's bra, using the moment to try and understand the complexity of the design.

The bowling alley isn't far from the cinema and we're joining the rest of our friends in lane four. It's Saturday night: it's busy, smoky, with every lane being occupied and the noise of multiple rolling balls smashing into wooden pins followed by ecstatic cheers or commiserative groans is distractive. I'm used to going bowling or playing pool when we had skipped off school in the week, and I'm not used to seeing it so packed. People are waiting for lanes to become free and our lane is on its last game with a group of lively young women waiting impatiently for the screen to display game over so they can invade our space. The pool tables are being used by a local gang of bikers and it looks like a table won't be becoming free for the duration of the night, so Jayne and I opt for walking to Ambleside beach which is just a short walk away on the other side of the mall and multiplex. It's not on the agreed list of places we're supposed to be but what the fuck… The others agree to meet us there when the game is finished.

Although Jayne and I have become close and nearly made love, I have never held her hand while we walk. We walk for about a minute with the backs of our hands brushing against each other until I grasp her hand in a kind of lazy handshake. She releases and I feel momentarily stupid, until she slides her hand over mine again, fingers wide open and waiting for mine to do the same so we can lock together, fingers tightly intertwined, and I can proudly show to the world that Jayne is my girl. Although I feel pride in walking hand-in-hand with Jayne, I can't help but feel a little awkwardness, shyness even. I've never openly displayed affection for anyone and nor do I feel that I have had the feeling reciprocated before. It's almost a feeling of unworthiness; like I don't deserve to be cared for. Two forces working in perpetual defiance: the heart draws me in, and my head is pulling me away. It's not telling me to run. It's telling me that

Jayne and pretty much everyone else in this world are too good for me. I'll try to go with the flow and block out the inner voice of my negative mind but it's always there, a feeling that I just don't quite fit in and one day, everyone will see that I don't. My heart is too strong to defy anyway and as Jayne and I walk onto the sand of Ambleside beach, it almost feels as though our hearts are living as one. She's smiling as we walk, looking first at me and then at the lowering mist starting to settle over the inlet.

We're still holding hands; *I never want to let go,* and our thumbs have been stroking each other's as we walk across the evening damp sand of the beach. In the summer, there would be desultory fires surrounded by careless teenagers, with their own brands of favourite music competing with the other ghetto blasters on the beach. Now, it is largely deserted and I can only see one other couple snuggling under a blanket leaning against a huge piece of driftwood facing the ocean; not looking across the inlet towards Stanley Park, but looking along the beach, westwards, towards Vancouver Island. It's not a clear night but there's still some light in the night sky, enough to see the silhouette of the island in the distance. It surprises me how close it looks to the mainland sometimes, almost as though it's a swimmable distance. The beach is scattered with driftwood which is logs that have broken free from the huge rafts of felled trees from northern British Columbia that are being towed into Vancouver daily. I make it a priority to pick up anything that might burn as we walk. There's plenty of medium-sized driftwood that was brought in by the tide, but it will be damp and it's too big to get a fire started so I'm scavenging up any bits that can be used as kindling. Both Jayne and I are now starting to build a good collection of firewood. Everything is damp but with judicious placing of kindling, the growing glow starts to ignite into a small flare with miniature flames grasping for more fuel to keep it going, as Jayne and I take it in turns gently blowing the infant pyre.

By the time the others arrive, we have a substantial beach fire burning and it's reminiscent of the ledge to see my friends' faces in a familiar light. I love the smell of wood smoke and at this point, it's about the only thing I can think of that I share in common with my family. My family, especially my father was heavily into the scouting movement which basically meant that Colin and I could light a fire with a piece of paper and a magnifying glass before we had even joined the cubs. My father literally burns everything. He's always got a fire burning in the garden and I'm surprised that there haven't been any complaints.

He came into the house about a year ago with his glasses stuck to his face and practically his entire head covered in grey paint because he had thrown what he thought was an empty tin of paint onto the fire. It was still half full, and as he stoked the fire up to raise the heat, it exploded in his face. He shook it off and was too embarrassed to go to the hospital but, really, he had a very lucky escape.

It's not long before the conversation around the fire turns to Donna and Mark. As we're talking and wondering, trying to make sense of it all, I still have this niggle in the back of my mind. It keeps occurring and I can't shake it. It's a memory but out of reach. I can feel something is there though… and I feel it has something to do with Donna because it only happens at the mention of her name. It's always just a flash; a brief burst of nearly something and then absolutely nothing again.

"Has anyone heard anything from Mark?" I ask.

"No," a staggered collective answer.

"He's probably beaten the shit out of half of Saskatchewan by now," adds Dennis.

"Talking of which, what happened with the man-mountain?" I'd forgotten about the scene at the cinema until Dennis spoke.

"Oh, nothing much. Dee punched him in the balls and called him a bitch, and while we ran away, he vowed to hunt me down until I'm dead. Just the usual Saturday night out… you know." Dennis is feigning irritation at Dee and she blows him a kiss.

"You're a feisty bitch, Dee," says Randy with a respectful smile.

"Dude! The last person who called her a bitch is still probably sitting on a bag of frozen peas." Dennis is still laughing from his own earlier joke and this just makes him laugh harder.

It seems like ages since most of us have been together and it's comforting to be with people I know and love.

"Maybe she's happy now," I say, turning the topic back to Donna. Maybe this is her version of running away, from something we all don't know about. Maybe she's the only one of us to have found the solution. I have been surprised at the lack of commitment from both the police and her parents to find her and I have been thinking that there's a bigger story that we have never been privy to.

That feeling of missing something in my memory floods over me again and as much as I try hard to grasp onto it and delve deeper into my thoughts to retrieve it, it remains elusive. I feel it's from the time spent on Granville Street and the following feverish blur, but I can't find enough of it to clutch onto it firmly. The more I try to find an understanding in my head, the more my mind seems to drift to other unrelated, insignificant thoughts and ultimately, it's gone... until the next time; like a *déjà vu*, but not quite.

"Maybe she just likes old cock," Dennis contributed.

"I wouldn't mind fucking an old dude."

None of us have had anything to drink but Randy brought a huge bag of weed so we're all very high and I have a feeling Dee might regret saying that at some point. Dee uses the opportunity to offer Dennis a glaringly overt message by spreading her legs and laying down in front of him on the sand, teasing him to join her.

"I'm not an old dude," Dennis says adamantly.

"Maybe not but your cock probably ain't looking so youthful these days... after your mishap." Randy is clearly going to get mileage at every opportunity.

"How is the little pecker these days?" Rob peels himself off Lisa to join in the conversation.

To Rob, everyone has a little pecker and we've all seen each other's peckers at some point to let it rest. Rob is abnormally well developed in that region and we all have to concede to having comparatively little peckers.

"You mean after the blistering and shedding of skin? It seems to be fully functional. Look!"

Dennis, without any sign of hesitation, whips out his fully functioning penis.

"Truth or dare," Randy shouts out the words while we were all shouting at Dennis to put his cock away. Not Dee though. Dee is transfixed, still laying with her legs receptively open.

Oh fuck. A double whammy. Dennis will never decline a dare and Randy will most certainly make this one count.

"Keep that on hold." Our eyes follow Rob's as he says the words.

We're sitting at the eastern edge of the beach which is very close to the underside of Lions Gate bridge, very close to where I had my erotic encounter last summer.

We're all looking up watching flashing blue and red lights bounce off a mountain mist that's hovering over the inlet. Looking up, we can all see the underside of the bridge that I walked over some days ago and we can all see the person standing on top of one of the towering abutments threatening to jump. A spotlight is on him or her and we can hear the metallic sounding voice of the police talking through a megaphone. The sound comes and goes as the wind and thermals continuously change their directions so we can't hear what they're saying. I should imagine it's something along the lines of what we're all thinking though, which is '*please* don't fucking jump'!

The mood amongst us turns very quickly to an uneasy one. Some of us are muttering; not really saying anything, it's more like a meditative hum to hopefully make the ugliness go away. Dennis has re-composed himself and if the rest are like me, then we've been sucked straight back into sobriety instantly, without a trace of the former high to cushion the blow of the scene unfolding very quickly in front of our eyes.

"NO!" Dennis shouts. "DON'T DO IT!" He's making a strong effort, but his voice will have trailed off into space long before it reaches the deck of the bridge, let alone the very top. He can't stop though. It's the only thing he can do to stop him from feeling completely helpless.

*

There were no screams nor hysterics, just a combined 'NO! NO! NO!' when he jumped. The silence was haunting as if the jumper were already dead before leaping. Their final journey seemed oddly peaceful but witnessing their peace with imminent death disturbed me more than the expected screams of terror. It didn't take long for the body to fall through the air but long enough to make me feel sick and then, a deadly thud and shocked whimpers from us when he landed. It's surprising how fast it all happened. I wonder if it was over as quick for them… or if it's as they say; and time slowed down for to see life flash before their eyes… whatever that means.

Jayne grips my arm tightly and pulls me close to her. Both too shocked to say anything. I have a feeling in my gut that I've never experienced before and I briefly wonder if the others have the same deep inner discomfort… not pain as such, but more like an internal ugly fist kneading my stomach, trying to empty the contents but not succeeding.

"Did that really just happen? Because it *really* feels like it really fucking did!" It's Dennis who breaks the silence. None of us answer him which is answer enough.

The sound was appalling. I'd closed my eyes and covered my ears just before impact but I still heard the wallop. Only seconds before, it was a living breathing person, now, just a broken and punctured sack of blood and bones, hidden just out of sight but uncomfortably close enough to feel its presence.

We're not supposed to have fires on the beach, but the cops help us to keep it going as they check we're all okay. They bring us blankets as they ask us briefly about what we saw. We're left alone after a short time and a young pretty police officer handed out her card to all of us if we want to talk to them about anything. The cold air is immediately noticeable as I remove the blanket from my shoulders to hand it back to the cops. The fire is doused and buried in wet sand as we vacate the area, all of us subdued and withdrawn into our own thoughts of what had just happened.

The press must have arrived soon after we left because the local Sunday morning papers are already covering the story. It doesn't say anything about who the man was or where he was from but there is an underlying message that PCP, (or angel dust as it's more commonly known) might have played a part. The picture of the scene on the beach only a few metres away from where we were sitting magnifies the constant gnawing feeling that still occupies my gut and I wonder to myself if it will ever subside.

The ordeal of witnessing the jumper has worked in our favour to a certain extent because we have been granted time together to help each other deal with it and talk about it. We decide to meet at the ledge because the weather is fine and we have our peace there. Word travels and it's not only the core who were present at the evening of the suicide jump, but faces old and new have turned up, with lots of beer. Jayne, Rob, Lisa and I sit higher up on a rocky outcrop big enough to hold all four of us if we sit tightly together. Looking down on the developing party on the ledge below us, I'm feeling that sense of euphoria that can only be achieved by being surrounded by the right people.

After the freedom party, we wrapped anything we felt we could leave behind in the waterproof tarpaulins and hid them away completely out of sight in little micro caves between big granite boulders. It's not raining so we're happy sharing two unzipped sleeping bags that we'd stashed to cover the four of us as we look at the sky changing from day to night. This is the only time that you realise the proximity of Vancouver to this wilderness. The orange from the city streetlights bounces off the forming mist giving the illusion of a distant forest fire.

This time, it's me who directs the conversation towards Mark and Donna.

"I have this niggle in the back of my mind we shouldn't be giving up on Donna, you know."

The others turn to look at me and I'm unsure where to go next with it now but I feel compelled to say the words and make sure she's not forgotten.

"I know what you mean," says Rob, adding, "I still think it's weird she just walked away from Mark."

"Yeah, but it's something more. Something I can't put my finger on and it's bugging me. I think we should look around some more."

"Where should we start though?" asks Lisa.

"Mark's mum," offers Jayne immediately.

It's clearly the best place to start and we decide to all go there tomorrow evening.

The fire is burning well on the ledge below us. Dennis has turned out the insides of his front pockets and is about to unzip his fly to do his impression of an elephant for the benefit of the girls who are visiting for the first time. Randy is walking off below the ledge with his new girlfriend Kathy and for a moment, everything feels perfect.

Chapter Six

I'm not enjoying working for my father, neither am I enjoying living by his rules, but comparatively speaking, life is running smoothly. So, when it's announced that we're all going to Vancouver Island in two days' time for me to attend an entrance exam for a private boarding school, it comes as a disappointing surprise. Boarding school doesn't worry me and I would normally be happy with the decision but now I can only think of an ocean and an illusory million miles between there and my friends. We haven't fought about it, but I'm carrying the discussion with me in my head as I walk to Mark's house. I'm still always unsure if Jayne will turn up to pre-arranged meetings because it all depends on her father's mood. I think her mum is having more of a say because I'm seeing a lot more of Jayne these days. If I go to boarding school, it will be the end of us and I can't bear the thought of that.

Mark's mum is stoned on something, probably weed or maybe even Valium. She's just on the verge of completely out of it with brief moments of lucidity but ultimately, no real information about Mark other than she hears from him once in a while and he's been looking for work in Alberta to keep him going. There's been no news of Donna and I get the impression from her derisive tone that she probably wishes Mark had never lain eyes on her. She also gives Lisa and Jayne a look of disdain as if all girls are trouble. With nothing really to go on, we decide to leave her in her bubble and head for Denny's. They have such a quick turnover of staff at Denny's, I'm surprised to see the waitress that Dennis was hitting on is still working here. She's serving a group of men who are also enjoying the view of her chest as she glances to our table to say she'll be here in a minute.

"She likes to work those tits of hers doesn't she?" Lisa remarks with no hidden envy.

"If you've got it, work it," Rob says grabbing his groin, smiling at Lisa and winking.

Lisa leans forward, tells Jayne that Rob has a huge cock and Jayne responds with a wry smile which makes me feel extremely insecure. I have been led to believe for as long as I have taken a deep interest in this, that the size isn't supposed to matter, and yet it clearly seems to have some significance. I really hope mine is big enough to raise wry smiles between girls. It would truly be a curse to have this level of horniness and not have anyone wanting to participate with me because my cock is too small. According to statistics, my erect penis is of average length but from what I've seen in porn magazines, it's distinctly below average and this does cause me some concern. I wonder if there are any exercises I can do to encourage permanent growth?

Lisa is very sexy. She likes to dress and act slutty, but just the right amount. She has a hippy kind of style and likes to wear a headband to help keep her long brown hair from falling down into her eyes, or maybe it's just for her fashion statement, either way, it suits her and adds to her sexiness. It's not just the clothes she chooses to wear to attract attention but it's her whole demeanour. Lisa just oozes sex appeal. She loves the attention she gets from guys of all ages and is perpetually flirty. Rob isn't bothered by it though. He's not interested in her for anything more than the sexual experience and apparently, she has an abundance. She told everyone that she's been fucking guys since she was thirteen, and I have seen her walk into a party, grab the first guy she saw and then head upstairs for what I can assume was a very nice surprise for him. I love Lisa but as far as sex is concerned, I give her a respectful wide birth. The extent of her experience is just too frightening for me to contemplate and any failure that might end up being shared amongst my friends around a bonfire is not required. Also, Lisa and I seem to have a different understanding of one another and we just never go there.

The waitress looks disappointed when she finds out it's only the four of us going to be staying and when she comes back with our orders, she drops a piece of paper next to my plate of fries with her number on it and asks if I will pass it on to Dennis. She didn't say his name because she doesn't know it, but she said the funny one with glasses and a crew cut, so it didn't take much deduction. I suppose my reaction is both surprise that she is interested in Dennis and disappointment that the number isn't for me. Even though I'm sitting with Jayne, it's always nice to get a number slipped to you. I like to think that because Jayne and I are now considered an item, I wouldn't stray into the arms of another girl but to be honest, I'm not so sure. In truth, there are very few females I would say no to if they are willing to finally take my cherry. Teenage gossip tends to revolve mostly around who's fucking who and according to a lot of stories, everybody seems to be getting some action apart from me. I touch Jayne's leg and I'm surprised to feel her jerk it away as if she's being touched up by a stranger. Then she laughs and relaxes to hold my hand that is now resting on her lap. I don't want to stray from Jayne. I won't stray from Jayne.

*

It's an hour and a half ferry trip from Horseshoe Bay in West Vancouver to Nanaimo on Vancouver Island and I spend all of it in the mini arcade onboard playing Asteroid and Space Invaders. I normally prefer playing pinball, but I guess because of the rock and roll of a ship, it wouldn't be practical to have a pinball machine on board, so I'm left trying to fathom the latest technology. It's addictive. I'm in the middle of a game of Space Invaders when the call to return to vehicles is announced. Colin never swears but he utters something under his breath as his game is cut short as well.

Colin and I are sitting in the back of Dad's new Buick. Mum is anxious, asking dad to start the engine long before the ferry's doors are open. She doesn't like water or ships and prefers not to recall the story of the two-week crossing from Liverpool when they immigrated in the fifties. Apparently, it was the only time she felt like she would prefer to die; and the feeling lasted two weeks until she arrived once more on land. Colin is in the back seat on the left behind Dad who's driving, Shaun, the red setter in the middle and me on the right.

Leaving behind the booming and clattering of the ferry unloading, we emerge into early spring sunshine on the east coast of Vancouver Island. Nanaimo is a small to mid-sized coastal town with a busy small port ferrying passengers either by boat or seaplane to any one of the Gulf Islands that are scattered between the main island of Vancouver Island and the mainland of Canada. An hour and a half to the south of Nanaimo is the major city of the island and although it's smaller than Vancouver, Victoria is the capital of the province of British Columbia. Victoria is so far south that it is below the forty-ninth parallel, the often-invisible border between Canada and the US. We're heading north, towards Duncan. We passed through Duncan when we went on a weeklong salmon fishing vacation at Campbell River last year. It was the only time the captain had lost a man overboard... and it was Colin. He was leaning against the waist-high gunwale when we hit an unnoticed swell, probably from one of the many ferries. I was standing talking to him as he was letting out a raspy laugh at his own joke and then he just did an inelegant backflip over the side. He was still laughing when we rescued him.

Duncan, to me, is a little drab. Apparently, it has a big drug problem and to be honest, I can see why. There is nothing else to do here. It's a decent-sized town really but it's struggling to make a mark and many of the shops give a temporary feeling, shop keepers sitting idly waiting for a much-needed customer whilst struggling briefly to breathe some life into the town's economy before having to give up the fight and leave another vacant shop front.

We're quarrelling over the best radio station to play as we're driving north, and because the argument is unsolvable and Colin is threatening me with violence, the remedy is to have no music at all. Mum tells me to shut up singing because it sounds awful and flat. She would never accept it but she's a lot like her own mother who can never seem to say anything to anyone unless it's a criticism. Other than that, she rarely speaks. So, I just sit quietly and look out of the window as I take in the surroundings of the increasingly pastoral landscape as we leave the outer limits of Duncan. I already miss my friends.

The school is impressive and considering I'm often hearing that business is slow, I'm surprised my father can come anywhere near close to affording it. I like it here and the other boys (it's an all-boys school) seem okay overall. I'm not prepared to leave my friends for it but had it been under different circumstances, I would probably quite like it here. The headmaster is an old authoritarian and my dad likes this. I personally don't like him at all, but it doesn't really matter because I'm not going to be coming here anyway. I've already been told to be ready for an entrance exam and that right there is the get-out clause.

I'm given half an hour to finish the exam, but it's multiple choice so it takes less than three minutes to circle random letters without even looking at the questions, and I'm now just sitting with my family, politely smiling as the headmaster officiously marks my paper.

It intrigues me how much emphasis is put on being successful in education and those who don't respond to a mainstream robotic way of teaching are deemed either stupid or losers without any future. The system disenchants potentially very creative children with hours and hours of uninteresting and unnecessary syllabi, rendering them with an overwhelming feeling of underachieving. These are some of the people who end up on Granville Street… but then, so do doctors.

The real problem is, the only people who can make any changes to an archaic system are the robotic blinkered-thinking products of that very same system and they see nothing wrong with it.

Everyone knows what I've done, including the headmaster but the fact is, I've failed the entrance exam, thus ending the possibility of me being deported. My dad is less angry about it than I had anticipated and is probably happy to save a lot of money. In my attempts to pacify him, I suggest that I will try to get back into my old school when we get back. I will have to be put in the year below where I should be but maybe it will be okay. He's appeased by this and decides to cancel his patients the next day and stay on the island in a motel for the night.

Sitting on the porch of the ramshackle motel, I roll my jeans up and dangle my bare feet over the edge, so, occasionally, I get a shocking cold blast of Pacific Ocean flowing over them. It reminds of paddling and eventually swimming amongst the phosphorescence in the summer. I'd never seen anything like it in my life before: I was camping on Galiano Island. I say camping, but really the summer was so amazing and dry, I don't think my friend Cam and I pitched a tent once on our two-week exploration of the Gulf Islands.

That night, I cast a fishing line into the water. It was a dark and warm night with a waning moon and the water looked black and moody, until it lit up into a magical display, as my lure entered the water. I'd never seen anything like it and I was mesmerised by the water in front of me – greenish spontaneous illumination… tiny sea creatures lighting up, reacting to being touched by the fishing line. Apparently, I've seen the northern lights on many occasions but I don't remember, and I've always wanted to see them. This though, I didn't even know existed and to dive into the water simultaneously with Cam made the water light up in a fairytale-like twinkle of millions of shimmering lights. And as more people from the campsite joined in the spectacle, the small lagoon turned into a glowing turquoise magical paradise, verging on the surreal.

I'd be quite happy living in a motel room forever with a view like this, but unfortunately, I doubt the building will survive another decade without some serious renovation work being done. It's quirky though, and even though Colin and I are sharing a twin room, it is partitioned with our own kitchenette. Colin's in there now warming up a tin of macaroni cheese for us. If Colin cooks, its macaroni cheese every time because it's his favourite. Anything with cheese is good for Col but macaroni cheese makes up about sixty percent of his weekly dietary intake. He hands me a bowl and it's piled high with steaming cheesy pasta with the bit he burnt on the saucepan lying on top. He sits down clumsily next to me and nearly spills his dinner into the ocean as he joins me with his shoes still on, dangling our feet in the water.

"I probably should have taken my shoes off."

Colin is snorting and laughing... cackling, as he stuffs a huge spoonful of food into his increasingly gummy mouth. As he's chewing loudly and messily on his dinner, he pulls out a ready rolled cigarette from behind his ear, stops chewing long enough to light it and then resumes to almost inhale the smoke and swallow the food simultaneously. This pattern is followed until the cigarette invariably goes out and he puts the remains back behind his ear. His shoes are saturated and a swell has soaked his jeans up to his knees, but he doesn't care. He feels the same as me. We don't need to say any words to just appreciate being with each other. Our parent's room is separated from us by one room and just that space gives us a little feeling of independence.

There's a bar around the corner and Colin manages (even in his squelchy wet clothing) to bring back a couple of pitchers of ale. It's nice just sitting with my brother, drinking beer. I'm smoking a joint as well, but Colin doesn't smoke weed because our father wouldn't approve. Col doesn't approve either but he doesn't stop me.

"Let's go fishing," Colin says excitedly looking at me.

"You mean from here?" I ask, thinking it sounds like a bit too much hassle.

"Nah, we can take out one of the canoes." He's pointing to the half a dozen or so canoes that share the same logo and state of repair as the motel.

Colin and I have spent many hours together canoeing. We used to go over to Bunsen Lake almost every weekend at one point, in his piss green Fiat with a canoe (that he painted himself) of a very similar colour, strapped to the roof (not a roof rack), with bungee cords coming through opened windows and secured inside the car. He had two cassette tapes in the car: Boomtown Rats and Scorpions. He only bought the Scorpions tape because it had a picture of bubble gum being peeled off a woman's tit and it turns out he doesn't like the music. Boomtown Rats are cool though, so the songs are joined by the two of us singing in unison over and over. We knew the words without having to try and remember them, we had sung them so many times.

I'd consider us to be competent canoeists on a peaceful sunny day meandering around the shoreline of a small lake, occasionally casting a fishing line over the edge in a lazy attempt to justify us floating around aimlessly. Taking a canoe out in the dark on the Pacific Ocean, which rarely gets warm on the hottest of days, and with strong currents is entirely different.

Colin grabs the empty pitchers and heads back to the bar, his shoes still squelching even though he's stopped dangling his feet.

"Get us a couple more," I shout after him. My feet are achingly cold now and I relish in the comfort of putting on socks even though the skin is still damp. I'm rolling down my jeans over my boots, still sitting on the deck as I hear the unmistakable sound of a small boat being slid over shingle…

*

"I gotta piss."

"NO, COL! DON'T!"

Before we launched the canoe, Col instructed me to get the two freshly filled pitchers that were on the beach. Half an hour later and the ale is pushing the boundaries of both of our bladders' capacities. Being surrounded by water and its increasing swell is making the pain intolerable and Colin has conceded to it, knowing full well we're both going to get wet. On the lake, it was fine to take an impromptu dip, but in the Pacific on a good day, you have ten minutes before hypothermia creeps in, so I'm not overly keen on going in.

"Piss in your pants." I'm about to do the same myself. Then, the canoe tilts in the direction of Colin attempting to lean over the side and the shocking cold of the ocean starts to fill the canoe, my bladder immediately releases the contents as I plunge into the water with the canoe turning over on top of me.

Colin's head pops up under the canoe to join me and I'm not surprised to find him laughing.

"What's so fucken funny, brother?" He's laughing so much he's struggling to speak.

"I still haven't pissed," he manages to half laugh and half say to me.

"You have to be fucking kidding me!" We're both laughing now.

"Fuck, it's cold. Shall we get this back upright and get the hell out of here?" Having been canoeing with Colin many times, we soon had to learn how to upright a capsized canoe in many conditions, including deep water.

When we were upright, before Colin's toilet call, he was in the front of the canoe and it was just assumed that if any movement was still happening whilst overturned, it would be in his direction, so the feeling of rocky seabed hitting the

sides of my feet as we are swept swiftly coast bound comes as a jolting shock…
then relief. I'm happy to be on land. I would be happier if one of us had a clue
where we are though. The currents are fierce around the shores and the time with
our legs spent underwater had allowed us to be grasped and pulled to a remote
piece of coastline without a single light in sight.

Colin considers himself a survivalist, one of the few who would survive an
apocalypse because he knows which berries are poisonous, which in my
experience appears to be the vast majority and I wouldn't trust my own judgment
as to which are which. We haven't got to the berry scavenging stage but, the little
survival kit that I repeatedly rip the piss out of Colin over has proven very useful.
He never leaves home without his travel soap box crammed full of everything
required to survive the end of the world; including matches that had been
waterproofed by being dipped in molten wax. Thanks to Colin, the fire is huge
and hot as we rotate our bodies, like meat on a kebab skewer, turning
deliberately; drying out slowly. Colin is absolutely loving this adventure and I
can tell he is loving being the big brother, bossing me around and telling me to
get more firewood. Looking at Col, you wouldn't consider him to be the
protective hero type, but he's a hero to me and I know that his acts of showing
off his survival skills are his way of telling me he loves me as much as I do him.

There are lots of small, relatively uninhabited islands in this area, only
accessible by boat, or in our case, an upside-down Canadian canoe. Some people
like to escape to some of these remote places because they are largely free of
bears which makes camping in the open much more relaxing. Some of the islands
do have bears though and we aren't sure whether we are on one or not. I'm not
overly concerned about any wildlife approaching the enormous fire we have built
ourselves though. Colin and I share the same excitement in building the biggest
fires possible whenever we get the chance, and this one is our best yet. Huge,
reaching flames, stretching high and disappearing to vapour as its replaced
immediately by another, performing a different dance to meet the same demise.
The embers are glowing so hot that my shins are starting to feel scorched. Orange
glowing sparks are being pushed rapidly skyward by the ferocious heat of the
huge fire. Smoke mixed with steam from our clothing illuminated by the flames
briefly suffocates the overhanging pine boughs that are swaying in the draft of
heat. There's no way we'd do this in high summer for fear of destroying the
entire island by wildfire but it's safe now and it's also drawing in a small

weekender boat that's mooching around the coast. The boat is a welcome sight and hopefully our way back to the motel before we're noticed missing.

The motel isn't that far away at all, as we found out from the young couple with the boat who are joining us around our fire. We hadn't floated to an unoccupied island; in fact, we had just drifted a little way down the coast we are staying on, but all sight of civilisation is obscured by a heavily wooded headland. We would have eventually figured it out for ourselves but we were both enjoying the spontaneous adventure. I'm not sure if it's our history in the scouts that makes us head for wilderness or if it's more of a desire to just get away, but Colin and I relish these times of being together and if we plan something together, it's usually something to get us away from civilisation for brief moments and although this was accidental, it had a feeling of the moment being created for us to enjoy. We share some more beer that our rescuers had on board their small fishing boat and sit around the fire. It's nice to know we are safe and that we have a way back to the motel but I can't help feeling disappointed that the adventure is coming to an end soon. Colin becomes even more awkward and clumsy around people he doesn't know and I've often seen glances exchanged between strangers at his peculiar behaviour, but Colin never seems perturbed by other people's opinions of him, so I ignore it as well. Despite his oddities, I'm perfectly aware that Colin is more than capable of handling himself if he needs to, so I never feel the need to intervene. Kim and Andy are the names of our new friends and they seem every bit as odd as Colin. Kim has no reservations when it comes to almost immediately removing all her clothes to hang them by the fire. She's not really that wet, nowhere near as wet as us and she tells us we should strip off as well and our clothes will be dry in minutes. Colin is nervous with a naked woman in his proximity, and to be honest, I'm feeling uncomfortable. I'm just not at all used to nudity and the casualness in which Kim walks around stark naked in the glow of the flames is both wondrous and alien to me. Andy just sits and smokes his cigarette as Kim seems to be enjoying the attention of two men admiring her. As exciting and erotic as the experience is to us, we just sit there quietly in our wet clothes and I don't know about Colin but I have no intention whatsoever of removing my clothes.

When we're on the boat and towing the canoe back home, it is a little embarrassing to see how close to the motel we are, but I am grateful for the tow, so we don't have to fight the currents on our return. Colin is sitting on the petrol can that fuels the outboard motor and is lighting up his emergency cigarette that he keeps in his survival kit. The wind caused by the increasing speed of the boat sends sparks flying off his pre-rolled smoke. He's laughing. I have no idea what he's laughing about. I don't know if his laughing is his way of dispelling discomfort and fear or whether he just is always happy. Kim has her clothes on again now but I can only see her naked underneath her faded jeans and T-shirt. I don't know if she arrived with a bra, but she isn't wearing one now. I've seen her breasts in the flesh, I know what they look like and now that they are hidden again under fabric, I have the feeling that we have shared an oddly intimate moment and I am one of the privileged few to have seen them. She probably flops them out regularly, but to me, it was a special moment.

As the boat nears the beach and the motor slows, the boat seems to sink a little down into the water instead of skipping over the top of it, then there's like a wash from behind that gives the boat an extra nudge forwards before it just starts floating aimlessly, being gently soothed by the irregular rhythm of the swell. As we get closer to the beach, the small rollers coming in from the ocean lift the stern and it seems as if the bow will be pushed under the water by the waves but it just slowly drifts towards the beach. It's shallow enough to get out and wade now.

Cold, wet and with our rescuers heartily thanked, and Kim is hugged by me for more than the usual appropriate time, we head back to our room to change and warm up.

*

Andy is naked and on top of an apparently regularly naked Kim next to a piece of big driftwood when I return to the beach to smoke a final joint for the day. I don't know if they know I'm spying on them, but I'm not exactly hidden as I watch him grinding his torso into her; it's not as though they seem shy about having an audience anyway. She is on her back, completely naked on the sand, her legs wide open and I can see her tits bounce as he keeps on banging into her. I can hear her. She's getting louder and I can see her nails digging into his back as they grind hard against each other. *I wonder if she'd let me have a go after he's finished.*

Shaun appears from behind the driftwood the couple are using to partly shield themselves. I suppose it's a dog thing to immediately shove an inquisitive snout in the region of different smells, and Andy has been brought to an abrupt halt as the dog has nudged his butt several times out of the way to try and get a better sniff of what's going on. I've never seen Shaun so animated. He's usually very docile as if almost half stoned most of the time, but the smell of sex seems to have awoken his basic animal instinct and has now firmly (if not slightly aggressively) grasped the hips of the escaping man with his claws. The scene unfolding of the dog desperately humping the man as he tries in vain to escape by crawling across the beach is both wonderfully hilarious and intriguing. *Why the man?*

If the dog's out though, then Dad's out and I wonder what he will make of the scene on the beach. With his presence imminent, I push myself closer into the driftwood, so I'm sitting against it to hide myself from view. I keep thinking about calling Shaun but I don't want to go through all the explanations of why I'm there so I keep quiet; now feeling a little awkward, and if I'm to be found, I can already feel the embarrassment building. I can smell his cigarette smoke before I see him, which panics me, but thankfully, it's just on the wind because I can see the orange glow of his cigarette glowing brighter as he takes a drag on it about thirty feet away, momentarily showing his face in the dark. He looks lonely. I always feel he looks lonely when he's alone. He's not comfortable in his own headspace. He can never just sit and think, and he criticises people who do. His mind must be perpetually occupied until he sleeps, never allowing himself time to inwardly reflect. He never talks about his childhood much, but I know he had a difficult relationship with his dad, and his mum by all accounts wasn't a particularly loving woman. His dad, my grandad that I never met because he died before I was born, was a drinker and a philanderer as a husband and father. He gave my dad a bike for his birthday one year, it was an old wreck of a rusty boneshaker in hundreds of pieces in various boxes. My dad was told that once he puts the bike together, they can go for a bike ride together. I think it took my dad three months to build it and, in his words, it was better than brand new. The promised bike ride went from their house to the pub which was at the end of their street in Leicester, England. My ten-year-old dad was told to wait outside… and he did; all afternoon, until his dad came out of the pub pissed and walked home, forgetting about his bike, the bike ride and his son. I don't blame my dad for being imperfect as a father, I just don't want him to expect his perception of perfection from me.

"You are disgusting people," he said as he retrieved the dog from the couple who are now scrambling around trying to find something to cover themselves with.

"Disgusting," it's all he can say. He seems very uncomfortable in the situation and is trying to get away as fast as possible; as if a terrible criminal act has taken place and he'd prefer not to be a witness. I didn't find it disgusting at all. I thought it was fun; arousing and exciting. I want to fuck a woman on the beach.

"DISGUSTING!" he shouts. He's down by the water now, finishing his smoke and I genuinely wonder if he's been traumatised by the event. He really seems to have a very big hang-up about sex; a naivety even, and I wonder what would have happened if he had stumbled across Colin or me, naked on the beach with a woman.

The couple have (not surprisingly) left the beach now and I want to go down to talk to my dad, but I know it won't go well. Firstly, he'll be embarrassed because he'll have been caught smoking but mostly, it's about his irritation at his morals being blatantly challenged. He's not in control of a situation that he really wants to have authority over but unfortunately for him, he can't discipline complete strangers so that frustration will be passed down to Colin and me. It's not a good time to approach him so I stay quiet until he heads back to his room. I notice him hovering outside our room, to see if there's any noise coming from it, but he seems satisfied that his sons are behaving themselves, so he goes back to his room. I don't like to think about my parents having sex, but with his extreme adversity towards it, I wonder if it plays any role in their marriage at all… more than twice anyway.

Shaun is panting vigorously and still has the odd hump against nothing as he walks; a bit like a nervous tick. It looks like he would have preferred that the party wasn't broken up as well.

Left alone now on the beach, in silence. Only the sound of the small waves rolling in to fill my ears. I wish the smell of the ocean remained as strong in the nose as when you first smell it in the morning, but sometimes a fishy, salty smell will drift on a warm thermal to remind me where I am. I'm comfortable with solitude and I sometimes think that Colin has the right idea about just heading north and building a cabin somewhere in the wilderness and living off the land. Maybe it will be how I will end my days, but I would like to see and do a lot in this world before becoming a recluse. I want to have an interesting life; a life worthy of many books, not just the apparent one that is in all of us. I wouldn't know how to write the books, but I would at least like to have gained enough content to fill them. I want to push the boundaries. I want to think for myself and not be swayed by others. I want to be unique. More than anything else, I want to find my own path to my own personal greatness. I don't want to fulfil anyone else's dreams but my own and although my dad speaks sense about job security and wealth, I feel as though I've not been put together for that type of existence. If we all have been given a special gift to enjoy while we live on Earth, I'm yet to find it, but I would rather dedicate my life to making its discovery than being in a job to merely exist until I'm too old to even know what true happiness is.

Colin's fast asleep back in the room and snoring like a pregnant walrus when I get back. He's still in his damp clothes lying on top of the bed with a copy of the latest Betty and Veronica comic covering his face… which I take. Betty and Veronica are like the two women in Abba: I rotate my fancying of them daily – as odd as it *is* to get horny over a cartoon character… then I fall asleep fully clothed with Betty and Veronica on my face.

Colin is playing solitaire on the ferry on our way back. He's got the cards laid out on the table in the *café* area and I love to try and beat him to his next move which really annoys him. We're not far from the area with the Space Invaders machines and I can see a kid about my age playing Asteroid. He's in the uniform of the school we'd just visited, and he has a very familiar head of curly blond hair.

"Jamie! Nice to see you," I say leaning against the video game he's immediately stopped playing.

"The way I see it is, you owe me twenty-five bucks and a job," I continue.

"I didn't know I was going to get you fired, Kev, honest, I didn't." He's clearly scared shitless, and there's nowhere to run.

"Bullshit. I'll have my money back now please."

He starts to fumble through his pockets and pulls out a bag of weed.

"I'll have that as well."

And he hands me the bag without question. I'm stuffing into my front pocket as a woman approaches and by the way, she is looking at Jamie, I'm assuming it's his mum. She smiles at me briefly, which quickly turns to a frown as Jamie tells her I'm trying to sell him weed.

"Is this true?" she asks me, looking angry.

"No, it's not true, but your son gave me his weed to pay back what he owes me." I'm glaring at Jamie as I answer her. I can see that the situation could get very bad, especially when I have no idea what trick Jamie will pull out of the bag next, so I back up, flip Jamie the finger and walk away. She gasps and calls me a 'rude young man' and I flip her the finger over the shoulder as well.

"I should call the police," she shouts after me.

"Do that and have them look inside your son's pockets for his pot pipes when you see them," I say. The family resemblance, symmetrically stunned, as I glance back at the pair. *Prick.*

At least I have a bag of weed for the weekend. It's not the amount I paid for but it's a small victory and a little consolation to prepare me for Monday when I have to try and kiss the school's principle's ass to try and get un-expelled.

Chapter Seven

I had to have a session with a school counsellor before I could have a meeting with the principle. The counsellor assigned to me is renowned for not giving a fuck about anything or anyone, so I was granted my appointment and I managed to appease the principle on the condition *as it's late in the year*, I join the class in the lower year. I expected it and accepted it, but sitting here now with these idiots, all glaring at me as if I'm a fucken freak, is wearing thin before the first lesson starts. It's just another societal thing: when you slip off the rails but decide to get back on, you might as well have 'loser' tattooed on your forehead… because it *will* stay with you for the rest of your life. There are only two ways to have the tattoo removed: work like hell and get back up to your normal class quickly or drop out before they have chance to firmly affix the label, and strangely, there is a kudos attached to dropping out but there is none attached to being a flunky. *He's the one who flunked grade nine… Isn't he the one who flunked a year at high school?* It sticks. If you're dropped a grade, it's widely considered to be because you're dumb. If you drop out of school, it's because you're rebellious and have your own agenda… it's cooler.

The teacher looks at me when she arrives behind her desk ready for the national anthem to be played through the school's PA system. It's a popular time to pass notes around and there's one that's heading in my direction that's causing a stir.

I've heard about David White. He's new this year and has been flexing his muscles amongst the lower grades. He's a low-level weed dealer and he likes to think he's a tough guy. He's sent me a note to meet at the cave at lunchtime. He's telling *me* to go to the cave, this'll be interesting. Clearly, his message has been interpreted as an invitation to a fight because that's his reputation.

When the national anthem finishes playing, the teacher (I don't know her name yet) announces that she's just here to introduce another teacher for the first few weeks because she has some personal matters to attend to. I'm already

100

uninterested and thinking about escaping to the toilet and eventually freedom when the substitute teacher walks in. She's clumsy, nervous and quite clearly the woman with the lumpy knickers in the bikini from last summer. She is still awkward as she moves and immediately has victim stamped on her back. Substitute teachers can suffer painfully at the hands of adolescents, and any sign of weakness will be immediately exposed and ripped to shreds until either another victim arrives or the permanent teacher returns… and normality.

This is going to be awkward.

She has been introduced as Ms Lloyd and she seems so consumed with anxiety that she can't focus on any of the class, let alone me. I'm worried that if she *does* see me, she could possibly have a nervous breakdown. After the main teacher says goodbye and leaves, Ms Lloyd takes the pressure off herself immediately and asks the class to take turns, standing up, introducing ourselves and telling her a little bit about ourselves so it will hopefully help her to remember our names. *I wonder what her knickers look like today.* I was hoping I could just keep a low profile and quietly sit it out until the end and leave. *My name's Janet and I like skiing.* I'm at the back in the corner and judging by the way she's working up and down the rows, I have time to think of something. *I'm Blair and I hate women libbers.* I lean back in my chair, against the wall behind me to sink further into camouflage, and whilst doing so, bang my head on the protruding metal fire alarm. *Bingo.*

In fairness, looking back on it, I didn't know the sprinklers would come on, nor did I expect more than half of the North Vancouver fire department to arrive so ceremoniously, and nor did I expect them to reveal the cause and position of the raised alarm with equally impressive speed and precision.

If there is one thing that came of it that could be considered remotely positive; as in a story to share with the grandkids: it's that I am now the only person in the history of that school to have ever been expelled twice. At least Ms Lloyd didn't have to suffer the humiliation of seeing me in her classroom. To my knowledge, she has no idea I was even there and I think it would be better for her, to keep it that way. I do still feel a kind of connection to her, maybe it's because, in my mind, we have sex at least twice a week.

So, having unsuccessfully managed to make it past morning registration, I am now cast out by society again. My parents don't know what to do with me, the school doesn't know what to do with me and I'm once again feeling as though there is something terribly wrong with me... a defected model; broken down, beyond repair.

I want to see Jayne, and I'm interested in what David White has to say, so I settle myself in the cave and wait to see who will come first. I'll face the consequences of my expulsion later.

Randy and Dennis are already sitting under the laurel, sharing a joint while the school is being readied for classes to start again. I feel as though I'm an outcast now, as if I don't belong to this existence anymore. I feel a stirring of envy for Dennis and Randy which they paradoxically feel towards me and my now permanent freedom. I am once again surprised at this freedom and how simple it was to attain. The system has simply washed its hands of me, not trying to assess why there is a problem with me responding to mainstream education. I am simply thrown out, without a chance to talk to anyone apart from a clock-watching counsellor with a twinkle in his eye for teenage boys. I'd rather sit in the cave with my friends.

"Fuck this, let's go to my place," says Randy, standing up with the joint still burning between his lips.

"Good call," says Dennis.

As we're readying to leave, Dee comes around the corner almost at the same time as Rob and Lisa pull up in Rob's dad's car. Then, two girls, we'd never met before pull up in a VW Beetle and ask if there's a party happening anywhere.

It's Dennis's birthday in a couple of days, so it's a good enough reason to celebrate and Dennis is making the most of it by becoming closely acquainted with one of the two girls that arrived in the Beetle and is currently seeming to have a problem with the bra fastening. Jayne isn't here and nobody has heard anything from her. I'm not allowed to call the house as both sets of patents have decided (although nothing happened), that we are not a good influence on each other. I suspect it's a clash of egos between the fathers, believing that neither Jayne nor I are good enough for each other and that it's nothing more than a teenage infatuation. Maybe it is infatuation and not love but severing all contact between us does nothing more than allow us to never know. And, if it is infatuation, what's so terrible about it? The fact that she is even too frightened of her dad to come to this party is making me want to go and rescue her from him immediately.

I decide to leave the party in full swing, not only because I want to find Jayne, but also because I'm curious about the note I was sent earlier this morning. If I leave now, I can meet this David White and hopefully find Jayne at the same time. Before I go, I remember the number from the girl that likes Dennis at the diner and I give the folded piece of paper from my wallet to him on the way out.

"Give her a call. She'll definitely come to your party if she's not working," I say to Dennis. "She's totally into you, man." I follow up as I head for the door.

"Is this the chick with the huge udders?" Dennis looks excited.

"Yeah, call her. She seems cool."

As I'm heading out the door, I see Dennis picking up the phone and double-checking the number.

Spring is in the air as I walk back towards the school and though my head is filled with a multitude of thoughts and worries, it's nice to feel the warm sun on my neck after such a long, wet winter. I even have in my hand the report card from last year. D E A D are the first four grades. The irony is equally humorous and worrying. The A is for music. It was the only subject that required no effort apart from learning a few scales I'd already learned years ago and playing an easy piece at a moderate tempo. I started playing my dad's clarinet when I was ten. I was told never to touch it, but he'd only played it once, immediately after unwrapping it as a birthday present to him from my mum. He mentioned he liked a clarinettist called Acker Bilk and especially a tune he'd written called Stranger On The Shore, so he was presented with a clarinet that would have gathered nothing but dust, eventually finding its way to the loft with all the other gifted extravagances if I hadn't dragged it out to practice my scales from the Tune A Day book that it came with. I saved my pocket money to buy books two and three and that was when I felt confident enough to ask the music teacher if I could join the school band. This was the school in Birmingham, England and it was solely a brass band until I joined. My dad got a letter from the school inviting my family to the school band concert and that was the first time my parents had any indication I was musically inclined. I was told off but allowed to use the clarinet until I'd saved enough pocket money to buy myself one. In fact, by the time I had saved enough money, I'd developed a painful crush on an alto sax playing girl in the Sunday youth orchestra I'd joined. When she let me try her gleaming alto sax, the crush was transferred and wholly to the saxophone and all my savings went to buying my first cheap beaten up old tenor saxophone.

David White is sitting in the cave when I arrive and this irritates me. He hasn't been invited to sit there. Sitting in the cave must be earned, not just taken. There are a few other people hanging around as well, not quite entering the vicinity of the cave but close enough to get a close view of any action if a fight breaks out. It's generally accepted that if David White gets word around that he wants to meet someone, it's to beat the crap out of them.

"You must be the Kevin that I've heard so much about," he says, a little bit overconfidently. I still think he's a cheeky fucker for inviting me to the cave and I keep pushing back the urge to administer some physical consequences. *The Kevin*. What the fuck is that supposed to mean?

"What is it that you need to talk to me about?" I ask, not even looking straight at him. I'm more interested in finding Jayne than talking to him.

"Mark," he says.

Now I'm interested. "What about Mark?"

"He's my neighbour so I've been hearing things that are being said between his mum and mine, and he's on his way back home."

He's standing up and swaggering towards me. He puts his right arm out towards me with the elbow bent to do a thumb handshake. I'm still a little irritated by him, so I keep my hands in my pockets.

"It's good to know Mark is okay and on his way home, but why the urgency?"

I'm still looking for Jayne as I speak.

"He thinks the guy who Donna was seen with is still here in Vancouver and he thinks Donna is still with him," he says with a sense of urgency.

"We've searched the length and breadth of the city looking for Donna. It's like trying to find a needle in a haystack, but I'm glad to hear Mark is coming back. Tell him to call me as soon as he does, okay?"

Just then, Jayne comes around the corner and gives me a huge smile.

"Nice first day back at school, Kev," she says laughing.

"It's a long story. I'll explain later, but do you fancy going to a party?" I ask her. It's funny, although my rendezvous with the teacher last summer was long before Jayne and I were even close to being an item, I am still uncomfortable with the thought of sharing the story with her. It seems so many couples go through their entire lives together keeping secrets and I wonder if this is supposed to be one of the experiences, I should just keep to myself.

"If the old man sees me even talking to you, I'll be grounded for an eternity and you'll probably get murdered, but fuck him, let's go." She grabs my hand and we start walking in the direction of Randy's house.

Yeah, fuck her old man. He's controlling Jayne's life to the point that she doesn't have one and the more she rebels against him, the more he tightens the reigns. We have talked about running away together but the reality is, we have nowhere to run to and no means to do so if we did. I'm enjoying sticking the finger up to Mr T as much as my own father because they are equally unreasonable; and frankly, unpleasant.

Jayne and I are walking hand-in-hand towards Randy's house, not talking. I'm a little tense after the talk with David White and I should have asked him more questions but I was just so happy to see Jayne, I put him on the shelf.

"Jayne, do you mind if we skip the party and got to Mark's house instead?" I ask, slowing down as we walk.

"No, it's cool. Why what's up?"

"I'm not really sure, but I think we should just go and check out how things are with him." We've already turned around and we have about enough time to smoke a joint before we get to Mark's house, so I pull one out that I'd rolled in the morning for lunchtime break and light it up with my left hand as my right armrests over Jayne's shoulders and I draw her into me as I draw on the joint.

We walk past the school and I have a strong wave of guilt flood over me when I see the pandemonium caused by my narrow escape with Ms Lloyd. I still think it was the lesser of two evils though; *Hi, my name's Kevin, and I snogged your face off last summer.*

Jayne and I are giggling from the joint as we walk, and she keeps grabbing my arse or pinching it. I retaliate by pinning her to a wall, grabbing the joint off her and giving her a blow-back which turns into a giggly snog in a cloud of Columbian Gold smoke.

"GET YOUR HANDS OFF THAT EVIL SLUT AND GET IN THE CAR NOW!" My eyes spring wide open and all effects of the high vanish instantly as I freeze to the sound of my father's voice ordering me to my fate. I should have thought of him being around the school. I should have been more careful and given myself time to work the situation out. Jayne and I are rigid, staring at each other with wide eyes.

"Denny's?" Jayne whispers at the same time as indicating with a slight nod and a glance away that we should run. My instinct is to spring into flight mode with her; she is like a coiled spring ready to go at the slightest sign.

"You know what old man; don't you ever call her a slut again." It felt good to defend Jayne. I also know running won't help. Whatever happens, we're fucked. We'll never be allowed to see each other ever again. This is reinforced during the drive back home when my dad tells me that if he ever sees me with her again, he will tell her dad. Her dad finding out that I have been smoking drugs and snogging his daughter at the same time will be the opportunity he's been looking for to throw me into a detention centre and get me out of his daughter's way.

"I don't know what I did to get two idiot sons," he says, as if he has the finest genes in the land. It does make me ponder the question though. Colin and I are very different, but both of us have turned out to be exactly the opposite, in our own ways from what our father would ever perceive as boast-worthy. There is absolutely no way I can tell him the reason for pulling the alarm this morning; that truth is really one I can spare myself the trauma of sharing with him. I would love to tell him. I would love that kind of relationship with him, but he has a wall that surrounds his thin skin, which is impenetrable, even to him. I say thin skin, because if his ego is damaged, deliberately or not, he will sulk and be a victim until an apology is extracted to appease him if the 'crime' is not acknowledged and atoned. I've seen mum and dad not speak to each other for days until she concedes and pacifies him until he rests firmly in control and once again superior overall.

We're following an old Toyota Corolla like Rob's. It's in about the same shit condition and the boot is held shut with what looks like a bit of garden twine. Once, Rob, Dennis and I went downtown, I can't remember whose idea it was, but Dennis ended up in the boot of Rob's car covered in ketchup. Whenever we pulled up at some traffic lights, Dennis would release the boot lid that he was holding from the inside to reveal what looked like a dead body covered in blood. The look on the faces of the people in the cars behind was priceless and Dennis and I took it in turns so we could each watch the reactions. A taxi driver took offence once and chased us halfway through the city for about ten minutes… with Dennis still in the boot, flipping him the finger every time he got close. He gave up eventually, which was lucky because I remember we were below the red line on the fuel gauge.

Colin is home and sitting at the dining table eating macaroni cheese. About half a fork full falls onto his lap as he gets up excitedly to greet me.

"I saw your friend Alan today," he says with food exiting his mouth and resting on his beard just below his creamy lips. I'm expecting to be sent to my room but because my father knows Alan is a vicar, I'm allowed to give my brother a quick hug and sit down with him at the table.

"He was asking about you and I said maybe I should bring him over one day, when you're home. What do you think?" he asks, excitedly.

"That would be cool, Col, yeah, thanks. How is he?" I haven't really thought a lot about Alan, but it would be nice to see him again, even if it is a reminder of a time I would prefer to forget.

"He's okay. Just doing his Godly work... he's a good guy." Colin is very religious, more so than my father so I had a feeling he would strike a bond with Alan. Dad is hovering, in the kitchen, as if waiting to pounce at any given opportunity. I can hear mum in one of the distant rooms, vacuuming. A day could never pass without the vacuum being run through the house. It's what Colin and I have been taught is women's work. Personally, I always found the floor polisher that my mum handles with ease infinitely more difficult to handle than a lawnmower though.

"Well, it looks like I'm pretty free again for a while so you can fix it up anytime," I say resignedly.

The opportunity is seized within milliseconds.

"You'll be coming to work with me again," my dad says, stepping into the room to gain full authority.

"I think it would be good for Kev to see Alan."

I couldn't believe Colin stood up to my dad so forcefully. It stunned my father, and it turned Colin into an immediate shivering wreck, which took another ten minutes to subside after our dad just walked away without a word.

Ding dong... and it really is Avon calling. My mum is an Avon lady and her regional supervisor calls in from time to time, for a cup of English tea more than anything else. She's originally from Liverpool, about forty and ridiculously sexy. It's always a treat for Colin and me to be home when she visits and I'm sure my brother's fantasies of her probably don't differ so much from mine after she's gone, and our bedroom doors are locked. I can see the outline of her suspender belt through her figure-hugging red dress. She has on American tan stockings with a seam running dead straight all the way up the backs of her shapely legs.

Her heels are insanely thin and high; deadly looking at the same time as heightening the full glory of her femininity. She's wearing one of those bras that push the tits together tightly and her breasts are more than ample to create an impressive cleavage. The fabric of her red dress is still thin enough to show a hint of firm erect nipples. It seems as though her nipples are always erect... *like chapel hat pegs.* The thought of her being aroused arouses me and I shuffle as discretely as possible to rearrange a growing situation. She wears just enough perfume to want to make you be just a little bit closer to her to take in the full aroma. There is a fine balance with perfume. Either too much which will instigate a flurry of sneezes from me, or too little is not noticeable and therefore rendered unnecessary. When my parents get ready for a night out, I generally spend a good hour sneezing after they leave. The Avon lady knows though; she knows exactly what it means to be sexy and how to wear exactly the right amount of perfume to entice rather than repel, and for a middle-aged woman she is terribly enticing.

Her makeup, although heavy, is impeccable and it's very clear that appearances are important to her. When she sits down on the couch next to Colin, I see him shift with an uneasy excitement, as she crosses her legs and leans slightly towards him to ask how he's been. He bounces up and down on the couch like a nervous child needing the toilet and just laughs as he shuffles off the end of the couch, around the corner into the safety of the kitchen. I never know if she's flirting or if it's just her nature but everything she does, every movement, every word and even breath is screaming 'FUCK ME', and I would dearly love to. I am dreaming of her taking me into my room and using me for her desires... *why is it so complicated to get laid?*

She's shuffling up the couch a bit, to be a little closer to where I'm sitting, in the armchair just off to the side.

"I hear you've been rocking the boat," she says, at the same time as closing one eyelid effortlessly in a very sensual wink.

"Flatjack?" Colin asks our guest. I don't know her name. She's just the hot Avon lady.

"Flapjack! You dozy twat," I correct him.

"Go sit on it and swivel," he retorts and it makes the Avon lady shift a little in her seat... just a little. *When I die, I want to come back as her couch.*

I've never understood why Colin can get away with using that phrase without question as if it's just one of those adorable Canadian phrases that the kids used to use back in the sixties, like: Catch you on the rebound or *neat* man... Now everything is rad, short for radical, I think. Launching a Toyota into the air at seventy is pretty rad, but then, so is hopping off a curb on a skateboard, so it's fairly universal. I never use it myself for that reason. I like to apply a suitable vociferation to each individual achievement rather than everything simply being washed over with a bland shade of rad.

"Well, to be honest, it's all a lot of something blown up from very little in the first place," I say, glad to have the opportunity to finally say what I feel to someone, even if she will play no role in the outcome of my future.

"My daughter switched to the school you went to at the beginning of the year. She has told me a few stories..."

And there was the wink again; as slow and as sensual as her elegant turn to face my mum who is now sitting next to her on the couch. I wonder if my mum has any idea her sons are infatuated with her boss. I'd love to run my hand all the way up one of her stockings under her dress, just to the point I can feel where the manufactured silk turns to the silky-smooth skin of her upper thigh. I've imagined that feeling so many times as I've lain awake stroking myself with a longing lust. It must be the most erotic feeling. It's like once I get beyond the stocking tops, I'm allowed anywhere, and she must want me as much as I want her. I think, given the chance, I would hover for a long moment at the stocking tops.

It's clear that it's time to leave as my mum sits on the couch and both her and the Avon lady turn away from us and wait for us to disappear. Dad is sitting on the deck out overlooking the huge back garden that runs gently downhill away from the house to a runnel of water that had been channelled through from the main creek at the very end of the garden which is completely hidden by woodland. It's a beautiful garden and it's where my father spends almost all his time when he's not working. Not for the simple pleasure of gardening, but to have the most talked-about garden in the neighbourhood. It also represents the vast proportion of my brother's and my weekly chores, along with washing the cars. Colin and I have a deal that if I wash his car every week, he will let me drive it sometimes. It's a cool trade-off because I quite like washing the Mini anyway. It still cleans up like it's just left the showroom, so it's a satisfying job and I'm getting pretty good at driving a car with a stick shift.

There's always an air rifle propped up against the side of the deck with an open tin of .22 pellets on the floor next to it. I sometimes like to set up a coke can somewhere down in the garden and endlessly shoot little holes into the thin metal. Dad uses it if he sees a rodent of any description; especially moles. Moles are his arch-enemy and if ever one has the gall to rise up on his lawn, it will become my father's obsession to kill it. He got lucky once. The same couldn't be said for the mole. My dad was turning over a patch in the area where he grows his vegetables with a garden fork and literally uncovered the snout of a mole just coming up from his underground labyrinth. He brought the fork down right into the back of the mole's neck, rejoiced and laughed at his victory and then just turned it over in the soil. Colin isn't allowed to use the air rifle because the last time he tried, he accidentally shot the neighbour's cat. The drama that followed that simple mishap has had long-lasting consequences and to this day, the neighbours to our left have chosen to ignore our existence.

"The lawn needs mowing, so you might as well make yourself useful while you're here," Dad's not looking at me when he speaks.

The thought of being at my father's beck and call is deeply disturbing and I recall a brief conversation I had with a guy at school this morning. He'd just quit his part-time job at a local restaurant, looking after their garden. With spring just around the corner, I'm thinking they might be looking for someone and I would rather be working for them than *him*. I lie and tell him I have an interview for a job in the afternoon, so once I've mowed the lawn, I'm off. Of course, he wants to know everything about the job, so I just turn what I heard this morning briefly into something more promising for his ears and briefly fill him in about the gardening job. He's not dissatisfied with the idea and says he will put a good word in for me. This basically means he will flex his muscles as a Rotarian and as a local dentist. It is the absolute last thing I want or need. I want to get a job on my own merits like I did with John and Ron. I don't need his help. Nor want it! This has been an issue since I can remember; my life is not for me to work out for myself, it's to be manipulated by him to show him in his own perpetual bright light. He's not happy with being asked to let me do it alone but does concede.

The two owners of the restaurant are two men. One in his mid-twenties and the other in his late forties stroke early fifties; I'm not very good with ages after twenty-five. The older one has a fair ginger complexion that has become a permanent reddish freckly brown from a lot of time outside in the sun. He even has white patches around his eyes where he's been wearing his aviator sunglasses and sun-bleached strawberry blond hair. The younger of the two has a more southern Mediterranean leathery dark complexion but still looks a lot younger than his partner. If they are related in any way, they haven't told me, but the age difference would suggest father and son. They haven't really told me anything apart from that I have the job, I can start now and they hand me the keys to the basement for all the tools I will need. I can come and go as I please, give them my hours at the end of the week and if the garden always looks nice for the diners to look out onto, the job is mine for as long as I want it, and I get paid every Friday.

It will be nice to earn some money again, especially with the release of the Zappa tickets coming up soon.

*

It's the best job ever! The bosses are cool and just leave me to it. I have always been a reluctant slave to my father's gardens, so I know how to keep a garden looking tidy. I've found a kind of new hobby as well.

I saw this guy hitchhiking on the main road that the restaurant is on and I decided to give it a try myself when it was time to go home. It's a real buzz, standing with your thumb out, completely at the mercy of a complete stranger's generosity. I've learned that putting in a little extra effort (a bigger smile) for cars with hot women drivers will often entice them to pull over. Anything that gives me a thrill will often become an obsession and it's always linked to sex. I'm worried that I think about sex too much but the thrill of being picked up by a random stranger is intensified if the stranger is a woman, so I generally do smile a bit more for women drivers.

After two weeks of meeting some fantastically interesting people, many of them more than once, my fantasy that keeps me awake at night, comes true by way of the Avon lady picking me up just as I've finished my afternoon shift at the restaurant. Climbing into her Cadillac feels inviting, almost how I imagine it to be sitting down in a plush opium den. She is wearing a different perfume from last time, this is a little sweeter; and a little more alluring, like she's either on her way to, or returning from a date. She's wearing a leather skirt with knee-high black leather boots, which leaves enough room to reveal about four inches of black stockings. *The Avon lady would never wear tights.*

A new but made to look old denim jacket covers a purple silk blouse covering a barely visible lacy black bra. It's subtle, but that's the Avon lady. Everything about her is subtle and that is what is so sexy. Even her voice is subtle, like it's

111

just above a whisper but still clearly audible. *I wonder how she sounds when she cums…if she cums.*

"Nice to see you, Kevin, but I doubt your dad will be happy to know you're hitching home." She does the wink again. That wink, that just makes me want her to devour me.

We small talk until the conversation drops off and I find myself looking at gardens as we pass them by. I never thought I would be looking for pruning advice in my life. My knee touches her hand which is resting on the bench seat between us and she moves it to put it back on the steering wheel. Looking back out the side window is all I can do to not keep looking at her leather skirt and getting aroused. We're just approaching the penultimate turn before arriving at my home and she asks if it's okay to go by the school to pick her daughter up. I'd forgotten she has a daughter and I'm happy at the prospect of meeting her. I'm hoping it doesn't seem weird that I'm sitting with her mum though.

Waiting outside the school, I'm about to suggest I move to the back seat to make room for her daughter when my door opens, and the daughter simply just slides in next to me pushing me along the bench seat to be quite tightly packed, between the Avon lady and the first girl I ever fingered. Just as I'm coming to terms with my awkward situation; as we turn the corner towards my home, I see Jayne just disappearing around the corner in the direction of her house with David White. *I'm sure I saw the cock sucker trying to hold her hand.*

"Hi!" says the daughter. She's bouncy and excited and uncomfortably unperturbed about me being there.

"Hi!" I return with less comfort and an added hurt of seeing Jayne with David White.

"I was hoping we'd meet again," the daughter says, smiling.

"You two know each other then?" asks the Avon lady.

"Tia?" she asks her daughter again and I'm grateful for the reminder of her name… if I actually ever knew it.

We just had a very quick rummage in each other's pants around the back of the church, on the swings. A kind of a: you touch mine and I'll touch yours situation, which we both ended up quite liking but, we had to abandon because of an imminent arrival of some noisy kids. There was no awkwardness afterwards and no exchange of numbers. We both knew what it was and we both left it at that.

Tia's even hotter now than she was then, and growing into a beautifully rounded woman, like her mum. *Do mums and daughters really seduce men together?*

I explain briefly that we met last summer which makes the Avon lady smile and glance at her daughter who is looking out of the side window now. The Avon lady does seem cool.

Tia has to get out to let me out at my house and as I stand by her outside the car, she grabs my groin very quickly and says she would like to meet behind the church again later. As tempted as I am, I have to decline with the legitimate excuse of having to take care of something.

When I turn the corner to see Jayne's house, I see that the garage door is open exposing all the unused trappings of middle-class success. Amongst the unused gym equipment and umpteen bicycles, the attention of Jayne is drawn to David starting the Suzuki 175 off-road motorbike that her sister, Pam, was given one Christmas and ridden once, in one gear only. When he fires it up, she gives him an excited hug and a kiss on the cheek. I'm guessing she has the house to herself because the Suzuki is strictly out of bounds.

I wait for David to ride off around the corner. He can ride. He pulls a wheelie as he speeds off towards the direction of the school and keeps the front wheel flying as he works through all the gears.

Jayne, of course, is surprised to see me and is pretending that it's dangerous to be near her house. She's saying things to me but I'm not hearing a word. The adrenaline that had been built up on the walk back here is blocking out any other thought than fight.

When I hear the sound of the noisy two-stroke engine of the bike getting louder, I know he's on his way back. Jayne is quiet and nervous, and I ask to borrow the helmet she has in her hand, which she reluctantly hands over. David isn't going so fast on the way back and he slows down to about forty miles an hour when he sees me. He's probably wondering what the fuck he should do now because he knows he's crossed a line, and it gives me great pleasure in solving his dilemma by smacking him square in the face with Jayne's helmet. He kind of stops in mid-motion as the bike continues under its own momentum and centrifugal force until falling to a heap in the road like its former rider; both of them separated by about thirty feet. One of them with some nasty scratches and the other is in a worse condition.

I heard that David suffered a broken nose and had a few stitches and a few days off school but I never heard anything from anyone about it. Jayne's dad apparently hasn't got past the fact that the Suzuki is destroyed, and Jayne has been grounded forever as a consequence.

Although the words haven't been said, I'm assuming that Jayne and I have broken up, even if we haven't, I'm not going to worry about straying anymore anyway. *I wonder if Tia's at the church.*

Chapter Eight

It's the Frank Zappa concert tonight and the bag of premium weed that John at the hardware store got especially for me is sitting on top of one of those fake logs wrapped in their own touch paper. The heat from the curious log is starting to make all the Columbian weed smoke vigorously and the sheer wastage is causing a knot to form in the centre of my gut. I'm trying to rescue it before the flames destroy it completely, but my dad pulls me back and drags me to my room with very clear terms that I will not be attending the concert tonight. Considering I've been looking forward to this concert for nearly a year and managed to save enough money to get the tickets, it's a bitter pill to swallow and I'm feeling certain inside, that one way or another, I'm going to be seeing Frank Zappa tonight.

I'm staring at my ceiling looking for a solution when I hear the hum of pleasantries and small talk as someone is welcomed into the house. It's difficult for my father to keep me locked up when the person who's arrived has come to see me, especially when he's a vicar.

Alan is looking tired. He looks more like the people he's caring for all the time and seems to have given up on shaving. His beard is long and dense, and his hair seems to have grown almost in perfect symmetry; framing his ruddy brown face in a doughnut-shaped vertical halo of black curly hair...*a Christmas wreath.* I even think bits of grey are starting to set in. He always seems a little distracted, as if something bigger is on his mind, so maybe he carries a lot of hidden stress with him, and it shows. He always looks cool on the surface, it's just when you get to know him a bit which Colin and I have, there seems to be a side to him that is firmly locked away from us... if not everyone. Alan really helps me out and talks to my dad privately on the deck about how important this concert is to me, and I expect the fact that he's a man of the cloth, it went a long way to my dad agreeing.

We've had a great day; shooting the air rifle, fishing in the river at the end of the garden, listening to music that I can listen to now because Alan likes it too and generally just hanging out. He really does not seem like a usual vicar at all. Colin is driving with Alan in the front and Dennis, Rob and I squeezed in the back of a mini, he surprises me further by pulling out a bag of top-quality weed, throwing it to us in the back while wishing us an awesome time at the concert. He really is the coolest vicar ever... He's even got a tattoo. A vicar with a tattoo, barely visible, but sometimes I can just see the top of an indecipherable design sticking out just above the top of his white collar. It's cool, an eccentricity or remnant from a former life; it still looks uncomfortably out of place next to a clerical collar though.

*

Frank Zappa and his band of world-class musicians gave the best concert ever! It was my first concert, but I can't imagine anything ever topping it. To be honest, the weed Alan gave us, was pretty lame but I don't think any of us thought about rolling up as often as we'd anticipated anyway, because of the magic resonating from the stage. We couldn't manage to get close to the stage but even mid-way back through the huge crowd, I could feel the vibration of the bass notes giving me a small kick on the inside. A perfectly struck syncopated offbeat hit in unison will always make my body jar as if I have an involuntary tick or the early onset of Parkinson's Disease. It just gets me right in the gut, like a punch, but a pleasant, almost slightly orgasmic punch. I can't help it. Even when I'm lying on my bed with headphones on, my body will frighten me out of my deep appreciation of the bass line or drum part by way of an involuntary spasm. The best I can liken it to is when the doctor twats your knee with a hammer to see if your reflexes are ok.

*

Mark returns the day after the concert, in the evening, and Rob and I go over to see him. I suppose he's been gone a long time but I wasn't expecting him to look so much older. His hair is longer and doesn't seem quite as blond as it was before he left, and he has a beard with a strong tint of red in it which seems to darken the hair on his head further. He's filled out, and his arms look thick from manual labour. He looks even tougher than he did before. Broodier too, quiet and even a little withdrawn as if nobody else but Mark is allowed in his own world. I can feel that he feels like an outsider in his own home, I can tell by the way he's not sitting as relaxed as he normally does in his bean bag. Something, in the few months Mark has been away, has changed him. He's grown up – mellowed into a more secure version of himself. He told us he'd done a brief stint working on the oil rigs in Alberta and then ended up working in a bar that he frequented daily. When he was ultimately fired from there because they found out he was underage, he somehow ended up being a personal barman for the local bikers that knew him from the bar.

"So, are you a biker now then? Like with a full patch and everything?" I ask Mark.

"No! Not at all, I'm not even close to a prospect. I was just a bit like one of their bitches really. The bitch with the beer."

Mark carried on telling us about the bitches, a little about the bikers, but mainly the bitches. Tattoos, leather and apparently an insatiable appetite for sex.

"I took a couple of weeks' leave and went over to Saskatoon because the whole Donna thing is still gnawing at me." Mark's starting to relax a little more even though he's becoming more animated. It's like he must force himself to relax but is naturally content when his adrenaline is rising.

"I have the feeling the piece of shit is still here in Vancouver…" Mark jumps straight into what he really wants to talk about.

"Which piece of shit? Do you mean the old Donna situation? Because we've all kind of let it go a bit now Mark." Mark isn't happy with this and lays into to both Rob and me about looking out for a friend.

"Mark, buddy, not even the police are looking. They believe she is safe. Let it go, brother!" Rob says, but Mark can't, and the more he gets riled the more he riles me, and I start to think things over in my head again.

"Fuck me, I think I know where to look," I cut Mark off as the blurred memory of the redhead on Granville Street starts creeping back.

"I don't know if it's anything, Mark, but I spent a night down around Granville Street just before I blacked out with pneumonia and I remember seeing a redhead, standing on that street a couple of blocks over from Granville Street. I thought she was a hooker looking for Johns. I remember her because she reminded me of Donna at the time but that's probably only because of the red hair. I don't think it was her really, but it might be worth checking out." I feel relieved to have finally recovered the memory that has been taunting me for weeks now.

"Why the fuck didn't you say something before?" Mark asks as he's immediately grabbing his jacket. I manage to explain the whole memory-loss story briefly as we all sit tightly crammed into the front bench seat in Mark's van, heading towards Lions Gate bridge and, then on towards the less photographed part of the city.

There are literally hundreds of beautiful women standing along the grid of streets east of Granville Street. All beautifully and erotically presented to win over custom ahead of their close competition. Skin-tight micro skirts with thigh-high shiny plastic stiletto boots in various colours stand out brightly amongst the equally alluring hot pants and fluorescent coloured boob tubes. Cars with excited and fidgety men drive slowly admiring the stock available tonight. The car in front of us has stopped and a beautiful blonde in a turquoise sequined micro dress, with classy looking stiletto shoes to match, is sauntering sexily towards the car. There's a quick exchange of words, she looks over her shoulder and then climbs into his passenger seat and I can see them talking and laughing as they turn off down one of the many back alleys in this area. *Lucky bastard.*

We've been driving around for nearly two hours and although there has been a steady movement and changes of the girls' shifts with new faces appearing all the time, there has been no sign of Donna nor a white pickup truck. What has been interesting is that every time we've slowed down for a redhead to take a closer look, none of them seemed to have been intimidated by the thought of climbing into a van with three young men in it and I can only admire their guts.

The new rule of the house is that if I'm not home by 9 pm, then the door will be locked until the morning. 9 pm? Most of my friends only start going out at 8. Rob and Mark don't have curfews and now it's fast approaching midnight, I think we all realise this is probably going to be an all-nighter, so Mark suggests we fill up on coffee at the diner that is lighting up the street like the first time I saw it in my dazed mind all those weeks ago. It's busy, with the main customers being the working girls having a quick break. They are all in high spirits and generally raucous, but they have a fun and perpetually flirtatious nature about them which is magnetic and even endearing. There are a few men scattered around the diner and judging by the way the girls act around them, I'm thinking they might be pimps overseeing their investment. I suppose it's not really an investment, more of a stocktake of merchandise is more accurate. We are all tired and sitting quietly as the buzz and clamour of the diner goes on around us. I have a fourth cup of strong coffee sitting on the table in front of me and despite the huge caffeine intake, I am starting to feel drowsy as Mark says we might as well call it a night and try again tomorrow.

By the fourth night, our patterns have changed and we have become night dwellers. Arriving back at Mark's basement at around six in the morning, we would all just crash out where we fell and this morning, I'm sinking deep into an overused corduroy bean bag. It's been used so much that my hip immediately hits the floor as I turn to lie on my side, but the feeling of being wrapped securely by the bag moulding to my body is comforting. I'll be awake in time to do my work in the garden at the restaurant this afternoon and then I'll wolf down a quick dinner prepared by the chef before Mark and Rob turn up for the next night of trying to find Donna. I think we're all starting to wonder if our efforts are pointless but at the same time, it's a bit like always wondering if your numbers will come up in the lottery if you don't buy a ticket that week. It's becoming addictive, and we're enjoying the whole night scene in Vancouver and have even found a bar where the barman has never asked our ages. So, in between cruising the streets like the other curb crawlers in the night, we rest up in either the diner or the bar, which is named simply 1365, after it's street number. It's said thirteen sixty-five, so it has a certain ring to it. *Meet you tonight at the thirteen sixty-five.*

It's generally always quiet by the time we get to the bar and I guess that's why we're allowed in. Tonight is no exception and we're the only ones pulling up around a table as the barman already pours us a pitcher. He's typically unfriendly, but he pours us beer without question and accepts our generous tips for allowing us to drink there. Other than that, he's never said one pleasantry towards us and I find it a little unnerving. He looks tough, with jailhouse tattoos running down his arms to a tattoo of a blue swift on his hand between his thumb and first finger of his right hand. I suspect his gruff exterior works well as a security measure during the late hours of a twenty-four-hour bar.

"Have you seen a guy in a grubby old white pickup truck?" Mark boldly asks the barman as he skilfully and gently places a very full pitcher and three large chilled glasses down on the table. His graceful natural moves, failing to be hidden by the rough exterior of his inked arms.

"I ain't seen no one nor no truck buddy. Never have, never will. Understand?" He's walking away as he answers Mark. Mark didn't bother answering him. It's clear he understood. This guy parts with no information about anything to anyone. It's a response to be respected. Not only because he's simply not someone any of us are prepared to argue with but more importantly, it's because we all agree with him. If it doesn't concern us, keep our noses out and offer no information to anyone. This *does* concern us though and it's frustrating when you want to be on the receiving end of any information to help us get past this endless cycle of fruitlessness.

"About two weeks ago, a guy came in here and put away a bottle and a half of Jack Daniels. He got up and walked out of here and climbed into his pickup as if he'd been drinking lemonade all night. That's the only pickup I remember seeing for a while and I only remember that because he was a priest or something and I thought it was all a bit fucked up." He said no more as he set down the second pitcher of ale that hadn't yet been ordered. "It's on the house, boys." And he walked away as if nothing had ever been said.

"Thanks, buddy. What do you mean by 'fucked up'?" Rob asks, feeling as though the ice has been broken.

"I'm just the barman, my friend. It's been that way so long now I'm forgetting my own name, and I prefer it that way." The barman isn't impolite, just straightforward. He simply wishes to be understood and left alone so we respect that and leave him to wipe more glasses that he periodically takes out of the long-finished dishwasher.

"So, the fucker is here," Marks says, quickly downing his pint and trying to drink the second pitcher by himself so we can get back to his van quickly.

"He was here two weeks ago, that doesn't mean he's still here. And what's up with the priest shit," Rob states a point rather than asking a question, and I have my own concerns rising. *Surely not...*

Rob and I help Mark out with the second pitcher and although we still don't know what to do or where to go, at least we have something to go on and it gives us a renewed energy to get back out searching the streets... *the tattoo...* I don't know if it's just me but I feel the fact that our guy might be in the area still has made me look much more closely at my surroundings. I'm looking into shadows and hidden driveways where a truck could easily go unnoticed. I'm much more determined, now that there is a stronger possibility of a result... *a vicar with weed?*

An hour of the usual block-by-block search of faces that are starting to become familiar and we have widened our search from redheads to hair of any colour because a lot of the girls are wearing wigs of various colours. No Donna though. Just as we approach the area of the diner for another top-up of coffee and to give Mark a break from the endless monotonous driving, I see Alan coming out of the side of the ramshackle chapel. He's probably been helping some other poor homeless kid out in the middle of the night and I ask Mark to head over that way so I can say hello. He's walking quickly and makes a quick left around the corner, out of sight and it's slightly reminiscent of the movie The Exorcist, seeing a nervous-looking vicar skulking around dimly lit street corners. As we turn the same corner, we see him fumbling with the lock of a grubby white pickup truck…

I can't believe what I'm seeing and I am sure there is an explanation because Alan is not the man we're looking for. He's a decent guy who probably saved my life. Mark is opening the door of his van and jumping out of the door while we're still moving and it's up to Rob to slide over to the driver's seat to put the brakes on.

"Mark! Leave him! He's cool," I'm shouting at Mark as I jump out the passenger door but it's too late. Mark's punch connected with such perfect timing and power that it lifts Alan off the ground, and he literally does a semi-conscious backflip into the back of the truck.

"Dude, reign in the fists. He's a friend of mine." I'm climbing into the back of the truck to help Alan as Rob pulls Mark back. Mark is still fired up and confused. He wants to finish Alan off without any discussions. Alan is looking frightened. There is fear in his eyes but something else as well. It's probably just the weirdness of the past few nights and a growing lack of sleep that is giving me slight feelings of anxiety and paranoia… *Alan is one of the good guys…*

After we all calm down a little, I start to feel more comfortable about Alan and definitely more guilty now that we've all taken the time to realise that he doesn't have Saskatchewan license plates. The tension eases and Mark starts heading back towards the church without an apology.

My head feels like a fruit machine with thoughts spinning simultaneously but randomly at the same time. It's beyond confusing and I am desperately trying to make sense of it. Mark is shaking, probably from a combination of anger and frustration. Frustration at me.

The pickup truck speeds off with Alan driving it. We had him. Mark had him and *I* let him go… *It's not Alan though, it can't be Alan.*

"I'm telling you, Mark, this guy saved my life. He's been in my house, more than once." I'm saying the words, but I feel my own confidence in Alan sliding.

Why did he run? It doesn't matter what I say anyway and by the time Mark has finished burning most of the rubber away on his rear tyres chasing an invisible truck, he slows down to take a pause for thought, which in turn provokes a thought of my own. Why is Alan always hovering around the chapel? I just realised tonight that the house he told me he lived in, the house next door, is completely boarded up and in a worse state than the church. It looked like it might be used, but by junkies, not a vicar. I'm feeling very uneasy and Rob sees it.

"You okay, bro?" he asks. "What's the story behind all this?" asking me for information I don't have.

"I genuinely have no fucken idea but I have a feeling we need to check the chapel again. You both cool with that?" Of course, the answer is a strong affirmative from both Rob and Mark and I think the same realisation has hit them as well. We only quickly checked the porch and had a quick glance around the outside around the scruffy yard area at the back of the church. Mark is gunning the van back in the direction we'd distanced ourselves from in the hunt for the truck. Rob and I are getting used to being tossed around the front seat as Mark drives in a state of perpetual acceleration regardless of any turns required to navigate our way back. I think he's slightly insane but he does get the job done. To be honest, I think the insanity mask that Mark wears is his armour against the world. He's not insane but giving that impression and having to perpetually live up to his reputation distracts him from his real life. A life in which he always tells us about what an amazing dad he has, but none of us have ever seen. He's definitely pissed off now and I can tell he's just looking for someone to punch. When Mark gets a rage on, I think he is more than capable of punching any one of his friends – us. He'd regret it and probably apologise afterwards, but it's definitely in him and at times like this, it's better to try and read his next move for self-preservation rather than aggravate him further. His erratic personality doesn't always make his next move easy to read though, so it's best to always keep at least an arm's length between him and you.

The timber at the bottom of the doors on the front of the chapel is starting to rot. The once planned to fit wood is now a jagged broken edge which has encouraged further destruction from rodents. The gap created by the decay caught my eye by way of a quick flash; the flick of a lighter lighting a cigarette perhaps. Mark and Rob didn't see it and had I not been looking into space trying to find an answer to what's happening, I would have missed it myself.

"I think there's someone in the chapel," I whisper to the other two. "In fact, I'm pretty fucken sure someone's in there," I say a bit louder than a whisper this time as if to bolster my first statement.

The lock is on the front, as it was the last time I saw it, so if anyone is in there, they didn't get in through the front door so we head around the back again. On the porch, the situation hasn't changed and the back door is securely padlocked too. Then, I think about the outside entrance to the basement at the restaurant and looking down through the slight gaps in the floorboards of the deck, I think I might have found our way in.

Nothing. Just a damp earthy smell and no doubt lots of rat shit. But no way into the chapel... *I'm sure I saw a flicker of light.*

"Fuck this." Mark starts heading back towards the van. "Wait, Mark, there has to be a way in..." But he's not listening anyway. He's already long gone around the corner of the chapel, not interested in listening to me or any reasoning.

I lean over the outer edge of the decking, the furthest away from 'Alan's house'. The whole street is run down, but it looks like there might be a light on the next door. The light is dim though and it's hard to tell if it might be just a reflection from the streetlights. Looking down the side of the church I can see the similar graffiti-covered timber walls with boarded-up windows. Running along the bottom of the wall are three windows that would have given a little light to the basement of the chapel, but no way in.

The loud smash of Mark's crowbar hitting the chain on the front door reverberates through the hollowness of an empty sounding chapel which, with a noticeable air of irony, amplifies it to the point of it not being dissimilar to the clang of a slightly worn-out village church bell. *Fer fucks sake, Mark...*

By the time Rob and I reach the front door, the lock is already lying on the floor and the double wooden doors are flung wide open, releasing a mixed musty smell of damp wood and general decay. The inside is lit up by the light of Mark's dying last match which he's using to light the little cardboard book the matches came in to prolong the light. Rob lights his Bic lighter and turns it up to full. The stale air is enveloping me, and it makes me feel uncomfortable. The chapel has been vandalised on the inside as well as outside, much worse in fact. Old wooden pews broken down into pointless piles of wood, scattered cardboard boxes, newspapers and a couple of grubby old mattresses pushed next to each other up against the wall on the left. Hanging poignantly above the makeshift bed is a two-foot-high crucifix with Jesus hanging, head bowed silently to the right as he bleeds from hands cruelly nailed to the cross. *Humans really are the most brutal in the animal kingdom…*

In its day, the crucifix would have been proudly displayed and brightly backlit to give it more presence within the small chapel. Now, just the odd mostly burnt out amber flicker of the virtually dead bulb brings the cross briefly to life. Fuck. That was the light I saw. Rob and Mark are kicking things around, hoping but not believing something will be uncovered to unravel another clue in the puzzle.

I remember the ground level basement windows and tell Rob and Mark to look for a way down. I go back outside to see if there's a way in from there. From the front of the church, the street lighting is more helpful to see than from the deck at the back and I can now see a padlock on the boarded-up middle window.

"Mark! Get the fuck out here with your crowbar." I'm trying to tug at the lock as I'm shouting for him, but it's firmly locked. The board has two new looking hinges at the top with a latch for the padlock at the bottom.

I don't know why but I expected Mark to jam the crowbar into the loop of the lock and lever it apart. His method of whacking it with impressive power and precision was probably the best choice though, as the lock easily splits into two pieces with both halves lying on the floor. Mark hauls himself through what was the basement window; just the lime green bottoms of his old Adidas trainers still in sight. Then not. Rob and I both head for the way-in at the same time and I hold the flap up for him.

"Ladies first," I say as Rob sticks his head inside. He doesn't say anything but he does flip me the finger just before he disappears.

The smell in the basement is different from upstairs in the chapel. It's not much more than crawl space really, with all three of us having to crouch considerably as we work our way slowly through scattered discarded objects from former Christian ceremonies. It smells used and not dissimilar to the smell that emanates from my brother's room on the rare occasions that his door is left open. It's a mix of stale sweat and old ashtrays. It's slightly more organised in the basement than upstairs in the main chapel and the vandals didn't seem to make it down here to mark it with their graffiti. It's still scruffy though, and damp. In the light of Rob's lighter, I can see that the back of the building has been partitioned off to make a separate room. Rob has seen it, as has Mark and we are all walking bent over in the direction of the door which is firmly closed but not locked. Once through the door, both Rob and I light up both of our lighters to illuminate the room enough to reveal a temporary home, of a kind. There is a torch on top of a cardboard box being used as a temporary table. Mark grabs the torch and lights up the small room which has the feeling of only recently been vacated and carries a musty stale air as if slightly stifled of oxygen. As Mark sweeps the room with the torch, he misses a flash of pink I saw briefly on the bed.

"Mark, over there. Point the light over to the bed," I say, and all of us recognise, simultaneously and immediately, the end of Donna's shawl sticking out from under the end of a grubby grey blanket.

"That son of a cock sucking whore has Donna." Mark is filled with rage as he's shouting the words but standing still on the spot, like all of us, not knowing what to do next.

"I will find that cunt and kill him if it's the last thing I do," Mark says the words convincingly, making a promise to himself.

I'm really wondering how much of Mark's anger is out of love for Donna or simply because he is now on a mission and he can't rest until it's completed. To be honest, now that the first clue has been uncovered, the lure of finding out what exactly has been going on is growing in me as well. Is this a life that Donna has happily chosen or is she being held against her will? I don't think anyone would really choose this life unless there is a hold over them. It's funny that the first thought that comes into my head is that Donna has a lovely home with nice parents so why would she choose to sleep here? But not so long ago, the same could have been asked of me. Donna was probably sleeping almost directly under me when I nearly froze on the deck above. If I'd have looked harder and tried to get into the basement for shelter then, the whole thing could have been long over.

Maybe Alan wasn't helping me. Yes, he warmed me up and helped me out but really, he was just luring me away from his hideaway and I'm starting to wonder how things might have gone if Colin hadn't turned up when he did. I'm also wondering why he felt the need to perpetuate the false friendship. The more that comes to light, the more I think it was Donna I saw working on the street that night and it's fair to assume now that Alan has some part to play in this. Was he grooming me by staying friends or did he know I am a friend of Donna's and he was simply keeping his enemy close? The whirring thoughts send mixed emotions running through me, and none of them good.

Mark is wanting to get out on the streets again to start hunting Alan down but Rob and I are trying to slow it down a bit. We've been hunting the streets to no avail for many nights now, so we have to start thinking more, instead of aimlessly driving around. He can't have got far yet but there are limitless places to hide even in the smallest radius in the city. He won't be blithely driving around the streets after nearly being caught. He will most certainly be holed up somewhere and he likely has Donna with him. He's kept out of trouble for a long time and is adept at hiding so we are wasting our time looking for obvious signs of him. Where would he go underground?

Just then, as we're taking a brief pause to decide what to do, the boarded-up window that we came through, opens slightly and Alan's voice penetrates the stale air.

"Bob? You okay, buddy?" he asks with his usual friendly demeanour.

Mark has his hands grasped on his thick head of hair and is pulling him through the window with nothing but brute force. He pins Alan to the floor and grasps him by the throat with one hand as the other is poised in a clenched fist ready to smash into his face if he doesn't tell him where Donna is within five seconds.

"Who? I don't know a Donna."

Mark's fist connects with Alan's nose in a bone-crunching blow and two thin claret coloured streams run immediately from his nose. If his nose hadn't been broken by Mark's first punch outside by the truck, it most certainly is now. Mark's fist is poised again, and he offers Alan another five seconds. I have never seen Mark so riled; completely out of control and Alan is the unfortunate victim of months of his frustration.

"Look, I don't know a Donna. I let the odd homeless person sleep here from time to time. That's all." Alan is clearly in fear of his life and is shaking in Mark's grasp and having to wipe the blood away from his mouth as he tries to speak as calmly as possible. "Maybe your friend stayed here. I help a lot of the girls on the street. You have to believe me. I help people. I don't hurt them." Alan is beginning to sob but Mark isn't loosening his grip and he looks like he's about to launch another hammering blow, simply because he needs to hit something in his rage.

"Mark, ease up, dude!" I'm glad Rob intervenes and goes over to yank him away from Alan who is now shuffling backwards, still sitting on the floor, backing away quickly from Mark. Alan's eyes are darting to the window and back at Mark. He knows if he runs, Mark will probably kill him or at least severely maim him, so he sits next to the wall on the floor with his knees drawn in tightly to his chest, securing them, as if creating a wall with his linked hands around his shins. He's still visibly shaking, and I imagine he's in a lot of pain.

Until this point, Alan hadn't seen me in the basement but now that he has time to speak, he starts to call out my name.

Mark is holding Donna's shawl in front of Alan's broken nose and is demanding he tells him where she is.

"Look, Mark. That's your name, right?" Mark ignores Alan. "I let homeless people sleep here when it's free. That's all. I have no idea who that belongs to. If she was here though, you can know that she needed the shelter and I helped her out. That's all I know. I swear to God. Is Kev in here with you? Let me speak to him."

I don't know about anyone else but I'm starting to believe Alan. He looks innocent, frightened and he *did* help me.

"Why did you take off in the truck so fast?" Rob is asking the question and it's in a lighter tone than Mark's previous interrogation.

"You really need to ask?" It's a fair point as Alan looks at Mark both with a questioning and slightly terrified expression.

Rob is shining the torch into both Mark's and Alan's faces and tells Mark to lighten up, which with extreme reluctance and strong persuasion from Rob, he finally does, and Alan resumes his curled up foetal position against the wall again.

"Kev?" Alan is asking me to talk and I want to hear his side of the story. Stepping into the light of the torch, Alan sees my face and I can see instant relief enter his eyes; even a faint smile.

"Tell me about your friend, Kev. Maybe I can remember when she was here and where she might have gone." Alan has his vicar mannerisms back and although I immediately warm to him, Mark just retorts by asking why the fuck we should believe a word he says... and why the fuck did he come back here after taking off?

"Mark! You've had your chance, now shut the fuck up and put your fucken fists in your pockets for fuck sake." I'm starting to get pissed off with Mark. He's out of control and very angry. He's going to end up killing someone if he doesn't get his rage under control.

I think most people have a certain level where a kind of switch in the brain occurs. The level that the switch is flicked depends entirely on the individual and maybe some people's switch is set so high, they haven't experienced it yet. I have. I remember, probably after watching a John Wayne movie when I was around five or six, I had an argument with my best friend Scott. I remember the rage in me to this day and if I had managed to catch him, I'm sure I would have twatted him over the head with my water pistol with the sole intention of killing him. This was a quick burst of anger and within an hour, we were laughing and playing in the puddles again. Mark doesn't seem to want to play in puddles anymore and his murderous rage is nearly constant. Even when he's amongst friends, he's perpetually edgy now. Hopefully, if we solve the mystery of Donna, he might resort to the old Mark.

"Fine! Have it your fucken way. I'm telling you though, this guy; this guy right there against the wall looking like a little boy who pissed himself in class is not telling us everything. I just know he's not."

With that, Mark walks off, heads out through the basement window, off into the night until we hear him starting up his van and driving away with tyres screaming on the road as he leaves us behind.

The walk to the 1365 bar is quiet apart from my remark about how empty the streets are. Alan tells us that there's a couple of American warships mooring for a few nights in town, so most of the girls are working in hotel rooms or hustling in strip bars. The men are let off the ships in shifts for all kinds of security reasons which keeps the demand constant for the girls for the entire four days.

"They make hay while the sun shines, face all kinds of men, one after the other for hours on end sometimes, rarely sleep but they hopefully make enough money to see them though for a few weeks at least. It's a good time for them."

Alan's smiling as he speaks and I can see he genuinely cares for the working girls and that they are making money to survive, at least for a while.

The bar isn't empty this time, probably because it's earlier than the time we usually come but thankfully, the usual bartender is working.

"Found him then," the bartender says nodding towards Alan as he places two pitchers and three large glasses on the table in front of us. I don't know if it's just him assuming that's what we want, or if it's all he's prepared to serve us.

"Oh, oh. Yeah," Rob answers, not saying any more. The barman doesn't ask any more questions but he gives Alan a wary look which makes him even more uneasy and Alan looks at me with a puzzled expression.

"We were looking for someone and, it turns out it's not you."

Alan is confused but satisfied with the answer and it's all I feel like saying for now. We all fall into silence, probably digesting all the prior events in our own individual ways.

"Not on the Scotch tonight then, Father?" the bartender shouts over to Alan from the bar with a straight face.

"Ha. No, better not. Thanks though." Alan looks at both Rob and I but stays quiet.

"It's okay, we know the story," I tell him. I don't need to hear the story again. Alan looks both embarrassed and relieved to not have to recount the night. Now, I'm trusting Alan again, I feel bad and I especially feel bad when I see the purple swelling increasing around both narrowing eyes.

"Why did you go back to the basement?" I need to ask Alan the question because he must have known we were there.

"There was an old man staying there; Bob. He's old and has a heart condition. The last thing he needs is that thug friend of yours roughing him up, so I had to go back to see if he was ok. I'm guessing he was lucky and went out before you got there," Alan explains. "Kev, that friend of yours... Mark? He's not quite right in the head you know. Be careful!"

Alan looks genuinely concerned for me as he says the words.

He's right. Mark does seem to have derailed and he was never particularly railed in the first place. He's always been hard to handle but now that his anger is untethered, it's a bit like the feeling of never knowing when the big one is coming.

The only other occupied table has two middle-aged men sitting opposite each other, laughing like school children; wheezing and coughing with red faces and identical shiny bald patches with thick rings of brown hair around the sides giving them the appearance of two monks hitting the tonic wine in a monastery's cellar. They look like old friends probably sharing the same jokes they have shared over and over for decades, but they will always be funny to them. One of the two men lifts the empty pitcher indicating they would like another one and the bartender starts pouring it from the tap immediately. The men are laughing, but it looks like it's only a brief respite in their otherwise fun-less lives. The way they are dressed and acting like boys let out on a school night, suggests that this is a rare moment of freedom for them and they are going to make a night of it. I'd hate to be forty-something and still have to live by a curfew and someone else's rules. I doubt I'll ever get married. I wouldn't mind a kid though. A son. I think a daughter would be more difficult. Our mum keeps telling Colin and I that she never wanted sons and always wanted a daughter so they could do 'girl's things' together. She always complains about being in a house full of men; even the dog is male she says huffily and frequently. I wonder what kind of father mine would have been, had he had two daughters instead of two sons. I will be a totally different dad from mine, that is for sure.

One of the monk type men gets up unsteadily, still chuckling at a previously shared joke. He's wobbly and pulling his trousers up under his huge gut. Pulling out a wallet from his inside pocket of his jacket hanging over the back of his chair, he starts to walk towards the bar and us. I pull my stool in closer to the table to give the guy (who is bigger than he looked when he was sitting down) room to get behind me. As he is directly behind me, he puts a hand on my shoulder.

"Got any ID, my friend?" He gives my shoulder a quick squeeze right after saying friend and I am frozen to the spot. *Fuck. He can't arrest me, can he? He's pissed.*

"How about you show the kid some ID first, you asshole." The bartender is coming from behind the bar and walking straight up to the guy.

"Here's the bill. Get your friend and get the fuck out you pair of cunts. Oh, and service isn't included, so be sure to tip your friendly barman before you fuck off." The barman points to the door as he speaks.

"Assholes."

He follows up as they start marching shamefully out, not even daring to look at us.

I'm still stuck in the same position as the two men scurry behind me and out the door like a pair of scolded boys, as two more men of a similar age to them walk in. These guys are different though; they have style. A childish prank like the other two played on me looks like it would be beneath them. The bartender ignores them as they walk in, so I guess they aren't regulars here. Having said that, he never greets us either, but these two look like they would expect a greeting. I am certain I heard Alan whisper the word fuck under his breath at their sight and when they saw him, they smiled and came over to say hello to him.

"Father Alan! My friend. Father Alan is good man, boys. Not many priests take you on piss, right?" says one of the men, winking and laughing loudly at both Rob and me. It's hard to pinpoint the accent but I'm thinking Eastern European, maybe Polish but I'm not sure. Russian? Rob and I exchange glances.

"Father Alan help people. Give bed to poor. You need bed? Priest give you bed." The Polish/Russian man then just walks away with his straight-faced friend following behind, towards a table just to the side of the jukebox that I have never once seen anyone put any money into. Even though his eyes are icy cold and empty of expression, I'm happy that Straight-Face makes eye contact with me as he walks past, still no noticeable expression though. He looks like an empty vessel. Both men make me nervous.

"I tread a thin line doing the work I do and mix with some unsavoury people sometimes. Those two are not good people," Alan tells us and moans as the two men start waving us over.

"We should leave," Alan says and he's looking nervous and willing us with his eyes to go.

"Hey, boys. Come drink, drink… here." I think he is Polish. "Hello! Man, at bar. Five Vodka please." Maybe he's Russian. He's holding up five fingers as he orders the drinks, probably because he's spent so much time being misunderstood. Straight-Face is noticeably staring at Rob. Rob knows it and is deliberately avoiding his eyes. He's very strange; intense. Five large shot glasses filled to the rim with vodka are expertly lifted individually from a tray and placed in front of each of us who are all now sitting around a large oblong table. The Russian invites the bartender to pour himself one. Actually, he said: "You! Man, at bar. You drink." It wasn't offered, more like ordered. The bartender pours himself a vodka and thanks the Russian with a nod. Then Straight-Face stands up, raises his glass, looks Rob directly into his eyes and simply says, "To my new friend." I'm surprised that he has an English accent. He hasn't said enough to decipher exactly what part of England, but I'm certain he's English. He throws the drink straight back down his throat, slams the shot glass down onto the table upside down and he looks up into Rob's eyes with an uncomfortable intent. His eyes soften though and his smile is as genuine as it is flirtatious. Rob quickly looks at me and I down my drink hoping to fuck the Russian guy doesn't give me the eye. He doesn't. He throws a hundred-dollar bill down on the table and Straight-Face puts a piece of folded paper on top of it, still, all the time looking at Rob.

"Keep change," the Russian says, and he nods respectfully to the bartender who respectfully nods back. I don't think he even knows that he's about to get a ninety-five-dollar tip, but then, I don't think the barman misses a thing in here.

"What *is* your name anyway?" I ask the barman as he slips the hundred from under the note without the hint of an expression. I guess sharing a drink with him makes me feel like we're bonding.

"I already told ya. I'm just the barman. Keep it plain and simple, okay, boys? And be careful who you choose as friends." The words are expressed as a friendly warning.

Rob opens the piece of paper that was left by the Englishman and it's just a name of a strip club on Granville Street. The bar is called Crazy Sexy, I've seen it many times before and thought what a stupid name it is. Alan takes the paper and tells us that it's the Russian's and Straight-Face's club and that we must stay away at all costs. He's adamant that they have only invited us for their own gain and that they have no friends in town, but a lot of enemies. They are absolutely not our friends is his clear message.

"If you boys don't mind, I really need to get some sleep. I'm more than happy to meet you tomorrow and help all I can though." Rob looks at me and we just shrug our shoulders and agree to all meet at the diner tomorrow.

I feel entirely too pissed to look anymore for Donna tonight and I don't know Rob's thought about it, but we're stuck downtown, both locked out and without transport. Public transport isn't running at this time, even finding a taxi will be rare and will cost a small fortune over to the North Shore. The prospect of a second night on the streets is only half as frightening when the experience is shared with a friend though, and it's a reasonably warm night in comparison to my first experience out here. There is everything we need for a comfortable night back at the basement of the church and it's going to be as safe as anywhere else around here.

Chapter Nine

There's a guy selling cocaine and weed in the men's room. I know nothing about cocaine but if his weed is anything to go by, it's probably mostly rat poison. There aren't any women customers at all, so I'm guessing the girls who we've all come to see have their own bathroom backstage. I'm reading a cartoon that's been stuck to the wall above the urinal at the perfect height to read when you're standing having a piss. I would dearly love to piss. I've been needing to go for a good hour now but every time I think it's going to be quiet; a crowd of men seem to descend all at the same time to relieve themselves. With all the pushing and shoving, shoulders rubbing together and quick appraisals of neighbouring cocks, I just can't break the seal and get a flow going. I'm still looking at the cartoon and thinking about waterfalls to try and get it started. "I've got one of these," says the boy in the cartoon, whilst pointing at his penis.

"Yes," says the girl, "but I've got one of these and with one of these, I can have as many of those as I like." You can't really argue with that.

I didn't know what to expect as the four of us turned up at the front the door of the club. I suppose I really expected us to be turned away as usual, but the closed double doors were opened for us simultaneously by two well-stocked men dressed in dinner suits and we walked into an overwhelmingly purple lit and overly mirrored entrance where we were asked to check our coats before entering the club. Then another man dressed in a dinner suit opened another door to reveal a beautiful blue-eyed blonde in gold hot pants so tight, you could probably see a pimple on her ass if she had one. Apart from the shorts, she is naked and I think she has the nicest tits I have ever seen, and that's including any I've seen in Penthouse. She has a cute wide smile that makes you fall in love with her immediately, as she asks us to follow her. I just don't know where to look as she leads us through the club. I'm feeling entirely underdressed and unkempt. Rob and I slept rough last night and still haven't freshened up. We've just been mooching around town most of the day since the brunch with Alan, still half searching but mainly just killing time before tonight. More than anything else, I'm impressed by Dennis's restraint. I look back over my shoulder to check he's okay and find he's not there. He's right up next to the stage trying to entice the stripper who's right in the middle of her routine to do something that provokes her to give him the finger. Then she turns her finger over and then lets another one join in as she does a walking motion with her first and index finger before bending over, pointing her scantily covered ass in his direction. Bent over double and looking through her legs, she tells him to shoo and waves him bye-bye. Some of the men in the audience start to chuckle and as Dennis starts to pick a fight with an American sailor, he's quickly swept away to safety and sat down with us in an out of the way booth, tucked away, as if purposely made for more private meetings. I'm questioning the VIP treatment we're receiving and I'm hoping Rob isn't going to have to sell his ass to the Englishman as the price for our night out. They only invited Rob and I but we decided to invite Dennis and Randy for backup. Neither hesitated in accepting, and nobody has objected yet.

A full bottle of vodka is placed on the table along with four shot glasses. The waitress with the world-class boobs smiles and happily tells us it's on the house. Dennis has the bottle and is lining up the four small glasses on the table and starts to pour into the first glass. *Nothing in life is for free.* It's a thought that is growing in my mind and causing concern now. Rob glances at me with similar suspicion and the worry in his eyes reminds me that the men who are schmoozing us are not men who simply want some new friends. They clearly have an agenda and Rob and I simultaneously try to stop Dennis from necking his first shot of vodka, but it's already too late and Dennis is filling up his second glass at the same time as saying cheers for the one he has just finished.

"What's wrong with you pussies?" Dennis asks.

We haven't really given Dennis or Randy much information about tonight other than it promises to be a fun night. Once we fill them both in on the full situation and who we're dealing with, Randy sits back in the plush almost completely circular orange sofa that is wrapped around the large round shiny black table in the middle of our private nook, and Dennis knocks back another vodka immediately pouring himself another.

"What?" Dennis looks at us with his hands held out either side of him, palms up like he's holding two invisible objects. "If I'm going to be molested by Russian gangsters, I'm not going to be sober. I suggest you drink up as well,

Rob." Dennis winks and smiles at Rob. "Helps to loosen the ole sphincter," he follows up unmercifully.

"I'm thinking we should just see if this leads us anywhere and get the fuck out before any of us get poked in the ass by a Kalashnikov. And fuck it, let's drink some free booze before we go," Randy says as he leans forward to grab a drink that Dennis has just poured for himself. It's noticeable by the way he struggles with the movement that he's put on quite a lot of weight quickly. Randy has been a well-stocked guy since I've known him and with the long hair, new beard growth and extra weight, he would look complete if he were sitting on a Harley Davidson Shovelhead. Randy pours into the other two empty glasses and Dennis slams his down to be filled again. He's drunk a third of the bottle already and is holding up well. Historically, Dennis and vodka don't mix well and I hope this won't turn out to be one of those nights…

Dennis told me he would never touch vodka again after divulging how he had drunk a skin full of cheap vodka with his brother Dave and a 'couple of others', and the only reminder that anything had happened the night before was the pounding head and the unusual feeling of a wax cock that had been inserted halfway up his arse… and left there.

There's lots of room around the table. Rob and I are sat at either end of the plush orange sofa with about a metre gap between us. Dennis and Randy are evenly spread, around the table, nearer to the wall. They are looking at Rob, as he's about to speak, when their two pairs of eyes raise to look high above Rob's head, and then to his shoulders, as the creepy English guy comes up from behind to massage Rob in a firm manly way.

"My new friend," he says with a convincing smile. "Friends," he counters himself, "may I join you?"

I move over to let him in but he waits for Rob to move which he tries to delay until he starts to feel uncomfortable, so he eventually stands up to let him in, but the guy only slides in enough to leave a small space for Rob to have to sit right next to him, so he remains standing.

"My friend, sit, please. I don't bite. What's your name? I'm William. Will for short."

"Mick," Rob replies and we all look at him.

"Short for Michael?" William asks politely with a smile.

"Short for Mickey Mouse. I'm not gay, okay?" Rob's getting pissed off now and I can see he's ready to leave.

"I don't care if you're gay or not. I usually find though, that any certain amount of money will make even the most resolute heterosexual question their sexuality. But that's not the game tonight. Tonight, my friend and I want to talk business with you all and I don't mix business with pleasure." He winks and smiles at Rob and shuffles along to offer more room for Rob to sit down within his comfort zone.

"I'm sorry if I made you uncomfortable. I am a terrible flirt and given the few gay men around, I tend to push my chances." William doesn't seem anywhere near as sinister now as the first time we met him. His cold eyes become more human when he smiles and the crow's feet give him a friendlier expression. He's dressed impeccably in a shiny grey suit and everything about him is neat and trimmed. He's in his fifties but is lucky enough to still have a thick head of well-kept business-like grey hair.

"Business?" Rob asks, not interested in his apology.

"Let's wait for Dmitri before we discuss business. Relax and have fun. Just try and keep a low profile though, okay? You don't exactly look old enough to be here; any of you." He looks at Dennis when he finishes his sentence and Dennis is looking unworried. I'm hoping his complacency isn't a head's up for something to come, and I'm really hoping he eases up on the vodka.

The next peeler is on stage and Dennis is removing himself from the conversation to give her his full attention.

Even though the cowboy boots and Stetson are missing, Dmitri has the appearance of a Texan oil tycoon as he struts in front of the stage in a smart white suit and string tie, nonchalantly putting ten bucks in the top of the strippers knickers. She winks and blows him a kiss as he blows smoke from his fat cigar into the brightness of the strips of multicoloured stage lights. He's greeting and shaking hands with random customers as he walks towards our table, sharing the odd joke. He turns and goes back to the stage, pulling out another ten-dollar bill from his pocket.

"Show big tits!" He waves the ten bucks in front of the dancer and she whips off her tiny bikini top to display yet another set of perfectly formed breasts. I'm thinking it must be a pre-requisite to work here or something. Dmitri stuffs the second bill in her pants and starts to applaud the stripper which is the lead for all of us to join him in showing our appreciation. Dennis isn't clapping and is counting his money and obviously thinking about following his lead in another way. He's got a lot of money too. His wallet is crammed full of bills and I can see a few big ones in there. His parents are earning more money than they know what to do with and they are working all the time anyway, so the kids are frequently gifted with extra funds to do with as they wish. He's found a way to spend some of it now.

"Boys, hello! You like tits?" he's gesturing towards the stage like a magician revealing an empty box as if she's a personal gift to us. He's smiling at all of us, remembering our faces like a camera taking a shot until he sits down next to me, making me shuffle closer to Randy who is remaining quiet but vigilant. As I move closer to Randy, Dmitri moves further in which makes me feel claustrophobic; I like a certain amount of space around me and I prefer to only let people into it when I'm ready.

"Dmitri. Please to greet you," he says, offering a hand to Dennis.

Dennis takes his hand and tells him his name at the same time thanking him for allowing him to come to his awesome club. Dmitri likes this and clasps his other hand over Dennis's as if hugging his hand.

"Welcome, my friend, Dennis Menace." Dmitri lets out a thundering 'Hah' from the back of his throat and spittle flies from his wide-open mouth onto the table, with a little landing on Dennis's lower lip which Dennis is rubbing frantically on his shirt sleeve.

"Dennis Menace." He repeats the 'Hah' and is looking at Rob and me this time, to see if we heard it the first time and we are still laughing, now falsely to keep him happy, though we are now the recipients of more of his spittle.

"Randy," Randy says as he shakes Dmitri's hand.

"Strong hand, Mandy," Dmitri says, still holding Randy's hand. "Very strong." He winks at Randy this time.

"I'm not gay," Randy says pulling his hand back swiftly as Dmitri reluctantly loosens his grip.

"Ha! Good to know, Mandy."

'Randy' states Randy but Dmitri is already turning to Rob.

"Pretty boy. What's name?" Again, offering out his hand in a friendly business-like manner.

"Oh, he's Mickey Mouse." William breaks his silence with the words and enough of a smile to accentuate the crow's feet again.

"Mickey," says Dmitri with a knowing smile and he is still happy to shake Rob's hand.

"Does that make you Donald Duck?" William asks me jovially.

"Just call me Don," I say, smiling, and for now, they seem amused and satisfied with our ridiculous pseudonyms.

The vodka bottle is empty and Dmitri calls over one of the waitresses, who happily comes with a spring in her step and a beaming smile.

Dmitri indicates for the waitress to lower herself so he can whisper in her ear. He puts a hundred-dollar bill in her hand and within three minutes, she's back with two bottles of the same vodka as before and six glasses. Then she stands by Dmitri, still beaming and slightly swaying her hips from side to side. She's trying to look coy but with her tits brazenly perched for all to see, the effect is ruined. Dmitri turns the bottle on its side and spins it fast in a clockwise direction in the middle of the table.

"Spin bottle," he announces with a beam to match the girl's.

When the bottle slowly comes to rest, the thin end is pointing directly towards Randy. When we have played spin the bottle before, the person the bottle points to would either remove a piece of clothing, tell a truth or do a dare, which generally means kissing another person in the circle.

"Hah. Mandy win." He looks at the girl. "What name?" She tells him but I couldn't hear her. "Mandy, fuck Angel. Hah! He win Angel. Who win next?"

Dennis is so focussed on the conversation now that he's starting to take over Randy's place by edging him out towards his prize.

"Let's get another bottle open, shall we?" Dennis says. He will never make it through to see a prize, let alone fuck one if he gets through another bottle with us.

"I don't know about anyone else but I wouldn't mind knowing what the fuck this is all about now," Randy's speaking the words and Dennis is worried his dream night is about to come to a disappointing end.

"Okay, Mandy, okay. Talk business. Drink. Spin bottle. Fuck after. Okay."

Even though Randy is still exasperated at the misuse of his name, we all decide it's time to know what the next step is and we sit quietly as William respectfully asks the waitress to come back in a little while.

"William, tell. Hah (spittle) William, tell. Hah Hah. (more spittle) Ahh, Canadians and English, not laugh. William tell business to boring Canadians, I go shit."

To be honest, it smells like he already has. I think farts were seeping out as he was laughing at his own joke and judging by the putridity of the stench, I think he's long overdue for a major evacuation. Dmitri drops another one as he stands to leave the table with absolutely no sign of an apology and certainly no embarrassment. I'm the only one aware of the perpetrator and when Dennis gets a whiff of the stench, he automatically looks at Randy with a frown.

"It wasn't me, fer fucks sake," Randy says adamantly. They remind me of two best friends on a long car journey home after a weeklong holiday together. Sitting behind a set of parents that agreed, but regret offering to take a friend along, rolling down a window without commenting at all about the smell permeating the car.

"No, was me," says Dmitri proudly. "I go shit now." Again, he says 'William tell' with another shower of spittle to follow while he gestures to William to speak. He's still laughing as he walks away and waving at a couple of customers who are beckoning him to go over and join them.

"No, I go shit," he shouts across the room to them, but still with no real urgency in his steps and judging by the waving of hands in front of faces, it looks like Dmitri is leaving a trail of noxious gas behind him. One guy is pointing at his buddy asking if it was him and I think he even paused for less than a second to consider claiming credit for it, but then deciding to vehemently deny it, and then, of course, turn blame on his friend. It pleases me to see that the humour and etiquette attached to farting doesn't fade with age. Grown men who are trusted to fight our wars are holding their noses and pointing fingers at each other, just like we do, and always have done. Farts are funny and I find it hard to trust anyone who doesn't giggle when someone lets out a ripper in the most tranquil of moments.

Once, when we were in one of the jazz band competitions, back in the junior jazz band at school, our leader, teacher and conductor, Reb, was introducing the next soloist who happened to be me and when he was about to announce my name to a hushed crowd of judges and other competitors, Dennis who was sitting at the end of the row of saxes with his baritone sax hanging by his side farted into his microphone that he had placed directly next to his arse for maximum effect. The effect was one of utter collapse of all order and decorum from the entire room, including all but one of the four judges. Reb had tears running down his cheeks from laughing and it seriously took a good five minutes for the last of the giggles to die down so we could start over. Throughout it all though and through my own tears of laughter, I could see the one unamused judge, the only judge not to award us full marks for a faultless performance.

The crowd is getting loud and a bit over-enthusiastic as one of the peelers has decided to auction off her underwear.

"They're really not supposed to do that," William says with a tut, turning back to face us. He doesn't seem too perturbed though. The women I've seen working here so far seem happy, so I suspect that there is a good balance of pay going on to retain the beaming smiles.

William leans forward, crosses his arms, and rests his elbows on the table. One hand comes up to stroke his chin, fiddling, like a reformed smoker.

"How would you like to have access to this corner of the club as many nights of the week as you like, boys?" Dennis jumps forward in his seat and Randy pushes him back.

"In exchange for what?" asks Randy with a surprising confidence.

"A little sales work. That's all it is. Let me explain…"

He doesn't have to explain and I should have thought of it much earlier. When it all comes to the surface, it seems so obvious.

Recently, organised crime families have been recruiting younger people to sell their wares. Often, they choose teens around our age and even younger because we are low on the police radar and if we are caught, we don't have to go to jail for long and can be back working for them sooner. It's not like taking a summer job at Safeway though. Once you take this kind of job, you're in, and you start at the level of being the most expendable, which, again, would not go the same way as quitting or getting sacked from Safeway. I might only be close to sixteen and I know I can sometimes be a bit gullible but I'm not falling for this and I'm already feeling stupid for letting things get this far.

At this point, William pulls out a small bag of white powder which I assume to be cocaine. He pours some out on the clean, smoothly polished table and separates out four lines of white dust with a credit card. He hands a gold tube to Dennis, who although I know he's never done it before, snorts up the line nearest to him. The rest of us decline his offer, so he sits back and gestures with his hand and a friendly face for Dennis to help himself. Dennis is rubbing his nose frantically like he's just sniffed pepper. He's half laughing, but fully fucked. He says he's got a funny taste at the back of his throat, so he washes it down with two shots of vodka and then he says he has to puke. Within a few seconds of William signalling her, a waitress arrives with an empty ice bucket and Dennis is heaving his guts up into it under the table at the same time as Dmitri returning to the table. Dmitri sits down and doesn't even remark on the vomiting situation.

I'm thinking that the vodka didn't even have chance to fully settle in Dennis's gut before being regurgitated and I wonder if it burns as much – or more on the way up again as it does going down. *I fucken hate vodka.*

The deal eventually thrown on the table is for us to be their street dealers selling shit coke. Obviously, it was dressed up to sound glamourous with earnings of a thousand dollars a week mentioned. Thankfully, Dennis is too wasted to hear the offer but the rest of us help him up as we start to leave the table.

"Boys, wait minute," Dmitri calls over the waitress who he slipped a hundred to earlier. She only gets halfway and recognises his signal. She's heading back towards us again now with a slip of paper in her hand which she gives to Dmitri.

"Big bill," Dmitri says passing the bill to Rob.

"Two hundred and forty-eight bucks?" Rob looks at Dmitri, shocked.

"Make it even five hundred, boys," none of us say anything. We're being shafted. I feel like such an idiot and I led all my friends right into the trap as well.

"Or you can simply work it off," William adds. "You'd probably have it covered by morning." Of course, they didn't expect a bunch of teens having that kind of money and I guess it's their common recruiting method.

"So, you're saying if we don't work for you, we have to pay you everything that you told us was on the house? I think you can go fuck yerself." Rob stuffs the bill into the pocket of Dmitri's white suit.

"Hah. Yes, pretty boy. Yes. Is understanding for you I think." Dmitri has his sinister look back, the one that his face suits best.

*

Randy and Rob are both supporting Dennis as he's slowly regaining some composure, standing on the pavement close to the curb, hopefully getting ready to flag a cab. Dennis is looking better than he was but not yet ready to be told I stole five hundred dollars from him to get us out of a situation that I got him into in the first place. My conscience is dealing with it because I will pay him back and if the roles were reversed, I would have expected him to do it to me to help us all out. William joins Rob and me and says in a low voice that I'm welcome to go to the police but, to think about if I would ever sleep properly again if I did, then he walks back into the club rubbing his hands together as if he's just evicted us.

There's a cab in the distance, about three blocks away with its roof light off, so the cabby's not picking up anyway. But then, the back door opens and his fare climbs out. A man and a woman, the woman is smaller than Alan and standing behind him so I can't see her face but I'm sure I caught the briefest of glimpses of a bit of reddish hair. In the light of the re-illuminated taxi sign, I can see the unmistakeable bushy silhouette of Alan's head darting side to side as he walks briskly around a corner out of sight; the woman slightly ahead of him.

Rob hails the cab that unbeknownst to him, Alan has just vacated, and Randy slides Dennis into the back seat, far enough for him to sit next to him and shove him further along to make room for one other. Rob's about to climb in the back next to Randy, when I grab his elbow and say we should check something out. Randy is looking a little concerned and a bit pissed off that we've left him to deal with Dennis, but I just have a gut feeling that we need to see where Alan is headed. Even though I've started trusting Alan again, I suppose once a level of suspicion is raised, there remains some time before it dissipates completely. The glances as he got out of the cab were glances to see if anyone was watching him and coincidentally, I just happened to be.

There is nothing to see in the immediate vicinity of where Alan alighted the cab. Just a short narrow alley with randomly placed overflowing steel rubbish bins with lopsided lids balanced tentatively atop the overflowing contents. An old light industrial unit is at the end of the alleyway with heavily locked steel double doors; everything is covered in urban graffiti. A cat is hovering around the bases of the bins and looks poised to jump up to the partly open containers to have a closer look inside when it's startled by the rough grinding sound of an old corrugated metal gate scraping over the pavement just a few feet away. Almost immediately, a young woman appears in a tiny tight leather mini skirt and bright red shiny plastic rain jacket. She's looking slightly disorientated and fumbling with her handbag as she walks awkwardly, in very high heels around the corner towards the red-light district.

She left the gate slightly ajar, just enough for us to see a pathway leading towards another (more solid) looking metal door on the side of a three-story old timber townhouse. There is still part of the decking left which comes off a room on the first floor but the steps that would normally lead up to it from the now shabby yard have been removed, leaving a gaping wound in the side of the house which has been blocked up with blue plastic tarpaulin. The steps have been stacked for firewood and covered with more blue tarpaulin. The house is partially lit but any view of the occupants is obscured by thick blankets of various colours and patterns placed over all the windows.

"Looks like a smack house to me," Rob says. It does. I agree.

I'm feeling quite content to leave before we attract attention to ourselves, but Rob has a very inquisitive nature and I join him peering through any openings in the blankets covering the windows. The only thing I can see is a small glimpse of tatty red carpet and the bottom of a closed wooden door that looks like it's seen better days. The place is condemned and basically ready for demolition. It's just a temporary shelter used by the homeless and drug addicts until it's knocked down and they move on to find the next place or end up back on the streets. We can't really see anything of the inside but it's clear that it's going to be rough and very likely dangerous to unknown visitors. The only access into the building is the heavy metal door we saw as we came through the gate and Rob feels the same lack of need as me to knock on it. We're starting to walk away and again I'm feeling guilty about dragging a friend on a wild goose chase, when the young woman we saw earlier heading out to work on the streets, returning with a youngish, scrawny looking man in his early twenties. He's wearing a baseball cap and jeans that are supposed to be tight, but his legs are too thin to fill them out and they're wrinkled at the top where his belt has pulled them in, so they don't fall down. He's a very small man and he definitely has some issues about his size because he's wearing football shoulder pads under his sweatshirt. I wonder if he really thinks it's not noticeable… and what happens when she wants to get him naked? The tiny man with huge shoulders looks a bit like a pint-sized replica of Superman. The girl in the mini-skirt doesn't seem to care though. He's got his hands dug deep into his front jeans pockets and she is linking her arm through his as if on a date. I suppose it is a date really. He's just paid to do away with all the usual courting and endless dates and probably saved himself a few bucks as well to get straight to the fun part. Mind you, he probably doesn't attract women all that well, and bless the working girls who are always willing to help a poor soul out for the right price.

She has a key. I really didn't expect her to have a key. I thought there would be a secret knock or something.

Rob manages to catch the door just before it slams shut and we wait for the couple to disappear around a corner at the end of a long hall before we slowly creep in. The floor is covered with the same tatty red carpet I saw through the gap in the window from outside earlier. The house is quiet apart from the sound of a door slamming someway off. Once we reach the end of the hall and as we start to turn the corner to the left, the door at the end of the hall nearest us, on the right, opens at the same time as the sound of a toilet struggling to flush. Even if we had time and a place to hide, we wouldn't have. I think both of us were equally dumbfounded and stuck to the spot at the sight of the pink and cute all in one pyjama suit, and the matching pink slippers with bunny ears, with Donna wearing them.

*

There are about a dozen girls living in the safe house that they created for themselves out of the derelict building that was once a proud family home for early Vancouverites. Apart from Alan, no men are supposed to know about it at all, so the woman who accidentally let us in was expelled from the house for being unsuitable and a risk to everyone else. Alan knows everything that is going on downtown and has been keeping an eye on them and helping out when necessary for months.

Sitting in Donna's room, we learned enough to understand it all and the parts that were left for the imagination are probably best kept that way. A tall, slim woman with long wavy strawberry blonde hair tucked behind her ears, joined Alan, Rob, Donna and I and told us she was CJ. The nominated leader of the house. I recognised her as the woman who got out of the cab with Alan. She stood in the doorway of the sparsely furnished room with a formidable presence and looked very dissatisfied that her safety perimeters had been breached; not angry, just perplexed. The speed in which the girl was evicted was swift. She and her ruffled client were marched out. He tried to hide his face behind an upturned collar of his faded denim jacket but he wasn't succeeding. The other girls, as if living by regimental order, didn't leave their rooms and I didn't see any of them the entire time we were in there. CJ was outside giving the two perpetrators their marching orders and I suspect a stern warning about telling anyone about the house. She intimidated me, not maliciously, but enough to not mention it and I think her demeanour had the same effect on the two that were cast out onto the streets.

"We're moving soon anyway," CJ remarks to Alan with a skyward tilt of her eyes, walking confidently back, this time, fully into the room. Alan and CJ told us very calmly and in a friendly manner, that the only right thing to do is to pretend the whole thing never happened. Erase it from our minds and do absolutely nothing that will endanger the women who are already scared.

My trust and bonding for Alan has grown beyond doubt, especially since telling us how he used to be a reckless drunk with only thoughts about himself. He told us about a particular night when he was in a bar in his home town of Toronto at 2 am which wasn't unusual and fairly consistent, when at precisely the same time, his wife was being raped in front of his daughter who was then also raped at the age of eight in front of her beaten mother, followed by both mother and daughter being suffocated by plastic bags being placed over their heads and taped around their necks. The attackers probably didn't even stay around to watch their victims die, for nothing more than a fucked-up TV set and about fourteen bucks that was in his daughter's piggy bank. Alan didn't even pack. After the funeral, he simply walked away, caught a bus and ended up in Vancouver trying to drink himself to an early death. He found God in time though, he tells us. He's never tried to push God and the bible onto me once and he knows my thoughts about it. I respect him for that. I respect him for what he's been through and survived as well. A life event like that would need a complete change of direction; a new beginning I suppose. I wish I had enough faith in someone or something to start afresh sometimes. Start afresh with the knowledge I've gained so far but not have to go back to repeat my life; I'd hate that. To be honest, if I were given the choice between going back and living it again or ending it now, it would be a tough one.

We're not telling anyone about it and I'm even reluctant to tell you, but Donna has never been happier. She's not having and never had a romantic fling with Alan. Alan never abducted her, in fact, it was *her* who was seeking *his* help. She was trying to get away from an abusive household and a boyfriend who was pimping her out on the streets; the boyfriend we had been searching along with in ignorance and vain. Mark has deceived us in the most horrific way, and we don't know how to deal with him.

*

"We know," is all Rob said. It's all we decided between us that he needed to say for Mark to shit his pants where he stands and disappear forever. Rob just hangs up the phone after saying the two words and we look satisfied with hopefully solving the problem of ever having to see Mark's face in the neighbourhood again. The rest of it, we try in our own ways to put out of our minds, but we both have a sense of achievement as well as huge disappointment in the level of betrayal someone is capable of. I know I'm going to spend weeks, months if not the rest of my life dissecting it in my head. *Why didn't I notice something sooner? Was he ever a friend?*

Chapter Ten

People do live here, but it has the feeling of being uninhabited. Bowen Island is only a couple of miles off the coast of British Columbia, but it feels isolated from the growing suburban sprawl of the nearby mainland. A short drive after the ferry crossing brought us to an empty oceanside campground with well-kept individual cleared pitches for each of us to have our own temporary oceanside property. Out here, we can hang out together or have as much space as we want. Even though the island is small, the surrounding fir forest with its numerous clearings seems to go on forever. We feel even more free and unreachable here than we did at the ledge. It's a different feeling altogether now as well. It's spring with the odd taste of summer heat in the air to let us know it's coming soon and the tension that was running so high then, is less intense because even though at home the pressure to succeed is ever-present, my job at the restaurant garden and the inability to get home before my curfew means I rarely see my father at all. I do sometimes make it home but I generally just go to my room and keep my head down and practise the sax for a quiet life. The other nights are mostly spent at Rob's and Dennis's. Scott's parents have been happy to have me stay as well. They love to have me stay with them. They feel they are on the wrong side of the tracks and for their son to be mixing with a dentist's son is something they for some reason hold onto with pride. Scott certainly doesn't hang out with me because of my dad. He hangs out with me because I'm the exact opposite of my dad, and it interests me – It's the first time (knowingly) I've been accepted into someone's home and honoured (embarrassingly so) as some sort of royal visitor who deserves the best China to come out of the cupboard only because of my father. For this reason, I tend to only go when other options aren't available.

Not everyone could come camping but the main core are here; my closest friends. Jayne couldn't come, of course. Her mum said she had too many commitments, but we all know the truth. Her old man has complete control over her now and until she fights it, he always will in one way or another. To be honest, I don't think I will see Jayne again after the incident with David White and although it hurts a little, I'm feeling over her. Lisa's here and although her and Rob aren't together anymore, they are still close and sitting on a log just watching the ocean lap against the pebbles only a few feet away from our tents. Randy is still asleep in his ridiculously small tent and it's unimaginable that his poor girlfriend is somehow crammed in there amidst the snoring, interrupted by impressively regular and powerful farting. I think the flies that occupy the organic toilet have migrated to more fruitful climes by the looks of it because there are literally hundreds of flies on their tent and nobody else's. I'd go and check if there are fewer flies at the toilet just out of interest, but I prefer to avoid going there unless it's absolutely necessary. I don't like public toilets at the best of times and this has really been pushing me out of my comfort zone. It's just a twenty-foot-deep huge hole in the ground with an equally huge mountain of shit piling up in it, ever closer to the oil drum-like looking thing on top to sit on. It's not a pleasant experience. Dennis and Dave aren't here yet but they're coming later today. They have to help out at their parents' restaurant but they're definitely coming and Dee has given us strict instructions that if we play truth or dare, the shit mountain is out of bounds.

I roll myself a joint and start walking along a trail that's marked 'lookout point'. It's starting to warm up, even though it's only eight in the morning and the air has the special smell of coniferous sap in the air. There is movement everywhere underfoot. Armies of red ants, marching in orderly lines, following their orders. Society and rules seem to exist in all aspects of life to a certain extent and I wonder if theirs function better than ours. When I think about the size of an ant and the distance it covers in such a short amount of time, it puts into perspective how slow and cumbersome humans are. Their speed doesn't alter either when the ants are ascending a cliff, which when put into perspective, would take a human two days to reach the top, whereas the tiny ant can scurry to the summit well within a minute. I wonder if they have huge meetings in their constantly evolving homes of dry needles piled higher and higher each day due to their tireless efforts. Every time I see the diversity and incredible beauty of all the species on the planet, I can't help feeling like humans are the ugliest and the stupidest.

The view is what my mum would call breathtaking from the summit and I roll myself another joint to sit back and relish in the amazing scene in front of me.

I can only describe it as a blue view. It's not masses of unhindered ocean, but more like a multitude of winding channels between umpteen blue-green islands and in the distance, the ocean just falls away over the horizon, giving me thoughts of what lay beyond. Ferries, yachts, speed boats, fishing boats and many other watercraft are leaving little white lines on the sunlit water, like random dashes of chalk on a blue canvas. I'm not an expert on birds but I know enough to see there are many different varieties circling the steep hillside rolling away in front of me towards the ocean. Some rising and circling on thermals. Some just sitting on boughs tilting their heads to look sideways down towards the ground waiting for a worm that might surface for the chicks that will be big and hungry now. It's early on a Sunday morning and I'm surprised to see so much traffic on the water, but then, Canadians do like to make the most of their free time and they truly appreciate the surroundings they are fortunate enough to live in.

I don't have a watch with me but my internal clock is telling me it's somewhere around eight-thirty and the tranquillity of the moment is interrupted by an enormous bang; enough to make me jump but clearly far enough away to not feel as though it's a threat. My immediate thought is it's the big one on its way, but it didn't sound like an earthquake. Just as I'm wondering if a wave is about to pass under me, there's another bang, followed closely by another. No real ground shake, and it all seems to have stopped now. Maybe it was a cannon going off on one of the islands – a maritime celebration or something. *Fucken big cannon.* My thoughts turn back to the things that have happened to me lately. It seems to have been a long year, a fight; a fight that seems to slowly be draining away in me.

Looking back, to the time on the Ledge when the determination was so strong in all of us for independence, it occurs to me that the ones that were making the most noise are all sitting here together on Bowen Island for a little escape. The one who remained quietest is free. Donna might not be living the high life that she dreamed of, but she had the courage and determination to get out of a situation she knew wasn't good for her. Her story is extreme in comparison to ours, but at some point, in some way, we have to find a way to leave a broken nest early in order to become strong and survive. Seeing Donna in her new life made me feel happy for her. She has nothing in the way of material artefacts, but she has friends who care about her and she was smiling; a real smile. Rob and I talk about her from time to time when we are alone and we both agree that we have done the right thing in keeping quiet about the safe house. We tend to avoid talking about Mark and he hasn't been discussed since he was ousted. I go over and over it in my mind, trying to understand why I couldn't have seen it sooner. Mark's betrayal has been a very harsh lesson and any trust issues I have had before, have been put on high alert for the indefinite future. He permeated all levels of our lives, became our friend, and to a certain extent, I believe he was a friend. He just got lost. In my life, he will remain lost. We told the others that Mark got another lead about Donna in Manitoba and has gone off looking for her. Nothing more has been said.

A breeze is starting to pick up and even though they are very small in the distance, I can see the yachts starting to keel over slightly as their sails fill with wind. A red ant bites me on the shin and I instinctively kill it with the usual following guilt. *Little fucker didn't have to bite me though.*

The wind is really picking up quite rapidly and the sky in the distance is taking on a dark squally look. I should imagine it's a sky to give the sailors below a cautious warning that something is on its way. The squalls that can blow up in the straights without much notice can be brief, but very severe and unless you really know what you're doing, it's best to find shelter fast.

The walk back to the campsite isn't as serene as the ascent and even the ants seem to have retreated somewhat from the impending storm. I wonder if the rain penetrates their homes. They don't look waterproof. Even though it's spring, a fir cone from last autumn is shaken loose by a gust of wind and lands with a menacing thud nearby. Trees are beginning to creek as they strain to remain upright in the gusts which are gaining momentum and very loud as they sweep through the trees, discarding more natural debris in their wake. The quiet chitter-chatter of birds and rustling in the undergrowth on the way up is replaced now by a roaring constant wind that seems to have built up from nothing to gale force with increasingly aggressive gusts on top of it. I'm guessing I'm about halfway back to the campsite and the wind has come out of nowhere in that time. If it keeps increasing in intensity at the same rate before I get back to the relative safety of a car, I think some of these trees might lose the fight. I hear loud snaps and cracks of boughs breaking around me, cracks and thuds as the wood hits the ground. Then the rain starts. It's an immediate deluge of huge heavy raindrops that can almost make it feel like it's hard to breathe. The rain is quickly turning to hail. The hailstones are not huge, about the size of a small pea, but the amount of them and the ferocity in which they are being spun around at speed in the air by the swirling currents of wind is making them painful on the face; like icy cold steel orbs coming at me from every angle at about eighty miles an hour on a gust.

It's really becoming unsafe now and I'm hoping the guys back at the camp are finding shelter because I doubt the tents are up to this. The only thing I can do is to go over to the only solid thing in sight and nestle myself as far as I can into the slight undercut of a huge granite boulder. I can squash about half of my body sideways under the rock, which is about the size of a small van, but half of me still remains exposed to the elements. The hail is getting heavier and bigger as the wind gains yet more strength and the noise is deafening; frightening. I can hear trees coming down now. The sound of huge trunks splitting and ripping apart is overpowering the tremendous noise of the gale, and as one goes, it opens up a little gulley for the next one to take the brunt of the wind, until they start to fall like endless skittles in an ever-widening alley. I've been in moments like this before, not exactly wind and hail, but in a situation where I wasn't sure if I'm going to get out of it alive. It's a strange residing feeling, convincing myself that if it happens it will be quick. A completely helpless feeling. There is nothing more I can do to protect myself because I certainly can't move from where I am. I think my friends probably will have headed for the cars and to be honest, I don't think they're enough protection against the size of the trees coming down, so I hope they're safe. *Fucken hell, I hope the boats below got to safety.*

Another bang that made me think my time really was up came at the same time as the lightning stuck the lookout point where I was enjoying the view not so long ago in the peaceful early summer sunshine. The power of the strike being so nearby made my ears ring and there is a general buzzing in the air around me.

As if the lightning strike were the grand finale, the storm ends as quickly as it began and the return to immediate sunshine gives the whole experience a spiritual aura; a kind of afterglow is definitely in the air... *a second chance, don't fuck it up.*

The brightness of the returning sunlight is intensified by the white landscape left behind by the hail, to the point that I'm squinting as I'm now standing, taking in the new view around me. The ants must be having a meeting now about who fucked up with the seasons.

The wind has torn open a wide patch of forest in the direction that I'm going and it's going to be hard work climbing over and crawling under the dozens of horizontal tree trunks. Most of the fallen trees have been snapped at differing heights, with only a few being uprooted; leaving a scene of destruction. As if cleared by mother nature herself, it's only the young saplings with their still supple stems that could bow enough to the wind and avoid being crushed, now having unshaded sunlight all to themselves. Climbing around the ripped part of forest means I gain some altitude again and I am surprised to find myself walking in ever-deepening wet snow. It's settled on warm ground and the sun is attacking it from the other side so it's melting quickly and I'm walking through unavoidable rivulets of meltwater and the ground underfoot is feeling unstable; boggy. Then I watch as the area that had already been levelled, slips away, in slow motion down the side of the hill, this time taking the saplings with it. The whole ground around me is rumbling and I'm worried the whole fucking hill might go, so my pace quickens whether I think about it or not. It's a simple 'get the fuck out' reflex which is, this time, inarguable.

Back at the campsite, the first thing I see is nothing. Everything and everyone is gone, and my first fear is that the whole lot have been washed away into the ocean, never to be seen again. It's amazing how quickly the feeling of panic can rise at a mere catastrophic thought and I can feel the inexplicable and uncontrollable anxiety starting to take hold of my body, but it quickly drains away, seemingly nowhere as I see everyone heading back from the direction of the car park.

"Kev!" They're as happy to see me as I am them. In fact, completely unexpectedly, Lisa runs up to me, jumps up as she wraps both her arms and her legs around me, forcing me to nearly lose my balance as I'm trying to adjust to holding all of her weight. My hands find nowhere else to gain a good grasp except on her ass and I'm surprised at how firm it is. Then she gives me a kiss on the lips; a really nice kiss. She kisses me hard but at the same time, I don't think the memory will ever fade about how soft her lips feel against mine and how her tongue tastes of bubble gum and cigarettes.

"I love you," she says it quietly, just for me to hear and by the intensity of the look in her eyes, I can tell she means it as more than friends.

"Kev!" This time, it's Rob who's shouting and I am still looking confused about what I've just been told on top of nearly dying and just stand staring into space as Rob gives me hug.

"We were worried about you, buddy." Rob is genuinely happy to see me and it makes me feel good. I'm still thinking about what the girl he's still crazy about has just told me and right now, I just want a beer and a big fat joint.

It's always the same and it's why I like it: whenever I get that hit off a good joint, all the thoughts and worries that are constantly whirring away in my head dissolve into a state of complete 'couldn't give a fuck'. My thoughts whir faster when I'm stoned but the feelings are never aggressive, and often creative. Alcohol makes me angry at all the problems that make me feel like shit but weed just makes them float away gently into the ether.

I have only recently seen the irony in my father (having just smoked a cigarette) slamming a healthy glass of single malt down on the table as he preached to me about the immorality of (in his words) taking cannabis. I think it's my father that makes me loathe hypocrisy. I've spent my life being told one thing whilst listening to him agreeing to someone he regards as superior and with very differing views and then condemning behaviour, not at all dissimilar to his own. Trying to understand my father is a minefield!

At times like these, I prefer not to drink, so I decline when the beers are being passed around our new campfire. Sometimes, a high can be ruined by mixing it with alcohol and I don't want to ruin this buzz I've got going on. Thoughts become deeper but the deeper I delve into them, I all of a sudden find myself thinking about something else completely, without being able to recall the thought from only a second ago. Depending on the weed strain, the thoughts can be uplifting and creative or at the other end, you kind of get a mind wipe and a capability of doing nothing other than sitting in a couch for at least an hour. I'm feeling quite uplifted at the moment and I hope that the joint that's being passed to me now is the same one. It's Scott's and I tell him I absolutely need to get some off him.

"I grow it myself," he tells us and I am wondering how the fuck he kept it quiet so long. "Actually, my dad does, but it's just between us, okay? Seriously, I'm trusting you guys, okay?" I can see that him sharing this information is a big thing for him. *He trusts us.*

"That's some very nice weed, man." Randy's just had his first toke and is getting the same nice buzz by the looks of it.

"Sativa dominant," Scott says as if that will mean something to all of us.

"A who the what the fuck?" responds Randy chuckling. It's a really giggly high.

"There are two main kinds of weed."

Scott is looking up to see if any of us are interested. All of us are waiting for him to continue, so he carries on telling us about Indica and Sativa which are two different types of what I thought was just weed. Apparently, it's the sativa that gets you being buzzy and creative while the opposite effect comes from Indica. The clever people who grow the weed have managed to crossbreed and start producing hybrids of both types which customise the effect to the growers' preference. THC is the part of weed that gets you high and the idea is to get the plants to produce as much of it is as possible. Scott tells us that the THC is really there for cross-pollination purpose, so, in reality, what the best growers are achieving is the very horniest female plants possible.

The banter that revolves around the horny plants starts and goes off on many tangents as I retreat a little into my own thoughts. I'm thinking about Lisa and what she said. I'm thinking that what she said to me has made me face up to the fact that I have been in love with her since the night at Cleveland Damn. I never knew if she felt the same as me as we were walking arm in arm after the events at the damn but now, with recent events and an adjusted hindsight, I think she wanted me to feel the closeness that I thought was in my own imagination. My thoughts are broken by the sound of contagious giggles trying to be kept under control and I look up to see Randy trying to get a breath and holding his hurting gut as he tries to stop laughing. The others, as me, have no idea what he's laughing at, but the giggling is contagious. Within seconds, the whole circle around the fire is in fits of laughter and Lisa leans into me and says I really love you into my ear as she starts to giggle again.

The butterflies are overwhelming me to the point of ecstasy. The guilt when I see Rob's face as she kisses my cheek is crushing. He doesn't get pissed at me or anything. He just smiles; the most painful smile I've ever received.

"I'm just going to go and talk to Rob," and I give Lisa a quick peck on the cheek as I start to make a slow stoned move to get up.

"I was worried you pussies might have run home to your mommas!" Dennis shouts at us on his approach. Dave smiling by his side, neither of them having any apparent gear for camping with them. They both even still have their waiter's uniforms on.

"Why would we want to do that?" Randy asks. "It's pretty cool here without our mommas." He answers in between laughs and just saying that makes him fall back into fits of giggles. I sit back down and decide to talk to Rob later.

"You've not heard then…" Dennis and Dave look at each other, Dennis pulling a pack of cigarettes out of his pocket and lighting one up before carrying on.

"Heard what?" I ask Dennis.

"Mount St Helens blew this morning. They're calling it the US's biggest natural disaster to date."

Dennis takes another drag on his cigarette and we're waiting for him to continue but he just sits there, apparently having completed his story.

Mount St Helens is in the US, but then, seventy percent of the Canadian population lives within twenty-five miles of the US border and Mount St. Helens is close to the Canadian border about seventy miles away from where we are now.

"And?" I press Dennis, eager to know more.

"Oh, it's no biggie really. Just loads of mud and shit. It's not like there's river of red-hot lava heading our way. Anyone got a beer?"

Dennis is totally uninterested in probably one of the most exciting things that have happened in my lifetime, apart from Neil Armstrong walking on the moon. I was only six, but I remember it vividly; a group of us watching it on a tiny black and white TV set with a snowy picture.

Fuck me, those were the bangs. I wonder if the freak storm had anything to do with it; earthquakes and volcanoes can set off some weird shit. I wonder if there is more weird shit to come. *Do erupting volcanoes trigger earthquakes?*

Dee is happy to see Dennis and quickly gets up to sit next to him as he takes up a place around the fire next to Randy. Dave, quietly and almost unnoticeably, sits on the other side of Randy.

The feeling I'm getting as I look at the best friends I've ever had; to see their faces glowing in the fire is more warming than the heat generated by the fire itself. I trust these people with my innermost secrets… except one. Only the one secret will remain between Rob and I not because we don't trust our friends, it's simply because the topic hasn't come up. If it does arise, we still won't mention it though, so as long as it's not talked about, we don't have to make awkward side shifts in a conversation to avoid outright lying to our friends.

"Fuck me, that's good weed." Dennis half laughs and half coughs as he prepares to take another toke before passing it along. "Oh yeah, I almost forgot…" Dennis leans over to one side and pulls out a tiny bottle, no bigger than one of those little eye drop bottles that easily fit between a thumb and the first two fingers. Why he makes the extra effort to lean over to *me* to pass it to, I don't know, until the words, truth or dare, come out as I take the bottle from his hand.

"Fuck sake. What is it?" I ask. It looks harmless enough, but this has come out of the hands of Dennis followed by the dreaded words.

I'd be a pussy if I said truth at this point, so I listen Dennis telling me to take the top off and breathe in a big breath and quickly put the lid back on.

"It's not going to send me on a trip to hell and back for a week is it?" I am genuinely concerned. I've never tried any mind-altering substances other than cannabis or alcohol. I don't like the idea of a trip that I have no control over, and I don't like the idea of an addiction to anything no matter how good the high sounds. I've realised from my short usage of cigarettes how strong the power of addiction is, and I seem to be low on will power to quit, so I'd rather stay away.

Dennis laughs and says to just trust him and nothing bad will happen. So, I trust him and take a deep breath on the strange but not totally unpleasant-smelling liquid and within less than a second, my mind is blank and the world I live in and all the people in it are momentarily gone. I'm just in a state of nothingness with a rising anxious feeling until the blackness goes leaving me with a very high, but not pleasant feeling that lasts a further couple of minutes. It's just too extreme and fast with no slow build-up or come down. It's literally a rush which is coincidentally what's written on the black bottle in bold gold letters. The unexpected side effect and aftermath of the quick rush is an impressive and uncomfortable erection that has appeared seemingly out of nowhere and for no reason that I'm aware of. It wouldn't have been so bad, even pleasant, but in my stupor prior to the aftermath, I hadn't been in the position to casually conceal it. There it is, standing proud, trying to escape the restrictions of my clothing and stretching the zipper's seams to the maximum for all to see and laugh at. Lisa whispers 'I want it' into my ear and it throbs enough for all to laugh even more at my increasingly vulnerable situation. Dennis now takes the bottle of Rush back and drops the filter end of a cigarette into the liquid until the cigarette is saturated. Once he's taken a huge toke on the unlit cigarette, he goes into an even deeper state of oblivion than I visited, and all Dee can do is look at his groin waiting for something similar to happen.

"I really want you, Kev," Lisa is whispering in my ear again and every time she does, I look over to Rob who has noticed everything.

"I'm going to talk to Rob now." This time, getting up is even harder than the first time I tried.

"Rob, wanna go and smoke one by the water?" I've got one hand on his shoulder and the other is waving a joint under his nose as I ask.

"Course, buddy."

"What's up?" he asks as we sit down leaning against the driftwood on the beach, he and Lisa were sharing this morning. It's an odd evening with a strange colour to the sky; like another storm might be looming in the distance.

All of us are blood brothers and sisters in the Cave. It's part of the process of joining; the final process before becoming a fully-fledged member and lighting up the ceremonial Russian cocktail cigarette. As Rob and I started, the latest member to join slices a cut, deep enough to bleed in their right wrist, followed by the new recruit who cuts their left wrist. They then join their wounds together forming the bond of blood brothers and sisters; an inseparable bond. Trust and honesty are paramount, and I know Rob well enough to know he wants me to get straight to the point.

"I've been making some moves on Lisa and she seems to be digging it," I say to Rob, feeling very uncomfortable in the situation.

"Fuck off," he says and I recoil slightly at his reaction. "I've seen her all over you. It's okay, brother, you dig each other and it's about fucken time you got your dick wet." He's laughing now. "Seriously, I still love Lisa but like a sister, so I'm cool with you two getting together." I'm not convinced that Rob is being completely honest with me about his feelings for Lisa because it wasn't so long ago that he was devastated at her breaking up with him.

"Maybe I'll have another crack at Jayne."

FUCK! JAYNE!

"Fuck me, are you two still together?" Rob could obviously see by the expression on my face that the mention of her name had sent my mind temporarily elsewhere.

"Well, we haven't exactly broken it off, but then again, we haven't even spoken on the phone for weeks and I sorta lost it in front of her a while ago, so I'm assuming we're over." Rob starts laughing again.

"Lost it?" Rob is eager to hear the whole story of me batting David White off Pam's motorbike and by the time I'm finished telling him, he's laughing his head off again.

But then, he realises that I have been wounded by the whole thing and still feel betrayed by Jayne even though I miss her.

"You did what you had to do, brother," Rob reassures me. "He's a cocky fucker who needed a pasting anyway," he follows up.

Rob does make me feel better about the whole thing, but it was another one of those moments that scare the hell out of me. I can't really imagine that Jayne will have been impressed by my actions, but in that moment, there was no other choice. There was nothing else on my mind than to severely maim a person, and thank fuck he had a helmet on, or I might have killed him.

We agree to never be arseholes about girls and that our friendship is more important. The words are said to each other, but I do wonder how much time I might have spent with Rob if I were allowed to see Jayne more over the last few months. I love Rob, but Jayne and Lisa are a different type of love; an alluring love combined with lust that is almost addictive and you just want to keep getting more and more, the more you get. I'm starting to think it's a shame that we try to find one person to be with for the rest of our lives when there are infinite varieties of love and lust to explore and enjoy.

When Rob and I get back to the fire, the wind has picked up a little again which makes me have immediate anxious thoughts about another storm like this morning's coming. The conversation around the fire has briefly halted as we all look at a fresh set of debris being swept around by the new gust, but that was it. A quick reminder, that's all.

Lisa has had a go with the Rush, and I don't know if it has the same effect on girls but she's pulling me on top of her and I grab her firm ass again as we fall together on to the ground in a passionately kissing embrace. She smells different from Jayne, a sexy scent as if she's been made to be especially pleasing to the opposite sex… God's gift to men.

Trust me when I say that losing my virginity is pretty much all I ever think about and with no disrespect meant towards Lisa at all, it's pretty much a given that unless a tsunami rolls in, I'm marked for getting laid tonight. But in front of Rob? He came here with Lisa because he still loves her. He knows she wants to move on and he knows she wants to be with me, but I just can't do it. It's just not cool. I merely say to Lisa 'I can't' and she stops, kisses me on the cheek and just says 'later alligator', walking, alone in the direction of the beach.

Dee is looking disappointed and telling Dennis his dick will probably never recover from the motel incident and that he might as well get a sex change. Then she starts to crawl on top of him and says that she wouldn't mind if he did with a naughty grab of his balls. Dee only took a tiny sniff on the bottle and her behaviour isn't out of character so it's still hard to decipher if it's actually only me who is feeling ridiculously horny. Rob and Randy both took huge draws on the bottle and are still looking a bit dazed, but as far as I can see, no hard-ons. Maybe I am just oversexed; it is always at the forefront of my mind with very little let up. Maybe it will lessen a little when I get laid. Seriously, since the beginning of puberty, getting laid has been my solitary purpose and goal in life. Yet with my sixteenth birthday around the corner, I'm a good step closer, but I'm still officially a virgin and it sucks. Maybe I'm really just a pussy; I mean, both Rob and Lisa are cool with it and yet I sit here with a throbbing boner and the invitation of a wanting beaver on the beach. *I'm being a pussy…I'm being a friend…I'm being a pussy…* Just as I move to stand and go to claim my woman by the water, Lisa screams from the beach, a shocking scream, then another one and we can hear her kind of crying and half calling for help at the same time. When we get there, Lisa is already in Rob's arms as he holds her protectively and caringly; lovingly. I don't love Lisa like that. I just want to have sex with her when all is said and done, and truth be told. When I see how Rob treats Lisa, I see how love really is, and I have no concept of that feeling at all, although I try to keep convincing myself I do. Even when I have a wank, the woman of my fantasy has no further consequence to me once the ultimate goal has been reached.

I'm happy that Lisa's okay and that it was nothing more serious than a leach that had latched onto her ankle that had freaked her out. A leach or an eel anyway. 'Something slimy and disgusting' were her words. I'm also glad to have seen her and Rob together and the realisation that I'm probably just kidding myself that I love her, just to fuck her, and the evening becomes much more relaxed now that the sexual tension has gone. I've decided to just sit around the fire and get high with my friends, have a few laughs and have an early night. Then Dennis passes me a soaking wet cigarette, soaked in Rush… followed by the dreaded words that have initiated many teenage mishaps… Truth or dare.

Part of my life went; literally disappeared, into blackness but the strange and worrying thing is that during the time in the darkness, I have travelled from the campfire to the beach and my painfully hard cock is in Lisa's firm grip. She has released it from the confines of my pants and is holding it tightly as she starts to wank me slowly. All my thoughts of being a good and decent friend have been wiped away by the sheer pleasure of feeling my cock in her hand. *I'm such an asshole.*

She leans into me and kisses me and as I push my tongue into her mouth, she teasingly sucks it in and won't let go of it. When she eventually does release it, she gives my bottom lip a little bite. I want to join in and be playful back, but at the same time, I want to feel helpless and let her do as she wishes with me. She senses my submission to her and her hand slides down to unbuckle my belt as she lifts my T-shirt to nibble on my left nipple. My cock is in her hand again and my eyes close as the ecstatic feeling of her wet tongue slides down my belly, over my belly button, lower, until she has the tip of my penis engulfed in her soft moist lips. She is slow and sensual as if savouring an ice lolly on a hot summers day. Slowly licking the end and then sliding her lips all the way down, to just come back and tease the end again. It's almost as though she's actually enjoying it. She's wearing black tight spray-on jeans and is sliding them over her own ass to reveal sexy lacy black panties with a tiny pink bow at the front, right above a tuft of black pubic hair enticing me to want to see more. I feel guilty watching her struggle so move to help but she pushes me back down firmly with a smile and a prohibitive wag of her index finger. Her jeans are off now and are lying in a discarded heap along with her boots and socks. She still has her panties on and sits astride me as she grinds herself against my desperate cock; gyrating like a cowgirl at a rodeo and giggling when she leans in to kiss me. My eyes are closed now and as I touch her ass in an attempt to remove her knickers, she brushes my hands away, then she pulls her knickers to one side so I can feel the wetness of her against the tip of my cock for the very first time. It feels so soft and I am trying to move my hips so I can push myself into her, but she keeps evading my moves… teasing me. She's still sitting astride me but is now leaning over to reach into her jeans pocket and I'm not only surprised but also disappointed to see the bottle of Rush appear in the palm of her hand. I want to decline and get on with the things the way they were going, and to be honest, I don't really get that much from the Rush anyway. Lisa is laughing and trying to keep her eyes focussed as she passes the bottle to me after taking a pretty big hit, so in the spirit of the moment…

I pass out for longer than Lisa is comfortable with and while I'm still out of it, she calls everyone over to help. When I come to senses, it's to a very different scene that I left; a scene that is back to square one because Lisa is fully dressed and helping to support me back to the fire. I don't need the support, but I like her arm around me. Dennis is on the other side of me and breaks loose as we approach the fire to throw another couple of logs on.

Thankfully, the seemingly endless painful erection has receded back to a passive state and I'm wondering if it was only me that it affected in that way.

After asking around, I learn that Rush is sold in sex shops to help with arousal and get partying. No shit! Although the other guys said they were aroused to a certain level, none experienced the boner situation, and the girls just said that they're always horny anyway. Randy's off somewhere with his girlfriend, Kathy. Rob's rolling a joint, Scott's knocking back a beer and Dennis is taking another huge suck on the bottle of Rush before settling back with a huge smile and eyes that seem to be slightly bulging as they stare at Dee dancing to an imaginary song.

"Let's get some sounds going," Dee is shouting the words at us excitedly.

"I don't know about sounds, but I think we're in for a cool light display," I say.

As Dee is dancing to her own singing and asking for music, a lightning display starts in the distance, probably in the US, but it's in the mountains close to the water and the amazing show in the sky is reflected in the water to double the wonderful display. It's constant. The natural exhibition of light is like masses of strobe lights illuminating huge expanses of the coastal mountain range. There is never a break in the lightning long enough for the view to dim completely out of sight and when I look into the darkness of the night elsewhere, I can see the image of the flashing horizon stamped onto my retinas every time I blink. The purple flashes in the distance are so regular that it seems as though we are watching the storm being sped up in a movie. Occasionally, we can see a clear fork of lightning pierce its way through the night sky to destroy something as close as possible to it on land. Mountain lightning is always fierce in my experience, and I've been caught up in the middle of some ferocious storms when I used to trek on camping trips with the Venturers not so long ago. I would never want to be camping in anything like the storm that is on the distant horizon and I hope it stays on the horizon.

The sexual tension that was sweeping through the camp earlier has gone and apparently forgotten about. All of us are sitting on the beach, lined up along a broken away log that has drifted to settle here. It's long enough to hold at least ten more people but I'm happy with who I'm with. I'm probably sitting in about the middle of the line, with Lisa on my left and Dee on my right. I haven't really looked beyond my immediate neighbours; mainly because of the lightning show, but also by Lisa trying to sneakily pinch me in various places which does nothing more than make me extremely ticklish.

A set of headlights pull into the car park where our cars are parked about half a mile away. I doubt it's new campers at this time, so it's probably either the police just doing a nightly sweep, some lovers pulling over for a quickie or maybe they saw the storm from the road and decided to pull over to watch from their car. I just hope they don't come and crash our party.

Now I have Dee sitting on my cock. I don't know if it's intentional on her part, but it feels intentional to me. She's straddling me like Lisa was but this time, facing away, as she's trying (successfully) to remove my shoes to continue the tickle assault that her and Lisa are inflicting on my body without compunction. I am so seriously hoping that while Lisa is practically sitting on my face and Dee is most firmly sitting on my groin, the return of my boner stays unnoticed. It's really becoming both a blessing and a menace of the trip so far.

"Oh!" Dee says with a playful wiggle of her hips. She's noticed. I was enjoying being past all this, but I am now under the complete spell of any touch of any level of sensitivity thanks to the intense tickling and I'm a slave to all and everything until the feeling subsides a bit.

Things could have looked better when Jayne and her sister Pam walked up to us on the beach. I wasn't really appearing in my best situation, with one girl climbing off my face as the other was still bouncing on my balls, giggling like a naughty schoolgirl. As Dee finally climbs off me, my boner has returned to its former glory which both Jayne and her older sister are looking at; Pam with a smirk, Jayne, well Jayne is walking away, back towards the car park, followed by me, with Pam closely behind. *FUCK.*

"I fucken organised a lot and went through some shit to come out here to see if you were okay, you fucken asshole." Jayne is sobbing as she speaks. I'm trying to catch her up, but Pam grabs my elbow and says it's best to let her cool down a bit.

"I'm such an asshole," I say to Pam. I don't really know Pam all that well, but Jayne likes her, and I suspect they both really did go through a lot of trouble and a certain amount of deceit to get here.

"Kinda," is her only response but she says it nicely. Like it's a forgivable mistake. To be honest, though, I'm not sure how I would react if I turned up unexpectedly to see Jayne getting dry-humped by two men, so I think she's (understandably) going to have to have some time to sort the scene in her head for herself. *At least we were dressed...* Dennis tried to dilute the tension by saying it was a dare.

"He didn't have to do it!" Jayne shouts back at him. Dennis looks genuinely perplexed at her statement as if he's thinking about telling her the rules of the game.

"Let it go, bud." I hear Randy say to him mutedly.

"You have to do a dare," Dennis shouts back to Jayne to a quiet chorus of 'fer fucks…' from the rest of us.

"Really?" Jayne stops and turns to face Dennis. "You absolutely have to do a dare, is that the rule?" she asks again and I have a really bad feeling about what's about to come next.

"Then I dare you to punch that asshole (me) in the face as hard as you can." I actually didn't see that coming and although I can understand Jayne's anger, I think making a friend twat another friend is too severe a punishment for a crime that hasn't even yet been discussed. Dennis of course refused, thus annulling his earlier argument and not strengthening my position.

"Assholes! All of you." Jayne is now practically running away and most definitely crying her heart out as she goes. This is the first time I've knowingly really hurt someone by my actions, and I think it's the worst I have ever felt about myself. I should never have let the scene unfold on the beach and I should never have started something with Lisa. Jayne's absence had weakened the bond I feel for her, and I assumed that the feeling would be similar for Jayne. With every thought about how I've treated her, I feel myself sinking in a rapid downward spiral into nothing but a dark pit of guilt.

The party is over, and spirits are low. Dee has apologised many times and every time I tell her that it wasn't her fault. Jayne and Pam have left and I wonder if I will ever see either of them again. I know she's not to blame and it's just her way, but I can't help feeling a little pissed at Lisa who is really acting as though nothing has happened and is openly flirting with Rob now that she feels the crisis has passed. I still love Jayne; I knew it the moment I saw her again today. Lisa is more of a lust thing and I can't help feeling that this reaffirms my thoughts that sex and love don't mix.

It was a joint decision to pack up and head home and we're all sitting now at the dock watching the last ferry of the day leave for Horseshoe Bay. One of the half a dozen or so cars on the ferry is Pam's new Pacer. I get out of the car and as I watch the first love of my life sail away, I have the feeling that it's not only Jayne that is leaving. I'm leaving a little as well; standing back, observing and noticing that nothing seems to fit quite right. Everything is a struggle, requiring will power and trust; and I'm noticing I'm running at a low level on both counts; I'm noticing that I'm disappointed in myself and that it still hurts far less than my father's displeasure in me.

We have seven hours to kill before the 6 am ferry leaves. Most of the others are trying to sleep in the cars but I get out to go for a mooch around the dock and smoke a joint when Scott comes to join me with a joint of his own burning between his lips.

"It really sucks, man," is all Scott says as we both stand on a small pebbly beach. Scott picks up a stone to skim it but it's not flat enough and just makes a loud plop and sinks immediately.

"Yeah, it sucks." I can't say any more than that because there's a huge lump in my throat choking any further words coming out. I can feel my eyes watering as I turn away from Scott.

Chapter Eleven

Bowen Island has changed everything. It just became noticeable that we all started to see less of each other as a group. Some of us would meet up from time to time individually to catch up, but there has never been another party or even a small group gathering. I have never again seen Jayne, Lisa nor Dee since the event on the island and the guilt I feel towards Jayne is yet to subside. It hurts me to know I hurt her so much and I don't know if it's ever going to be a forgivable offence. Maybe one day it will become less significant and probably even pale against worse crimes but for now, it still stings a lot, and I still get a lump in my throat if I let myself think about her for too long.

Nobody knew, but my brother had done the unthinkable and asked for a night off the moment he heard about Mt St Helens blowing and he drove down there and somehow made it close enough to the disaster zone to return home (none of us having known anything) in an unrecognisable, mud-covered and mostly destroyed version of the former Mini Cooper. He was laughing his tits off when he climbed out of the wreck, and he had a fistful of polaroid pictures in his hand that he was waving about in the air. Although every one of the pictures had value to Colin and a story attached to each one, to the layman, it was nothing more than the flash bouncing off the reddish-brown dust occupying each and every frame in his collection of around twenty snaps. I think my brother is slightly mad... *I wonder if it's genetic.*

It's high summer now and my old friend from Birmingham in England is coming to visit for a couple of weeks. He's an old mate who's coming to see me but, for my father, anyone visiting from England has to be given the grand tour. It's always the same tour; Jasper, Banff, The Rockies, Lake Louise... etc. It's all very beautiful but also very touristy with visitors from all over the world being unloaded constantly form grubby Greyhound busses. I suggested just taking it easy and I would show Davis around Vancouver and maybe take him on a wild camping trip up Black Tusk which Davis liked the sound of, but the trip was booked and paid for already, so no choice but to go.

The most fascinating thing I find about the Rockies is that they are still growing. In geological terms, it probably means they are still young mountains and I wonder how big they will be when fully adult. The constant movement of tectonic plates, the formation of rocks and the array of wondrous crystals that form under intense heat and pressure interest me. When I mention that I might like to go back to school and study geology, it's dismissed as a worthless job with no status. I'd just spend the rest of my life shovelling rocks apparently, and if I'm not going to be a doctor, dentist or a lawyer there's not really much point in wasting money on education and I might as well train to be a dental technician. I do not, and I never will be a dental technician. I have a better, more exciting life than that ahead of me.

The second week of the tour is new to me. We only normally do a week in the Rockies and then return home but probably because Davis's dad is quite important in the Birmingham police force, my dad feels he needs to make an extra effort to impress. We're staying at a beachside hotel on the lake Okanagan in the British Columbian interior. We came here a while ago, thinking about moving here and I loved it then as much as I do now. It's hot, dry and sunny, with endless fruit orchards. I can only eat peaches from this area. They are sweeter than candy and so juicy, and an entirely different experience from anything I've tasted from a shop. The climate is so warm and sunny here that they've started turning some of the lands over to growing grapes, and from what I've heard, the British Columbian wine is good. The only wine I've tasted, was a sip from my mother's Liebfraumilch and it felt like I was having my gums stripped back before I'd even swallowed it, so I'm not particularly interested. I'll happily eat the ripened grapes before they're trampled though.

There is the most beautiful aboriginal girl with a deep tan in a tiny white bikini playing with a white family in the water right in front of the motel. Her body is the essence of feminine perfection for me. I'm fixated on her and I think I'm experiencing love at first sight. Seriously, I'm not just talking about the amazing figure or the way she is bouncing around in the water, also to the delight of a few men slowing down their pace, as they take their morning stroll around the lakeshore. I'm talking about the bit I see that nobody else sees. I am seeing what I feel all the time. I see a girl totally lost in this world and having no idea where she fits into it. I see this every time she looks at me with the same intent in her eyes as she sees in mine.

We meet secretly in the games room and agree to meet later by the boat rental place down the road because if her dad sees me with her, he'll probably kill me. If my dad sees me with a native girl, he'll probably kill me as well. He has taught me on many an occasion that all 'Indians' are lazy good for nothings that don't deserve the land they've been given because they just trash it. My mother will agree all the time and say that they are the same as the 'wogs' in Leicester, and I'm left wondering if it's only me who sees how ridiculously stupid supposedly intelligent people are. Where does this arrogance, this supremacy come from? Are we evolving, or merely masking a hidden monster inside of us that is gated by society?

Davis has been homesick and insecure on the trip so far, but I was hoping it might have abated a bit so I could meet my date. I don't expect him to hang out with my parents but I thought he might enjoy a little alone time for a couple of hours; I know I'd appreciate it if I was staying with another family. It's decided though, that he would rather chaperone me on my first date with Rose, and I feel like a bit of a twat turning up with a friend. Rose is totally cool with it though and she and I walk hand-in-hand as Davis follows us to the store on the corner that sells ice cream. There's a table outside and we're all silently enjoying our ice creams as Davis surprises us with the suggestion of renting a speedboat. I've seen them out on the lake and they look and sound awesome; fast too.

The lake is long, the weather is fine, and Davis has the throttle fully open and the boat is absolutely flying. It's more in the air than on water and every time it hits a swell, we all three whoop with excitement on impact. It's so bumpy it's hard to let go of the handrail and then Rose says we should all try to stand up. Then standing up no hands.

Thankfully, Davis manages to grab the steering wheel before plunging overboard like Rose and I. One either side. Simultaneously flying through the air and landing on the water at about thirty miles an hour. The impact is harsh. It's no different from falling off a skateboard onto the tarmac at this speed and my arse has hit and bounced once as I'm poised for the second impact. It hurts a bit, but it's fucken hilarious and I can't stop laughing as I skim across the top of the water before finally losing momentum and sinking. When I bob back up to the surface thanks to the life jacket, I'm happy to see Rose is laughing as much as me and just floating on her back enjoying the moment. It's a good feeling when you're at the end of something you weren't wholly comfortable with halfway through; nervous relief with an instantly added feeling of new inner strength.

Rose's bikini bottom has slid down and I can't avert my eyes as she climbs directly above me out of the water back into the boat. She's pulling them up with one hand to retain her dignity, so I push off and go for a quick swim while she gets in the boat and wraps herself in a towel. It will never take away the image though. I won't let anything cover the image in my mind for as long as I live. I think it's the fact that I wasn't supposed to see it that makes it so much more exciting. *I want her...*

Rose is going out with her family tonight and Davis and I want to go and check out a fair that we saw from the boat earlier, so Rose and I agree on a secret rendezvous at 6 am on the beach on the other side of the road.

Fairs at night-time are infinitely more fun than during the day. The noise, lights, people, smells of candy floss and toffee apples everywhere in the air. Screams are coming from the direction of the bumper cars and that's the direction we both want to go. Davis and I grew up in the heart of Birmingham and it was really only the very hardened fairground families that would occasionally brave the neighbourhood around bonfire night. They are called bumper cars there and if you weren't quick-witted, it wasn't too uncommon for a kid to lose a tooth or two when ramming each other at high speeds. The whole fun was trying to time the longest and clearest run for the highest impact head-on crash. At the fair we're at presently, they're called dodgems and it's not until now that both Davis and I have been kicked off them for scaring other kids, that we see everyone trying to avoid everyone else, with the odd scream when someone gets 'accidentally' sideswiped.

Where's the fun in that?

The ghost train is as uninspiring and uneventful as expected until Davis lets out a hideous fart. More commotion is stirring in the carriages behind us due to that, than any of the plastic puppets that have seen better days. "Phooff."

"Pwaw, who farted?"

It's unfortunate timing as well because the train has stopped for us all to revel in a glow in the dark skull about to shoot out from behind a curtain sideways and I hear someone say thank fuck for that, at the back of the train as we start moving again. I don't think anyone was really certain who farted but both Davis and I are getting strong looks as we move on to the next ride.

I'm not sure what it's called but for some reason, we are the only two people on it when it starts up. We didn't even look to see what it was before climbing into an empty car and we only chose it because there wasn't a line-up. It starts almost as soon as we sit down and it's then that I see we're sitting in a plastic boat that's been moulded to look like a carved-out log, with surprisingly strong high-backed seats that an attendant has efficiently buckled us into. Something latches onto the boat underneath us and we immediately start climbing, rising, slowly upwards to a height that didn't look so high from down on the ground. As we come out of the spiral, I can start to see a view of the lake and the people that are starting to gather at the bottom of a very steep piece of track that is falling away on the other side, almost vertically from the summit that is about five seconds away from us on our steady climb. As we reach the top, my adrenaline levels are through the roof and even more so, when the log leans slightly forward over the precipice towards a plunge pool not too far off directly below us at around eighty feet in distance, I'd say. Both Davis and I have been quiet all the way up but we both say fuck at exactly the same time of seeing our fate, and then the exclamation turns to a unified scream as the log simultaneously turns on its axis at the same time as dropping off the vertical edge backwards. The picture taken of us on the way down depicts in clarity the extent of our shock and fear as we try to deal with a complete fuck up of all senses and then the gentle sweep into the pool at the bottom which not only slows us down but cools us down by way of a complete head to foot drenching. That's why the crowd was gathering and they are all cheering us as we climb out, completely soaked and trying not to look too shocked. It's another one of those experiences to gladly have behind me and we're both shaking as we walk back to the motel, shaking as the adrenaline is still being washed through our bodies. A couple of girls are shyly following us as we leave the fair, giggling behind us, but keeping enough distance to pretend that they aren't interested.

"Hey! Cowboy!" She's talking to Davis because he's wearing the ridiculous cheap straw cowboy hat that he won at the shooting gallery. Davis is trying to ignore her but she's starting to run after him now with her friend in tow.

It's funny, Davis was kind of a nerd at school who tended to get picked on because of his thick glasses and trousers that were always too short for him. He has very sticky-out ears as well which earned him the unfortunate nickname of

Wingnut when we were at school. But now that he's grown his hair over his ears and started wearing contact lenses, and most importantly, wearing jeans that are the correct length, he's turned into a bit of an eye-catcher for the girls and he seems quite used to it; to my slight irritation. Still, I have a date with Rose in the morning.

The girls want to party and they have a bottle of something with them that they are trying to entice us with. Davis grabs the bottle and takes a healthy gulp. I fail to see how he didn't wince when it went down. It's disgusting! It's like drinking fire and it has absolutely no definitive taste apart from repulsive. Davis grabs the bottle back off me and takes another big swig before handing it back to the swooning girls. They are annoying, giggly girls who are trying to look and act older than they really are. I suspect that they are only fourteen, maybe even thirteen and they are really starting to annoy both of us with their girlish screeches every time Davis says something not even remotely funny. He grabs the bottle again and takes another swig, then he hands the bottle back, now a bit pissed and puts the cowboy hat on the girl nearest to him and lunges into a full-on snog with her. This, of course, makes her jump back in absolute horror.

"I'm not a slut!" she says as she pushes herself firmly away from Davis.

"Girls are really weird," Davis says as we continue our walk back to the motel with all four of our feet making noticeable slushing and squelching noises in our wet trainers as we walk. To be honest, I don't feel the same way and keep quiet. I think the whole human race, regardless of the seperate sexes is weird.

I didn't know this and it may shock some of you as well, to learn that in the sixties, in Canada, aboriginal babies were taken from their birth mothers and put into the social system for adoption, largely by middle-class white families. Rose was one of those babies and now at nearly sixteen, she is yet to meet her real mum whose identity has been kept classified. I'm still just a kid myself and I can't fathom what would be going through a person's mind to think that this was a good idea. Many people must have thought it was a good idea for it to happen and this is even more worrying to me. Does anybody ever stop to think about the peaceful and natural existence these people had before the arrogant European decided to conquer their land and transform their ways; to the 'correct' way? I'm genuinely lost for words and thankfully, Rose makes it easier by pulling me into her and telling me it's okay, and that she's used to it now and there's nothing more to be done. I hear the words but those are the words merely escaping her mouth. In her eyes, I see the fury; I see that one day she will fight back against this abominable inhumane act and with the rage I feel against the system inside me right now, I would fight proudly alongside her. How could I ever conform to a society that agreed such a thing only a couple of decades ago? If I am to conform to such ideals then I am happy to be an outsider, even if it's not the easiest road.

Rose fits so perfectly into my arms, it's as if we've been made especially for each other and I love that she is as happy as I am to not say anything anymore. We just sit and watch the early morning wildlife starting out on its separate journeys for the day. Looking over the still misty lake, the odd ring of water will appear out of nowhere as a fish disturbs the surface. Rose feels smooth. She's warm on a chilly morning and I feel comforted in her presence because she says wonderful things like: I want to make love to you in a wild hot spring next to a glacier. She dreams like me. She looks beyond what everyone else sees and sees the fun part; the part where you can make up life as you go along. She is my soulmate. The first time we kiss, we are both smiling so our lips are tight which makes us laugh and bang our teeth together and laugh even more. The second time, she kisses me like I have never been kissed before and tells me that she fell in love with me the second she saw me looking at her. I feel stupid saying I felt the same way, but the truth is, I really did. I suppose you can't really totally love someone only on a first glance but you can certainly love what you know so far and it opens up the gateway to finding more and more to love and that is how I feel about Rose with every word she speaks and every kiss we share. She's deep, creative, smart, sassy and very much her own woman with her own thoughts that are held strongly by her and it's just another thing to love about her. We've known each other for less than twenty-four hours and have spent less than two of those hours together alone, but already I feel that I could never live without her and how is it going to be when the holiday is over? She's just calm and serene about everything as if knowing that everything is mapped out for her anyway and there is no point in fighting life. I feel peaceful in her presence. I feel comfortable being simply in her presence, knowing that she will lead when she wants things to go further. I'm in no hurry to ruin things as they are right now.

"You can touch me anywhere," Rose tells me as she pulls away from a kiss.

I look down to see a very hard nugget like nipple poking very strongly at the cotton T-shirt that is the only thing keeping it hidden from the elements, and as my hand slides up under her shirt to cup her breast, the hardness seems to pulse in the palm of my hand. Rose asks me if I've been with anyone before and I answer 'no' without shame because I'm happy for Rose to be my first. I'm disappointed to hear that Rose is a bit of a dab hand at it and started young but I suppose it's better than two novices fumbling around, so, again, I'm happy to pass the lead back to Rose. As I'm kissing Rose and still cupping her right breast, a shadow passes over my closed eyes and I open them to see an old man, probably in his sixties just openly standing there watching. I'm expecting him to tell us how disgusting the youth of today are but then I notice he's got his hands in his pockets and one of them is clearly having a tug.

"Fuck off, man! Seriously, get the fuck outa here," I say, getting up to shoo him away, but he just keeps tugging at himself until the inevitable happens and with a quick orgasmic grunt, he wipes his hand on the inside of his pocket and briskly walks away.

"Did he just do what I think he did?" asks Rose laughing. "That'll be you when you're his age." She keeps laughing as she's pointing at me. And falling back to lie on her back on the sandy beach. It's funny now, but maybe I *will* end up like him.

When I fantasise about my old age, I'm either a gentle old pothead grandpa that the kids love to hang out with, or I'm a rich playboy with my live-in female beach volleyball team. Maybe I'll even find a way to combine the two.

"I better get back before my dad gets up," Rose says, kissing me on the cheek. I take her hand and pull her up off the sand and we walk back arm in arm to a motel. The place still seems to be in a deep slumber, and I wasn't prepared for my father walking around the corner of the building. He's smoking a cigarette and pulling a reluctant dog on the end of a lead. The end to a near-perfect start to a wonderful day.

We've both had a lecture about mixing with 'native' girls. We've both been told that we should understand that they are not as developed as us. They are the same as the blacks and are just not capable of living in a civilised society. They will get pregnant and trap us, so they can try and live in our world, but they can't. I did try to tell him that Rose has said quite clearly and definitely that she doesn't want kids, but he dismissed it with a 'poof' and a facetious laugh.

"Stay away from her!" is all he said, as he walked away.

Although the words were intended to threaten us, and to some point, Davis has been threatened, I have no intention of stopping seeing Rose and I advise Davis to just block the old man out of his mind and try to forget it... it's the only way.

"Your old man is a bit of cunt, really isn't he?" Davis says.

"A bit? You think?" I answer.

"A racialist," Dave is saying, seeming quite stunned.

"My old man is a lot of things. I tend to bundle it all up and put it under the simple title of arsehole. Trust me, just ignore him. I do."

Davis smiles again, but I can see he's been scarred. The words we heard and the attitude in which they were expressed leave a scar, and when the words come out of the mouth of your former role model, the scars sometimes seem to never heal. Davis's scar will heal. Mine will take more time. This just makes me want to see Rose even more than I already do and I sort of have the desire to rub my dad's nose in his own attitude a bit.

Mum has suggested us all having a barbecue on the beach at lunchtime and although Davis has a date and I'm meeting Rose, I agree to be there even if Davis is giving me a look of *what the fuck.*

"Dude, it's okay. Invite your chick along for the barbecue. I'm going to invite Rose."

"Are you fucking mad? You heard your old man." Davis is looking worried again.

"I'm going to invite her family as well," I say with a smile.

Davis knows what I know, and what neither of my parents know, and it's that Rose's parents are white middle-class professionals. It's an opportunity not to miss.

My father is in his element and as embarrassing as usual as he shares age-old jokes with a new captive audience. To the naked eye, we look like a normal group of holidaymakers sharing beers and burgers on the beach, but really, it's a volatile catalyst of a racist and an overprotective father of his only daughter trying to remain civil, at the same time as keeping a very close eye on the four of us playing with a beachball in the lake.

"You are fucken nuts, Kev," Rose is cautiously keeping her distance from me even though I keep throwing the ball closer and closer to me so I can grab her and dunk her.

"I think it's a stroke of genius," I retort. "Watch this."

I walk out of the lake and straight up to the group of parents and Rose's younger brother, and when I ask them all directly and politely if the four of us can all go out tonight, they fidget and fumble for words before settling on a reluctant 'yes'.

When I go back into the lake and tell everyone that we're cool to go out tonight, Rose jumps up and straddles me standing waist-deep in the water and kisses me right on the lips. I don't even want to see what our fathers' reactions are, and I'm bracing myself for a pair of hands dragging me away or at least a shout to get off her, but nothing came, so we keep kissing... and I feel very awkward. I really don't like kissing a girl in front of my parents and I'm surprised at how relaxed Rose is in front of hers.

My father dilutes his defeat by saying it's okay as long as it's just a holiday thing. "Just make sure she doesn't make you get her pregnant!" are his last words before Davis and I leave to pick up our dates.

Once I've knocked on the door for the third time with no response, I look over to Davis who is waiting for me on the beach and then peer in through the window to see that the room has clearly been vacated.

The happy rotund woman working in the motel's office gladly hands me an envelope with nothing but a heart drawn on the front and SWALK over the part that had been stuck down. *Sealed with a loving kiss.*

I'm thinking of Rose's loving kisses as I read about her being taken home early because her brother is sick. She has given me her address in Edmonton and her phone number with a note underneath saying to pick her up and run away together, forever... "my one and only love". *Her brother looked fine at the barbecue.*

I'm trying to convince Davis to not stand his date up, but he says he was only meeting her to hang out with us and that she's a bit full of herself anyway.

"It will do her good to be stood up," he laughs.

Once the ice had been broken about the weed, Davis and I spent much of the rest of the vacation stoned on the beach and trying to avoid my father as much as possible. The note that Rose left me was left on the table and has mysteriously disappeared with nobody apparently having a clue as to what I'm talking about. It doesn't matter though; I memorised her number the moment I looked at it.

Chapter Twelve

The view in front of me, from the roof of the train, is the epitome of a Canadian picture-postcard scene. Reaching snow-capped mountains with a deeply carved canyon in the foreground. Chalky green glacial water at the bottom of a steep and narrow gorge is thundering hundreds of feet below the trestle bridge we have come to rest on. We've been stuck here for the last two hours, apparently because there is a bear on the tracks ahead of us, and I'm grateful to it for providing me with this unforgettable extended view.

Although I'm sixteen now, I'm still below the legal age for drinking but the waiter seems happy to keep slipping me the odd whiskey because he's seen me drinking one with my mum. She's downstairs in the tiny cabin in which she's spent almost all of the journey so far. The bar which is a glass dome perched on the roof of one of the train's carriages is mostly full of men drinking whiskey and smoking heavily, so she probably feels out of place. One guy who had clearly had a skin full tried hitting on her last night and she hasn't been up here since. To be honest, I think she quite liked it but was clearly uncomfortable with me being around as it was happening. *I wonder if my mum has ever cheated.*

*

I'm being shipped to England. It was a sudden announcement that came out of nowhere: pack your bags, we're leaving.

It's all my fault. I've been told so on a few occasions now by both my mum and dad. Even though things have been going quite smoothly and I've decided to get my act together and get back to school, the decision has been made.

I didn't even have time to say goodbye to my friends. The train was leaving that night and my mother and I are now halfway through a three-day journey to Winnipeg. We will stay with the family... and the boy I tried to twat over the head with a water pistol before we fly to London. Back to the grey. Scott will be fifteen now, a year and a month younger than me and I haven't seen him since he was five.

I miss my friends already and it was cruel to take me away without being able to say goodbye to them. Jayne still probably hates me, I miss her and I would have liked to have seen her once more at least. All my closest friends that I went to hell and back with, just pulled from under my nose. In fairness, I did have the opportunity to stay. Gary has been coming over to my place and vice versa in the last couple of weeks and he called me this morning to ask if I wanted to hang out. When I told him what was going on, he was so shocked that his mum came on the phone and once I told her, she said without hesitation that I am welcome to go and live with them anytime. It was a very kind and generous offer and I'm not going to say I didn't think about it, but this is my family and for bad or worse, I will stick with what I know until I'm free to go. I would feel very awkward living with another family as if part of it, and it makes me think about whether Rose feels that way.

The third scotch is starting to make me feel a bit pissed and I'm happy to join in and learn how to play poker with a few guys in their fifties and sixties. One of them hands me a huge Cuban cigar and places another scotch in front of me with a wink and a shush signal as he puts his finger up to his lips. I feel like one of the men. The fucken cigar is disgusting though. I know I'm not supposed to inhale, but that's the whole enjoyment for me. I don't see the point of puffing like the others and I'm happy to suffer the consequences of coughing up half a lung every time I take a draw if that's what it takes to gain some satisfaction from it.

"You're not supposed to inhale it," One of the men says, and the others start to laugh as I keep coughing.

The game, drinking and smoking continue quite late into the night and the darkness outside is only occasionally lit by the flicker of a car's headlights or a distant town. I am completely shit faced and having difficulty negotiating the tight spiral staircase down to the cabin deck. I managed the staircase impressively well, but the moment I open the door to the cabin that I'm sharing with my mum, the train jolts slightly and the lights go out as my face hits the floor.

It's not through any strong bond that I feel for her but when I see the guy from yesterday sitting with my mum in the buffet carriage for breakfast, it pisses me off. It pisses me off because he knows I'm here with her and that she's married. He's had all this brought to his attention and he is still overtly trying to get into my mother's knickers and I don't like it. It's not as though she's firmly forcing him away either and that also pisses me off and I wonder why. I guess it's because no matter how different we view life, no matter how much we can't sometimes bear the thought of it, genes will always somehow invisibly bond us and make us feel protective over our family. I am yet to feel the parental bond and protection a father must feel but I think that there is a fine line between protection and outright control. My father has crossed that boundary too many times and my pull towards wanting to protect him in any situation is there, but heavily doused.

My mother excuses herself from the table, politely thanks him for his company and stands up. He remains seated which, again pisses me off. I don't know if it's the regimental upbringing or not, but at least stand for a lady. Then, he shuffles his seat back and stands up to offer to walk her back to her cabin but sits down again when he sees me with very tightly clenched fists coming to get her. My mum is truly helpless without my dad and it's really not her that is keeping an eye on me anymore. It's really quite shocking for me to see my mum alone and how utterly uncomfortable she is without being guided every step of the way by my father. Even though my mum and I aren't really speaking much, I feel like I'm bonding with her, a little; as much as either of us are capable of.

We're pulling into a station, I'm not sure which one, as I missed the announcement but it's probably Regina which is a half-hour stop. Enough time to get out and walk on solid ground for a little while. It starts feeling a little claustrophobic after many hours on a train and I look forward to the long stops to get a little fresh air, even if I do smoke a cigarette at the same time.

My dad bought my mum a camera last Christmas. She's never used it to date, which is a shame because it's a nice one. I'm thinking of it because as we pull into the station, someone is running along the platform waving one at us; not taking pictures just waving it frantically around as if showing it off to all the passengers arriving into the station.

"Fuck me, it's Dad!" My mum is so astonished she let the bad language go and then fall into a state of a complete loss as to what is happening.

"W…Wh…How…?" She's lost, so I head to the door and let her figure it out as she follows me.

"I thought you might need this for the trip, sweetheart," he says.

I am beginning to think that I am now part of an insane family and it is definitely best to start making my own future plans. My father has flown from

Vancouver to Regina to intercept a train to deliver a Christmas present that my mother had forgotten about by Boxing day. He must have studied the schedule of the train quite closely, so I wonder why it hasn't occurred to him that the most picturesque part of the journey is a good day behind us and that unless we want an album full of endless flat prairies and big blue skies, there was very little point to the whole exercise. I know what a complete and utter arsehole he can really be, and generally is, so why would he do this? Does he love her that much? I haven't seen an awful lot of evidence that he's capable of love so it's hard to accept that this is a true act of kindness as opposed to him checking up on her, which has entered my mind. It's pretty fucken extreme though, and if it *is* the case, then it's disguised impeccably to make him appear like the proverbial shining chivalrous knight. Now, more than ever, I can only see my father with a perpetual question mark floating over his head. I know nothing of him, and it saddens me that he knows even less of me. We will never be close; how can you be close to someone who you never know is telling you the truth or not? I will accept what he is, fight him and ignore him when it's necessary, accept that it is what it is and take what I can from the situation until I'm eighteen and walk away permanently.

Its's raining when we land in London; of course, it's fucken raining. It always seems to rain here and it looks just as grey as when we left it three years ago. I've never seen my mum smoke a cigarette before, but she smoked about half of mine during the flight over and never refused a drink. I spent most of the time trying to find one decent inflight radio station to listen to without success whilst waiting for the film to start. I fell asleep at the beginning of the film and woke up during the credits at the end and that was the only sleep I managed to get.

I don't have a driving license and I'm driving a brand-new red English Ford Cortina along the M4 motorway towards Devon in the southwest of England as my mum snoozes in the passenger seat. When I offered to drive the rental car (because I'm sure mum was feeling groggy after the flight) I didn't expect her to agree. It was just one of those 'can I drive?' questions that I've been trying for as long as I can remember, and I never expected to hear an 'okay'. Ever.

She's not quite so calm when she wakes up though, and nearly causes a multi-car collision when she tries to grab the wheel off me as we're travelling at seventy miles an hour in the fast lane.

"Seriously, Mum, let go." I'm trying to keep the car under control as she releases the grip.

"I'll pull over at the next services and you can take over. I'm getting tired anyway," I lie.

"You don't have a license. Are you trying to get me put in jail?" she shouts at me.

"I *did* ask if you wanted me to drive and you said yes." She was obviously out of it after the flight and that explains why I got away with it so easily.

Now she's being her usual really annoying nervous passenger and telling me to slow down and watch out continuously and to be honest, the fun has gone out of it, and I'm happy for her to take over when we pull up for a quick rest and a greasy bacon and egg sandwich. *I miss McDonald's.*

After driving from one service stop to the next, my mum concedes to being terrified and lets me drive the rest of the way to Torquay and I'm surprised that she falls asleep all the way to the hotel that I found by asking directions from local good-looking girls.

Life is easy when it's just my mum and me. I just say I'm going out, and there are no questions about where I'm going and when I'll be back. She just says 'have fun' and she gives me some English spending money. She's lost without my dad, but she is altogether a much more relaxed woman on her own.

He's coming in another two weeks, with Colin. They stayed behind to finish things off and I am still reeling from the urgency in which I have been deported. How can everything be sold up and closed down to start a new life in another country so fast... and why? The only answer my mum offers is, that they think it's for the best.

It's raining. It rains differently in England from Canada. The rain in England seems permanent. It's the default setting for weather and anything else is, whether it be the odd flurry of snow in the winter or sun in the summer is always cause for excitement and sometimes chaos in the otherwise general grey dampness. The people are grey as well. English people seem to emanate their climate from their pale washed-out complexions and dim clothing until there is the odd day of sunshine and regardless of the temperature, the presence of a warmish sun will encourage people to strip off to a level of nakedness that should really be thought about carefully even in the confines of their own bathroom.

I spend the pocket money my mum gave me going ice skating. I say ice skating, in fact, the ice is made of plastic and although I grew up on ice skates, this shit does not feel right under the blades and the opportunity to try and show my Canadian prowess on ice in front of the local talent is quickly halted as my blades seem to be sticking to the plastic every time I try to glide. I finally start to get a little bit of a feel for the surface and make jerky attempted glides in the direction of two girls around my age, clearly looking for a boy to come and hit on them. In fact, I hit them, quite hard, as one of the blunt blades of the rental skate gouged into the plastic and flipped over my own feet to land at theirs after banging both of them against the boards.

"Clumsy git," one of the girls says. She's laughing though, as is her friend.

"Not seen you here before," the bigger of the two girls says, in fact, she's very big, round, with huge tits that seem to defy gravity as they poke straight out towards me and jiggle when she giggles.

"Where you from then, clumsy?" It's the big one again and it looks like the other girl, who happens to be the one I want to talk to is leaving so she can leave her friend to get chatted up.

"Vancouver," I answer.

"You American?" she asks.

"Canadian," I answer.

"Same thing," she retorts. *Fucks sake, retard.*

"I like your accent." She is making a move for me and regardless of her not really being my type, I might have accepted if it weren't for the 'American' comment.

"Do you know where I can buy some weed around here?" For me, this is just a straightforward question that most teenagers will ask when arriving in a new town, but when I ask her, she pales and looks at me as if I'm a murderer on the run. Then she went over to her friend and starts whispering to her as they both appraise me disapprovingly. I better leave before they call the cops or something and I'll make a mental note to be careful who I ask about weed. There is clearly a different view towards it here.

When I get back to the hotel, there is a man sitting at a table with my mum in the bar area. When I sit down to join them, he makes it quite clear to me that he fancies my mum and keeps telling me how beautiful she is. It's clear that no matter the age, if a woman is sitting alone, a man somewhere in the room will consider her fair game. It is a bit like a game too; a game of conquest. Seeing my mum in this different light brings the question of monogamy, sex and relationships again. Is marriage really an exchange of vows to announce their love for each other or simply proof of ownership? It's a big ask to marry someone and never have permission from your owner to experience another fruit from time to time. It's, to me, verging on inhumane. I've never seen my mum as a catch before but now looking at her, she *is* quite a good-looking woman, and she is definitely enjoying being complimented so I leave her to it and head for the pool. I'm thinking about how my father would handle the situation if he were to walk into the hotel right now. As much as I think, I really have no idea how he would react because it all depends on who's mindset he's chosen to follow at the time. When the dog misbehaves, he tells us that it has to know who the boss is and he beats it over the snout with a chain lead. When I misbehave, well, you know some of it. I wonder how he would deal with a misbehaving wife.

I don't know what my mum did to upset him, but I recall a time when we were living in Birmingham: I was about ten or eleven and it's uncommon for my parents to row, simply because my mother is so submissive but this time, my mum was screaming and crying as she hauled me out of bed to plead with my dad not to leave in the middle of the night. To be honest, I wasn't really that bothered and just wanted to go back to bed, but the scene went on for hours, while we had to pacify him and make him feel superior and needed again. I remember it because it was unusual and because I got the cane the next day for falling asleep in Physics.

For many weeks now, I have wandered the streets of Torquay, and in contrast to the norm, the weather has been pretty sunny for most of the time. I don't like it here though. It's tiny and boring in comparison to Vancouver and the kids seem, well very provincial with little other interests than going skating on plastic or going to arcades on the seafront. It's boring, I miss my friends and I feel like I will never meet or have friends like those I left behind ever again.

I've been having extra biology lessons from a tutor, which is fairly pointless because I haven't been going to any of the classes at school. The tutor is one of my dad's patients and he will seize any opportunity to have me educated to a higher level than my cohort. She gave me a test to do last week to discover the level of my intelligence and apparently, I'm quite smart. I have a definite leaning towards creativity and should consider this area as a career option.

I was pleased with being told that my intellectual ability is advanced for my age and that I'm in the top two percent of the population. I was actually beaming a little with pride when I gave *him* the information about a school catering for the arts nearby and about my IQ result. I remember looking at my mum and Colin both back and forth looking for some support as both pieces of paper landed in the bin. He was furious that the money he was paying my tutor to teach me biology had been wasted on trivia. No support came, which was no surprise and my mum is back to her old robotic shadow of my father. The next time I went for a biology lesson, I was told not to unpack my bag and that she's very sorry but due to unforeseen circumstances, she will have to stop tutoring me. I can see that she is genuinely upset and I'm not sure if it's just an old person thing or if she has a slight tear in her eye. My father, and sadly my mother, both believe that I did something to annoy my tutor and that's why she quit. I have racked my brains for weeks now and I still can't think of a single thing I could have done to upset her. I didn't really have a great interest in biology even though I enjoyed her lessons and I did actually learn something. *I didn't do anything wrong. I'm sure I didn't.*

I failed another entrance exam; this time to a technical college that my father thought would be a suitable grounding for an engineering degree. He will settle for an engineer as a son but would still prefer a doctor. I didn't fail the exam on purpose this time, I failed it because it was sheets of paper full of diagrams of things I didn't recognise and asking me the best way to fix them. I remember one of the questions being about headphones and my thoughts were at the time that I don't know, or even care how my headphones work. I just want to listen to music through them and not have to think about all the intricacies that bring me my pleasure.

So my dad lined up an army of tutors and I attend a sixth form college on the edge of an old farmers market town in the heart of mid-Devon; the head of which has been informed that it is his job to get me into medical school. Engineering was taken off the table after the test failure.

Day after day goes by at the new school with me attending about five percent of the classes and the rest of the time in the boys' toilet, which is really the smoking room. I'm used to being the new kid in school, but this time is very different. I've been through some shit in my life now. I've had some scary and even near-death experiences. I've felt love and I've been lied to. I've been beaten up and tossed around like I've been living in a washing machine for the past year. I've learnt more about me, and I've learnt that a first day at a new school is a piece of piss in comparison.

With a strange accent, newfound confidence and wild stories to share, I soon find friends, those friends introduce me to English pubs that don't ask for ID and every time the girls that come to the pub with us have a little too much to drink, they get all giggly and start teasing me about when Dawn gets back from holiday. Dawn is depicted as a maneater, and I don't have a chance.

Although I've snogged a few of the girls in the boys' toilet, I have told them that I have a girlfriend in Canada. Rose and I spoke on the phone yesterday. I was lucky to have picked up because if my dad picks up, he tells her that I don't want to speak to her and puts the phone down on her. I know this really upsets her and I have told him so, but it doesn't stop him. The arguments between my father and I are becoming more and more heated, but the violence has stopped because the last time he went to hit me, I said, go ahead, but this time I'm going to hit you back! He could see I really wanted to, so he retreated and has never lifted a hand against me since. It's still a different story for my brother though. He will never stand up to him. He went back to Canada last week because he doesn't like the 'English mentality'. I think it was because he'd had enough of fighting and knew he could never win. I miss him but to be honest, I haven't seen much of him since we got back to England. We both seem to have been doing our own things. My dad found Colin's porn collection when we were unpacking after the move and had a huge bonfire in the garden at the same time as shouting out how disgusting it is. The neighbours must think he's insane.

This time last year, I walked away from my family in jailhouse overalls, so in comparison, life's rolling by quite smoothly and now that I have my own moped, I am never at home. Whatever the weather and whether I've got a specific destination or not, I just love the freedom of riding the little 50cc step through which is nothing more than a bulky bicycle really. It's my independence though. It has zero street credibility, but I am insanely proud of it and it has no trouble keeping up with my friends' cooler looking bikes. They're still only 50cc and mine keeps up fine, but theirs look more like motorcycles than a pregnant push bike.

With the way things are going, I think I can stick it at home for another year or so and then, maybe I'll join the Marines or something. The careers guy at school said I should think about the police. Twat!

My father still baits, and I bite, but I'm getting better at calling his bullshit, but only a little. It's still a big thing to call your father a liar and my mother gives me such a disappointed look every time I do, that I tend to just whisper 'bullshit' under my breath as I walk away from him. I am walking away from him. I am walking backwards to see who he really is and now that I have a clearer understanding, it's easy to decide that avoidance is the best option.

I have brought home a few girls but even though I'm allowed in their rooms at their houses, it's absolutely forbidden for unmarried people of the opposite sex to be in a bedroom in our house, and my father has no idea that I go in their bedrooms. I'm still in love with Rose and if I'm to be really honest, Jayne too. The English girls are different; a bit annoying in a way. Not quite as slutty as I like. So far, I've only managed to get a hand job (not allowed to finish) and a regular fingering of Sue in the boys' room. Dawn has turned out to be amazing and we totally have fallen for each other, but Dawn is young, beautiful and has a tendency to fall for a lot of guys so we are perpetual flirty friends and nothing more.

I'm playing pool with two of my new friends, Mark and Roger. Mark and Roger have been mates for a long time so I'm thinking that Roger is still checking me out as I've started hanging out with Mark a lot. I'm thinking about when Rob, Dennis and the rest of us would go and play pool back home. I still call it home but to be honest, it's not so bad here. My friends are cool. A bit tame compared to what I'm used to, but they still like to have fun.

The letters and phone calls to all my friends in Canada are becoming less frequent from both sides and I guess we're all moving on with our own lives in our own ways.

Because I left in such a hurry and didn't have time to say goodbye, it's been promised that we will have the greatest return party as soon as I get enough money to return. They talked about pitching in and getting me a ticket, but I told them not to. I think I still miss them too much to see them again yet.

Dawn has come into the pub and is totally flirting to the extreme with me.

"Let's go and watch the band," she says as she pinches my ass. She always pinches my ass, ever since the first time we were introduced.

"Dawn, this is Kevin."

"Mmmmmeow, Kevin," she purred in my ear as she pinched my ass for the first time. She did it almost every time we met ever since and repeatedly during physics where she sat next to me. I still get flustered when she does it now.

The band are good. A three-piece with an old dude in his thirties on bass, with a miserable looking drummer, and a pretty boy singer/guitarist both in their early twenties. They're playing standard rhythm and blues classics with a few heavy numbers thrown in, by request of the drummer by the looks of the energy he puts into it. He's good. He's an unfriendly twat though and pretty much offers me to fuck off when I say, I hear you're looking for a sax player. I didn't hear it,

I just thought it sounded better than are you looking for one. Maybe it's what pissed off the drummer and it's certainly been a bumpy start with him to get to the stage of playing in the band long enough to know that this is what I want to do with my life.

It's never been accepted that anything considered enjoyable is work so when I announce that I want to be a musician it's immediately disregarded.

The man playing the piano in a late-night bar or the musicians in the theatre or circus pits are insignificant to my father. He thinks that to be successful as a musician you have to become famous. I wouldn't mind a taste of fame but that isn't my driving goal. My goal is to do something I enjoy and to do something that is absolutely nothing like being a fucking doctor. The idea is laughed at derisively, however, and he doesn't need to say the words that are clearly implied:

"You're not good enough."

Forty years have passed since the story I've just told and there are many more to tell.

I can say I tried. I tried up until the very last two weeks of his life, and that was when I finally had the courage, the strength and no other choice but to finally walk away.

THE END